TRAVERSE
The Last Heir of Arthur

Traverse

The Last Heir of Arthur

A novel

by

W. A. HOLDSWORTH

Adelaide Books
New York/Lisbon
2019

TRAVERSE
The Last Heir of Arthur
A novel
By W. A. Holdsworth

Published by Adelaide Books, New York / Lisbon
adelaidebooks.org

Editor-in-Chief
Stevan V. Nikolic

For any information, please address Adelaide Books
at info@adelaidebooks.org
or write to:
Adelaide Books
244 Fifth Ave. Suite D27
New York, NY, 10001

ISBN-10: 1-949180-97-2
ISBN-13: 978-1-949180-97-8

Printed in the United States of America

To Kris, Anna, and Sarah – the loves of my life

Prologue

"There is neither happiness nor misery in the world. There is only the comparison of one state with the other, nothing more. He who has felt the deepest grief is best able to experience supreme happiness. We must have felt what it is to die that we may be able to appreciate the enjoyments of life."

– Alexander Dumas

"What comes next?" he wondered aloud, his words rolling into each other.

A disheveled looking man of averages with wavy dark brown hair flecked with grey, William Cameron MacCrarey swayed gently back and forth as he stood barefoot and staring out his sliding patio door. Behind him, a half-empty bottle of Bombay Sapphire gin and an empty vial of something with a part chemistry, part marketing name sat on a coffee table. The books on the shelves lining the walls of the living room were mainly historical novels, contemporary thrillers, and non-fiction tomes on western philosophy, religions, and history. A few impressionist prints hanging between the shelves broke the chromatic monotony of the room's black-lacquer furniture and gray carpet.

He let the tumbler he'd just emptied fall from his hand before sliding open the door and stepping out onto the deck. The cold evening breeze swirled about his pale face and sent a shiver through his torso. Stumbling towards the railing, he gazed out at the ridge of hills on the far side of Traverse Bay and then at the countless stars firing up for their nightly run. It had always been his dream to have a home overlooking the bay. But with the loneliness and mounting disappointment he struggled with day in and day out, the house might as well have been in the middle of the bleakest desert or endless prairie.

He tried to cut through the thickening fog in his mind with a shake of his head, but time was against him now. "How many people lose hope?" he asked the stars. "How many decide that life is so difficult…or disappointing that death becomes a release…for them…a place where they can finally find peace?" His words and thoughts were slowing down, and his limbs were growing heavy. "Wasn't there something…something else I was…supposed to do with my life?" He tried to steady himself but his legs buckled and he fell to his knees. "Wasn't I destined…to be something more? Wasn't there a reason…a purpose for me…being here?"

Mozart's Requiem Mass in D minor was playing through its final movement on the CD player in the living room as he grabbed hold of the railing and tried to pull himself up. But, it was no use. Staring out through the bars at the black, quiet water of the bay, he wondered, "Would death…be black and quiet? Will the end…be painful? Will I…even know…when it comes?" A tear ran down his cheek as he laid back onto the deck, arms outstretched. "I guess…no one has a choice…who…or what… they are." His breathing slowed, and a sense of peace began to envelope him. He closed his eyes knowing it would soon be over…no more pain, no more disappointment, no more losing…

An explosion of light tore through his mind, and swirling flashes of color danced around him. He felt as if he were being lifted off the deck and something akin to a rush of adrenaline coursed through his body. At once the night became day. Billowy clouds filled the sky and weeping willows, pines, and elms materialized around him, swaying in the yards of turn-of-the-century houses. He knew at once where he was – two hundred miles away from his deck in Traverse…and nearly forty years in the past. He was watching his childhood self playing outside the house of Mrs. Lee with her son, Robbie, who would become a lifelong friend. Not yet seven years old, Mac – his nickname for as long as he could remember – was laughing and running about without a care in the world, while Mrs. Lee sat on the front porch steps rocking a baby carriage back and forth.

Adult Mac slowly turned around. Three other small, two-story houses crowded around the gravel cul-de-sac of the dead-end street, including his childhood home, already the worse for wear. It sat in the middle of a larger block of similar houses, which, in turn, was part of the working-class neighborhood north of the railroad tracks in Downers Grove, Illinois. Then, he turned to look down the lonely street to where it ended at a busy intersection. That's where it happened…where it would happen again…soon.

"Mac! Mac! Where are you?" his four-year-old brother Clark called from the next street over.

"I'm at Robbie's!" little Mac yelled back. Clark didn't answer and soon, lost in play, Mac forgot all about him.

"No!" adult Mac shouted. "Go get him!" But, his six-year-old self didn't hear. These were but shadows of things that had been, and the events written in the book of time would once again play themselves out.

A siren began echoing through the neighborhood, urgently growing louder, and soon flashing lights appeared at the end of the street. Mrs. Lee herded the boys together and headed off with the carriage to join a knot of onlookers. Little Mac and Robbie slowly rode their bikes down the street, unsure of what to make of the commotion and too young to be scared.

Then, Mrs. Lee gasped and raised her hand to her mouth. "It's Clark!" she cried.

Little Mac looked over at her and then turned to see what she was staring at. There, in the middle of the intersection sat a car...and under it lay his brother. Without a word, little Mac swung his bike around and peddled as fast as he could back to his house.

A moment later, adult Mac was standing in the kitchen of his childhood home.

"Mom!" little Mac screamed as he burst through the back door. His mother met him in the doorway between the kitchen and the dining room. "Clark got hit by a car!" he cried.

Without a word, she put her arms around him. Mac watched his young self wrap his arms around his mother in turn, but noticed something curious, something he hadn't noticed back then.

She didn't cry or ask how and where. She didn't say anything at all, she just held her child — who would recall the last few minutes nearly every day for the rest of his life — and stared straight ahead, her face emotionless.

In the living room came the voice of Dan Rather on the TV, "President Ronald Reagan was shot today as he was leaving the Washington Hilton hotel..."

The kitchen faded away and a stream of vignettes from his school days played out around him, one quickly morphing into the next. Many were of a small, quiet boy observing others, trying to be invisible, afraid of being wrong or laughed at. Others were of schoolmates and playgrounds, Sunday school and classrooms. Then, there were those of his parents – his father drinking his scotch in an arm chair in front of the TV after dinner, his mother scolding him again and again for not doing something the way she wanted it done, and one of him brimming with pride and hope as he showed her his report card filled with A's yet again. Knowing what came next, adult Mac's heart sank. His mother took the card out of his hand, gave it a once over, and without a word handed it to his father. Taking it from her hand, he tossed it in the wastepaper basket without so much as a glance on his way to the cupboard where he kept the scotch.

Mac never showed them a report card again.

A moment later, he found himself standing in a cemetery on a sunny summer's day. Beside him was his 17-year-old self staring down at Clark's gravestone. Engraved on it were the words, 'He wanted to see God.' In young Mac's mind, a mix of emotions swirled about – sadness, frustration, anger, guilt. A four-year-old wouldn't want to see God. He wouldn't have wanted to die. It was his fault Clark was killed. He should have gone to get him when he called, he could have kept Clark from running out into the street.

Again, the kitchen of his childhood home formed around him. He heard the sound of a car door slamming, footsteps on the back stairs, the screen door opening, and in walked young Mac. He spied a letter addressed to him on the yellow Formica table and yelled, "Mom?" as he picked up the envelope. He noted there was no return address as he tore open the envelope and slid out a single piece of parchment-like paper. 'Dear Mac,' it began, 'I hope that you will be pleased to know that

I've arranged for you to attend the University of Michigan this Fall. Arrive no later than August 25th. Your major is up to you, but we have taken care of your tuition, room, and board. I and the Clan are very proud of you.' The letter was signed, 'K.D.'

Young Mac noticed a presence and looked up to see his mother standing in the kitchen doorway, exactly where she'd held him all those years before when he'd told her about Clark. She stared at him, arms crossed, as he held the letter.

"You're on your own now," she said coldly and turned away. Tears welled up in his eyes, but a quick shake of his head and wipe of his sleeve sent them away. By nightfall, he'd packed what little he had in a beat up '68 Mustang and, without saying good-bye or leaving a note, walked out of his home – and his childhood – forever.

He got into the car and turned the key. The engine roared and at once the Mustang faded away. In its place formed the front porch of his high school sweetheart's home. Crickets chirped and fireflies floated about in the warm thick evening air. The two of them were facing each other, holding hands, and young Mac was telling her he'd be leaving for Ann Arbor in the morning.

"I'll come home on weekends," he promised her, wiping a tear from her cheek and trying to make his words sound heartfelt. She'd be a senior that fall. He'd be two states away and now there was no place for him to come home to.

"I love you," she whispered.

"I love you," he said softly. He did love her, and he'd miss her terribly, but it had to be this way. Besides, he knew, she'd be better off without him.

He never saw her again.

The porch replaced itself with a stage and it took adult Mac a few moments to realize he was at his college graduation.

It was customary for the Engineering School's honor society president to give the commencement speech and in the fall young Mac had been elected. From stage left, he peaked around the curtain to scan the audience for his parents. He'd barely spoken to them in four years, yet he'd written to tell them when and where the commencement would be. They'd not replied, nor were they there. The all-too-familiar feelings of sadness and undefined guilt welled up, but he was getting quite good at shunting away his emotions. The Dean began introducing him from the podium and the stage morphed into the sidewalk outside West Quad.

His roommates Mark and Duron had just finished helping him pack up the Mustang. Everything he owned in the world was inside it, and in his wallet was all the money he had – forty-dollars – and a nearly maxed-out credit card.

"I'll write when I find a place," he told them as he hugged each goodbye and got into his car. Waving as he drove off, he pushed Van Halen's *1984* into the cassette player.

A letter sat on the seat next to him. It was written on the same parchment as the one four years earlier and read, 'Dear Mac, you've done very well at university, as I and the Clan were confident you would! I hope you will be pleased to know that you have been enrolled in the master's program at Harvard University. You'll be staying at Kennedy Hall, classes begin July 7th and your major, as before, is up to you. Also, as before, your tuition, room, and board will be taken care of. Good luck, lad.' Once again it was signed, 'K.D.,' and the envelope it came in had no return address.

The music rolled out of the speakers and faded away as the car reconstituted itself into a table and wooden chairs, and the blue sky and buildings on either side of the street became the cathedral-like graduate library he'd spent many an hour studying in.

Young Mac was reading a history textbook, elbows on the table and head in hands, his knees pumping anxiously up and down. Older Mac remembered well the discomfort he'd felt that day. It wasn't the first time either that his readings made him uneasy, and it wouldn't be the last. The humanities and philosophy classes he'd taken in undergrad made him feel as though the warm, mental cocoon of his youth was being ripped open, and for the first time he was seeing the world for what it was. The calming beliefs he'd learned in primary school, at home, and in church were being challenged with every turn of the page. Had everyone – teachers, parents, minister, even friends – purposely misled him? Had they simply chosen to believe what made them comfortable and ignored the rest? Or had they never learned the things he was learning? Whatever the answer, it seemed to him that mankind was capable of great cruelty and self-delusion, that every aspect of life could be rationally explained, that what people mistook for truth was relative, that maybe there was no greater purpose to life, and that there was no One watching out for us.

The bookshelves and arched ceiling rushed towards him and suddenly he was sitting at a tiny kitchen table in his Cambridge apartment. Young Mac and his roommates, Damon and Dwight, sat around the table, beers in hand, staring at two pieces of paper. Damon was enrolled in the Engineering College, and Dwight was writing his political science thesis.

The parchment-like letter read, 'Dear Mac, Congratulations on graduating with honors! I have arranged for you to enter the PhD program at Oxford University. A British Airways ticket will be waiting for you at Logan Airport September 1st, and Dr. Robert Helmbold shall be your doctoral advisor. However, should you choose to begin your career, we have also secured a position for you with the firm of Dumas & Dickens of London. Whatever your choice, I know you'll do well. We are, as always, very proud of you, lad! K.D."

"Who's we?" Dwight asked.

"Don't have a clue," young Mac answered.

"Who's K.D.?" asked Damon.

"No idea," Mac admitted.

Damon chuckled as Dwight asked, "What are you gonna do?"

Young Mac sighed. "I think I'm tired of being a student… and being broke."

Damon, who was working on his third bachelor's degree and had little interest in gainful employment, said with a grin and a swig of beer, "What's wrong with being a college student?"

"Living like one," young Mac answered with a wry smile, picking up the other sheet of paper. "I've been offered a position as a management and technology consultant. Apparently, the managing partner of Dumas & Dickens is 'a friend of the Clan,' whatever that means."

"The Klan?" Dwight, who was African-American, exclaimed, grabbing for the letter. "You're getting mixed up with the KKK?"

"No. Clan with a 'C' not a 'K,'" Mac chuckled.

"So," Dwight said absently as he scanned the piece of paper, "stay in school and get your PhD, or join the real world and make some bread."

Mac nodded thoughtfully, breathed in, and sighed again. "The real world," and at once the table changed its shape and hue as the kitchen morphed into a coffee shop just off Michigan Avenue in downtown Chicago. There he'd spent many an evening and weekend afternoon sitting at a corner café table doing paperwork.

The bell above the door jingled and an attractive woman with a little girl of maybe three or four walked in. Younger

Mac had seen them there many times and noticed the mother didn't wear a wedding ring. She always ordered the same two drinks, a caramel latte and a hot chocolate. Younger Mac had indeed become quite the observer as the years went by, and less the participant. He was the audience watching the players on stage act out their lives.

The drinks were ordered and while they waited for them to be made, the mother smiled at the younger Mac. He smiled back and quickly returned to his paperwork.

Taking the drinks from the barista, she guided her daughter towards the door and turned around to push it open with her backside. She caught Mac watching her and smiled again as the bell jingled. Then they were gone. He slid his paperwork away as regret and relief fought for the high ground of his mind. How safe and small his life was getting – hardly seeing his friends anymore, no love interest to speak of, 60-hour work weeks, the idealism and passions of his younger days abandoned – and then everything went black.

Mac heard the faint tinny sound of music. A bedside lamp turned on and a Mac looking much like him rolled over in bed and pressed the snooze on the clock radio. The glowing green digits read 5:30. Outside it was still pitch black and the windowsill was dusted with snow. A dream of his high school sweetheart faded from his mind and the dread of another day rushed in to fill the void, another lonely stretch of time watching everyone else live their lives until he could come home and crawl back into bed.

The room flooded with sunlight and a rush of noise. When his eyes adjusted, Mac realized he was standing in the carnival midway of the Cherry Festival in Traverse City. It was hot and humid, and rides and game booths stretched along the beach in both directions. Grown-ups passed by laughing and talking while children and teenagers ran this way and that. The sun was high above the bay and sailboats crisscrossed the water all the way out to Lake Michigan. The smell of popcorn, cotton candy, and elephant ears carried on the warm breeze as his younger self meandered through the fair watching everyone and everything. Ever the detached but eager observer, the world was a theater in 360 and he was an audience of one.

Older Mac realized what was about to happen and smiled. He turned expectantly and there she was. Genevieve, talking and laughing with her friends as they tried their luck at a nearby game booth. The breeze from the bay was gently blowing her long auburn hair about her shoulders, the sky matched the blue of her eyes, and the copper sundress she wore perfectly accentuated her shapely figure.

In that fleeting moment, he could feel the essence of his life returning.

Beside him, younger Mac stood dumbly staring until she began to move further along the midway with her friends. Instead of his usual cautious analysis and decisive inaction, he ran to the nearest fresh-squeezed lemonade stand, ordered two, and before the cups could touch the stainless-steel counter, grabbed them and ran off, leaving a $20 bill behind.

When he was within a few steps of her, he stopped and collected himself, trying to look as cool and casual as his racing heart would allow. He tapped her on the shoulder and when she turned around, he handed her a lemonade and said, "Hi. I'm Mac," a bit too business-like he decided. Her smile said this sort of thing happened to her all the time, and the way she said, "I'm Genevieve," told him he didn't have long to prove himself. So, he started up a conversation, suggested a stroll along the midway, and they ended up talking and laughing until afternoon became evening. They found a romantic dockside bistro and afterwards took a bottle of wine and two plastic cups to the beach and watched the sun set over the bay.

Scenes from the few precious years he spent with her played out until he was standing in the foyer of his condo on a rainy evening and Genevieve was walking out the door for the last time.

The latch clicked behind her and at once Mac was lying on the deck.

But, something was different this time. Not the past, for the only aspects of the past that can change are our perception and acceptance of it. Yet, despite all the sadness and loss, hopelessness and disappointment, he sensed a vague feeling of...

The same brilliant, dazzling light exploded in his mind and gradually dispersed into a vibrant, swirling rainbow that gelled into still more scenes from his past. The first was of a very young Mac lying on a blanket next to Robbie in the back yard late on a spring night. Side by side they stared up into the heavens, and young Mac wondered if anyone was staring back. There had to be someone, he decided, there just had to be. If only he could find out who...

The night sky lit up and a moment later he was playing in the school yard with Clark. Butterflies flitted about, songbirds sang in the trees, and a train whistle sounded in the distance. School was out for the summer and they had the whole playground to themselves. It felt as if they had all the time in the world together...

The sky closed in around him and soon he was standing in the gym of his high school. The teacher was taking attendance on the first day of spring term. He looked around to see who else he knew. "Hey, who's that?" he said to Robbie, pointing at a cute blonde wearing a t-shirt and shorts, and talking animatedly with a clutch of friends. "That's Ricky's kid sister, Cheryl," Robbie said. Then, the highlights of Mac's time with her played out – their first date at a Baskins-Robbins; their first slow dance at homecoming; walking in the park near downtown holding hands; saying "I love you!" for the first time; going to a late-night show at the theater on Main Street; learning to make love in her bedroom…

The walls and ceiling of the room dissolved into a white mist. A cool breeze came up and carried it away to reveal Mac's not-so-much-younger self standing on a dock. He was sipping steaming coffee from a handmade ceramic mug he'd purchased from an artsy little shop on Mackinac Island. It was early on a clear, chilly morning, and stretching out in front of him was a small northern Michigan lake. The remnants of the white mist lazily wafted over the water and a lone seagull cried as it flew low searching for its breakfast…

The trees around the lake rushed forward and became the walls of a dimly lit living room and a crackling fireplace. A Christmas tree stood in the corner complete with twinkling lights and presents underneath, and the scent of pine needles hung in the air. The holidays were his favorite time of year – great food, visiting with friends, time off from work, carols on the radio, Scrooge on DVD, driving through neighborhoods of homes decorated for the season, the ball dropping in Times Square, Auld Lange Syne playing at midnight…

The room faded into a night sky and he was standing on a stretch of beach. The smell of burning wood from a nearby campfire came and went with the breeze rolling off the great lake. Waves lapped onto the beach and slowly rolled back into the black lake. Several old friends of his were sitting on blankets looking up at the stars, laughing and clapping. Plastic wine glasses and open coolers sat on the sand. Shooting stars streaked overhead and the shimmering northern lights arched above the horizon…

The dome of the sky brightened, and Mac was standing just inside his patio door looking out at a doe and fawn eating apples off the tree in his back yard. Beyond was the dark blue bay framed by hills colored with the many-hued leaves of fall. He motioned for Genevieve to follow him and quietly slid open the door. Stepping onto the deck, he breathed in the earthy scent of burning leaves and felt Genevieve's hand slip into his...

Once more the sky darkened, and he found himself alone, lying on his deck as Mozart's Requiem finished playing. The cold wind rolling up the hill from the bay and over the deck cut through the haze of booze and pills. He could feel again the crushing loneliness and disappointment that had driven him to the edge, yet he sensed they no longer held sway over him, and that maybe, just maybe, this time he'd be alright.

The reds and yellows and oranges of dawn appeared along the horizon, and with them came...not so much as hope, he decided, but of...of longing. Longing for the passion of mind and spirit, of life and companionship.

And he sensed he wasn't alone anymore.

1

"I have a creed…the way to be happy is to make others so."

— Robert Ingersoll

*"Until God grants us the ability to read the future, all human
wisdom is contained in these two words: wait and hope."*

— Alexander Dumas

Dr. Angela Fuentes gazed out at the gray waters of the icy bay
and the words of Melville came back to her – "Those grand
fresh-water seas of ours possess an ocean-like expansiveness.
They yield their beaches to wild barbarians, whose red painted
faces flash from out their peltry wigwams. They know what
shipwrecks are, for out of sight of land, however inland, they
have drowned full many a midnight ship with all its shrieking
crew."

She sighed. There may be no ebbing of tides, no grand
worldly currents, yet there is still something of the seas in the
Great Lakes. Sitting at her usual table in the beach-side café,
she glanced at the mounds of broken ice pushed up onto the
shore by the winds and waves. How odd, she thought, that in a

few short months they'd be gone and, in their place, would be sandy beaches, lapping water, volleyball nets, and sunbathers. She sighed again and looked back down at the papers and case files strewn about her table.

Sandra the waitress brought more coffee and another cinnamon roll to the table. "Thought this might help," she said. Looking at the papers and folders, she added, "Another long Saturday afternoon, huh, Dr. Fuentes?"

Angela nodded and said, "Please, Sandy, call me Angela."

She smiled. "Anything else…Angela?" A shake of the doctor's head and a warm smile told her no. "Okay. Just let me know if you do," Sandra said as she headed for one of the other occupied tables.

Angela glanced about the café, a popular hangout in the summer, which was now nearly empty. "Back to work," she sighed and opened the next case file.

The name printed on the tab read 'William Cameron MacCrarey,' but everyone at the hospital called him by his nickname, Mac. She scanned the medical report and her case notes – overdose, possible suicide attempt, brought to the State Hospital two weeks ago after being found at his home unconscious, remanded into her department's custody for observation by the court, declined meds, lives alone, one of the brightest patients she'd ever treated, even a step ahead of her at times. She pulled a blank release form out of her satchel, set it on the table, and looked out the window again. There was no medical reason not to release him, Angela knew, but still she hesitated.

He hasn't let anyone visit him at the hospital, doesn't want to go back to work, nothing interests him besides his books and their subject matter tends to be heavier than I'd recommend for someone suspected of attempted suicide.

She considered extending Mac's observation period but dismissed the idea. The Hospital's budget had been cut time and again in recent years. The state had fallen into the hands of a political party who'd begun dismantling the government without regard for the consequences. One of the first programs to go was the state's Department of Mental Health. Funding levels were slashed and every state hospital but one – Traverse City's – had closed practically overnight. The assumption was that non-profits and churches would take over the care of mentally ill residents. But, what actually happened was the population of county jails and state prisons rose to capacity, drug and alcohol addiction levels soared, and suicide rates quadrupled.

So, it was nearly impossible for Angela to provide every patient with the mental health care they deserved. "Stabilize and release," was the policy – her staff cynically called it, "Drug 'em and shove 'em" – and in this case, it meant the hospital wouldn't allow her to keep someone like Mac a moment longer than they had to.

Sandy dropped the check on the doctor's table as she whisked by.

Angela closed Mac's file, picked up her pen, and began filling out the release form.

The speed of sound, Mach One, and Merrill MaGeah could barely feel a shudder. He took a sip of champagne from a crystal glass and marveled again at being on a private supersonic luxury jet. This was way beyond his means by the coin, but the Clan had wealthy friends. After learning of William Cameron MacCrarey's attempted suicide two weeks before, Michael Abrams placed his jet at the Clan's disposal.

Merrill had convinced the Clan Elders the time had come, and they'd entrusted him with the mission. In a millennium-and-a-half, the Elders had never been so bold, but they understood how critical it was to protect Mac.

He took a deep breath and let it out. "The lad's not going to take this well, I'm sure of that."

The supersonic jet proceeded along its Arctic-arch toward America. The champagne made him feel warm, though all Merrill could see out the cabin window was dark blue water, ice flows, and the craggy, snow covered coast of Greenland.

He wondered what the weather would be like in Traverse.

Built at the turn of the last century, the old State Hospital had that look of sinister intent and unseemly things. Its two-dozen buildings were once set in the countryside on two hilly, tree-covered square miles of land west of Traverse. At one time there'd been a farm, stables, an orchard, a steam plant, a railway spur, a water tower, cottages for staff, a dining hall and kitchen – everything necessary to be completely self-sufficient. Now there were only a handful of buildings housing patients with every conceivable form of mental illness, and the campus was completely surrounded by neighborhoods and industrial parks. On its southeast side near US-31 was the newly constructed Traverse Bay Medical Center, a primary care hospital with an emergency room that had received William Cameron MacCrarey late one evening two weeks before.

Just after eight o'clock Monday morning, Angela walked into the anteroom of her office in the campus' administration building and without so much as a, "Good morning," or a smile, Gertrude Van Theiss – the frumpy, 59-year-old administrative assistant the hospital had assigned Angela – tossed a handful of messages at her boss of eight months.

"Thanks," Angela said perfunctorily as she walked into her office.

She dropped her purse in an empty file drawer behind her desk and leafed through the messages.

"Gert," she called out, "do we know who this Merrill MaGeah is?"

"No, we do not," Gert replied curtly.

Angela rolled her eyes. This was her first position since her residency, giving her the least seniority among the medical staff and the worst secretary.

"Does he want a psych consult?"

"We do not know."

Angela looked up at the empty doorway, "Do we know anything?"

"You're the shrink," Gert snapped.

Angela shook her head, flipped open her schedule book and said, "I have a cancellation at eleven. Schedule him in then…please," then threw the message slip away.

Curiosity, however, was not so easily discarded.

"Senator, your grandfather is on the phone," Gerald, his man Friday, said from the doorway to the mansion's darkly paneled and well-appointed study.

Jack Abrams waved him away and reached over to the end table next to his overstuffed leather chair and picked up the receiver. "Good morning, grandfather."

"Good morning, Jack," Michael Abrams replied as though talking with a business partner. "Listen, I want you to meet with an old friend of mine, a Clan Elder named Merrill MaGeah. It's important that you two talk before the confirmation hearings."

Closing his eyes and trying to keep calm, the younger Abrams muttered, "Damned Clan," under his breath. He was tired of his powerful grandfather meddling in his affairs of state and believing in that ridiculous Clan fantasy.

"Grandfather, if this is about the position you brought up last week, the White House already sent my committee a nominee –"

"I made a few calls," the elder Abrams said dismissively. "The White House has, shall we say, reconsidered their decision and withdrawn their nominee's name from further consideration."

Senator Abrams jumped up from the chair, his anger rising. "I…you…Ambassador Tanner will be furious!"

Ignoring the expected outburst, Michael said simply, "Dulles, 3 PM, Hangerover Bar. Merrill will be there with a man named William Cameron MacCrarey. Be respectful to him…very respectful. Is that understood?"

The Senator sighed and closed his eyes again. "Yes, sir," he said through clenched teeth, tightening his fist around the receiver.

Mac closed the door behind him and sat down.

"Where's Earl?" he asked, referring to the orderly who'd escorted him to and from the doctor's office for the past two weeks. "I waited but he never showed up."

Angela held out the signed release form. "The state says you're free to go, so it doesn't make much sense to treat you like a patient anymore, now does it?"

Mac suspected as much. "No…I guess not." He hesitated before getting to his feet and taking the form. "So, I just –"

"There's always Genevieve," Angela suggested.

Mac looked down at the floor.

"You know she came to visit you. Several times. Why didn't you see her?"

"It's better for her to be out of my life. That's why she left me."

Angela sighed. This wasn't her fight anymore. "You have a visitor," she said resignedly.

Looking up anxiously, Mac asked, "It isn't –?"

"No, it's not Genevieve," Angela assured him as she stood. "Your visitor is someone I hadn't met until today, and neither have you. But, I think you'll want to see him. If I'd been a writer instead of a psychiatrist, I doubt I could've written a better story than the one he has to tell."

She held out her hand and he took it. "Come by and let me know how you're doing, okay?"

"Uh…yeah. Sure," Mac said. He gave her a weak smile and turned for the door.

He found the bleak, sparsely furnished visitor's room with its worn-out orange carpet, yellowed plaster walls, and humming fluorescent lights. He spied a man who looked to be in his mid-fifties, a bit overweight, and with a somewhat rumpled appearance. His wavy salt-and-pepper hair hung down to the collar of his white Oxford shirt, over which he wore a dark brown wool sweater and a tan Harris Tweed jacket that together with his khaki pants and loafers gave him a rather professorial look.

"Sit down, lad," the stranger told him, gesturing casually to the plastic chair across the dingy white table from him.

Mac hesitated but did as he was asked. "So, you have a story to tell me, huh?"

"Aye. That I do," the visitor replied with a smile.

Mac knitted his brow, trying to place the accent. "Scotland?" he asked.

"Not a bad guess. Me sainted mother was from Melrose, not far from Hadrian's Wall. But I'm from England…like you, laddy."

"You're misinformed…whoever you are."

"My name is Merrill MaGeah, and 'tis *you* who are misinformed."

"Look, Mr. MaGeah, I don't want to waste your time or mine, so since you obviously have the wrong guy, I'll just be –"

"No, I don't, and I know more about who you are and where y'are from than you do."

Mac shook his head slowly and began to stand up. "You don't know a damned thing about me or my life, pal, so if you'll excuse me –"

"Sit down and take that bloody chip off your shoulder. You ended up here because you think life's been rough on you, eh? Well, isn't that too bad. I've met men and women from your own family who faced the end of *everything* they knew and loved and *still* refused to give up. Air raids night after night, V-1 attacks, sons and fathers coming home in coffins –"

"Look, mister," Mac interrupted, still half-standing, "I don't know who the hell you think you are, telling me about my family, but my relatives are all from Chicago, so why don't you –"

"I'm talking about your *real* family. Back in England. Your biological parents died when you were a wee lad. That's when we gave you to the MacCrarey's."

Mac fell back into his chair, his eyes never leaving the visitor's. His mind raced, struggling with the enormity of what this stranger had just said. "You…you gave me to my…they never said anything about…you're saying…I'm adopted?"

"Well," Merrill answered sheepishly, "you weren't really adopted by the MacCrarey's. We didn't want any records of your whereabouts."

"Why?" Mac said, still in a daze. "And who's 'we?'"

"All in good time, lad," Merrill replied, glancing at his watch. "Right now, we've a flight to catch, so go get your things. We'll have plenty of time to talk on the plane."

"I walked in here, what, two minutes ago and in that time you've said I'm someone I'm not, told me you arranged things you couldn't have, and now you're telling me to get on a plane with you? Forget it!"

"You're no ordinary man, laddy," Merrill MaGeah said quite matter-of-factly, standing up. "I suspect, deep down inside, you know that. Y'are about to learn why." He grabbed his overcoat. "I'll meet you out front," and with that, he walked out of the visitor's room.

Without once looking back over his shoulder, Merrill strode purposefully towards the main entrance. Reaching the door, he held it open for a slim attractive woman in a long black overcoat. She had big brown eyes, alabaster skin, and straight black hair down to the middle of her back. "Thanks," she said distractedly as she stared at her phone and passed through.

"A gentleman always holds a door open for a lady," he grinned. With a quick glance back, she gave him a curious smile and continued on. Merrill walked out and called to his cabbie. "Let's get a cup of tea, lad. Me mate has to pack."

A stirring in her lap drew Genevieve Boujeau's attention back to the present. Looking down at her sleeping daughter, not yet three days old, she whispered, "Cameron Kristine –" and a tear trickled down her cheek. She glanced at the unfinished birth certificate form on the nightstand beside her hospital bed, gave a sad sigh and said, "– MacCrarey. Cameron Kristine MacCrarey. You should have your father's last name."

Looking out the window at the gently falling snow, she said softly, "I'll take you to meet him someday, Cameron… someday."

Someone knocked on the open door to the room. "Hey, you."

She looked up to see her best friend Stacey walking in. The long winter months had faded her summer tan and the whiteness of her face and long black hair emphasized her pretty brown eyes. Genevieve, in contrast, had wavy shoulder-length auburn hair and bright blue eyes. "Hey," she said, wiping the tears from her cheeks.

Stacey crossed the room and wrapped her arms around mother and daughter just as the maternity ward nurse came through the door with a wheelchair.

"Ready to go home, sweetie?" cooed Stacey, brushing Cameron's cheek with her fingers.

Handing her the baby, Genevieve picked up the pen and finished filling out the birth certificate. Handing it to the nurse, she gingerly transferred herself from the bed to the wheelchair. "I can't believe I'm a mom," she said, her voice quavering.

"You'll be a great mom," Stacey assured her, a mother of two herself with her partner, "and you're not alone. Remember that, okay?"

Genevieve took Cameron from her and, as the nurse wheeled them out into the hallway, said, "I know you'll be there, but –"

"You're not alone," Stacey repeated, "and you'll meet some great guy soon who loves babies and who's crazy about you and you'll wonder why you ever worried about a thing."

Genevieve tried to give her friend a brave smile. "But…he won't be Mac."

Stacey nodded, trying to think of what to say next. "Well…no, but…maybe that's a good thing, you know? I mean…he was kinda not there at the end."

"I still love him," Genevieve whispered.

"I know, sweetie. I know."

They passed the visitor's room where two men were drinking tea from Styrofoam cups, and exited through the main doors. The nurse took Cameron while Stacey helped her friend into the back seat of her idling car. Kissing the baby's forehead, the nurse said her good-byes and handed Cameron back to her mother.

As Stacey walked around to the driver's side, Genevieve fiddled around with the baby seat trying to make heads or tails of the straps and latches. "You'll be home soon, my darling daughter, and we'll have a wonderful life together…just you and me," she said as the tears came again.

Merrill finished his tea as he stood watching the flat screen TV mounted on the wall.

"A ceremony was held today," a stunningly beautiful reporter with auburn hair, large brown eyes, and shapely figure was saying, "in Cross Junction, Virginia. The Reverend Johnny Swaywell broke ground for Williams Jennings Bryan College, an evangelical Christian school named after the famous lawyer, three-time presidential candidate, and chief prosecutor in the Scopes Monkey Trial." The caption said the reporter's name was Jan Roberts.

Jan had worked her way through a BA degree from the University of Michigan's School of Journalism ten years earlier by taking modeling gigs on weekends in Chicago and summers in L.A.

The picture on the screen switched to a broad valley framed by the rolling, tree-covered Appalachians. "Plans for the campus resemble a small city, complete with lecture halls and office buildings, residence dorms, restaurants, libraries, stores, a hotel, and a new 10,000-seat cathedral for Swaywell's Church of Eternal Vigilance. Its total cost is a closely held secret, though it's rumored to exceed a billion dollars."

Merrill spied Mac, garment bag slung over his shoulder, crossing the lobby. He smiled to himself and called out, "Here lad." A moment later, Mac was standing beside him. "You'd better watch this," the Elder told him.

"Here's what the Reverend had to say during the groundbreaking," Jan Roberts was saying, and the screen switched to a video of a portly, well-groomed middle-aged man wearing an expensive charcoal gray suit and red silk tie. He was walking purposefully up to an outdoor podium waving and smiling at the hundreds of people who'd gathered for the ceremony. But, no sooner had he adjusted the microphone than his brilliant smile faded away. "This is America today, my friends," he boomed, his words spoken with a sing-song southern drawl. "Pornography, abortion, homosexuality, the liberal media, the ACLU, a Jew-controlled economy, Blacks shooting Whites, drug abuse, activist judges, illegal immigrants flooding across our borders, pagan Muslims killing God-fearing Americans, and public schools conspiring with secular humanists." He paused to look at his audience. "That sounds kinda nice, doesn't it? Secular humanism. But, don't be fooled by the name! It's atheism pure and simple, and the god of atheists is Charles Darwin. Its cathedrals are lecture halls and classrooms and government buildings. It preaches that we e-volved, that we're not moral and spiritual beings, but *animals.* Its sinister mission is to destroy our culture, our families, and our country, and take over our government, the UN, the media, and everything else necessary to control the minds of our people!"

Applause and shouts of "Amen" could be heard from the crowd.

"Don't be fooled about the Constitution of the United States either. We're not beholden to a federal government. We're beholden to God. We're not bound by the Bill of Rights. We're bound by the Ten Commandments. We're not free to say or do or believe what we want. Only God is! There's no separation of church and state, only a separation of good and evil. Our nation was founded by persecuted White men who wanted to create a Christian country in a new world, and it's time to retake that nation and place it back into Jesus' hands!"

More applause and cheers of encouragement.

"Joseph Stalin had it right when he said, 'Death solves all problems. No man, no problem,' and purged his country of evil doers."

Some in the audience laughed, others clapped.

"If you're a believer in Christ, then help evangelicals and conservative politicians *rid* America of evil doers. Impeach secular judges. Send abortionists to jail for what they're doing to God's babies. Send immigrants back to whatever third-world, Godforsaken hole they crawled out of. Ban evolutionary science and genetics. End welfare. Disband the U.S. Department of Education and Environmental Protection Agency. Terminate the broadcasting licenses of liberal TV and radio stations. Revoke the business licenses of liberal newspapers. End funding for PBS and NPR. And get the U.S. out of the United Nations!"

Enthusiastic cheers and a chorus of "Praise Jesus!" were his response.

"I am the messenger of God," he bellowed. "Hear me and believe! Lucifer is creating an evil, secular new world order. It's taking root in the United Nations General Assembly, the International Court of Justice, the World Bank, the Jew-infested International Monetary Fund…and one day there will be a world army…an army so vast that no single nation will dare stand up to it…an army led by Satan's spawn, the Evil One, the Antichrist foretold to us in the *Book of Revelations*."

Gasps and cries of "No!" rippled through the crowd.

His voice went suddenly calm and he continued, "There is good news as well, people, for *Revelations* tells us that the times we're living in today are the Tribulation and God's most glorious blessing, the Rapture, will soon be upon us." His hands and face turned to heaven and he cried, "Oh, come Jesus. Come!"

Music began playing, the choir behind him sang softly, and the Reverend bowed his head in prayer. "In the name of the Father, and of the Son, and of the Holy Spirit, I consecrate this ground so that all who teach and learn here shall forever be God's soldiers. Amen."

The TV turned off.

Merrill set the remote down on the dingy table next to his empty tea cup. With a worrisome shake of his head, he gestured for the cabbie to bring the car up and said to Mac, "Let's go, lad. We've a long trip ahead of us."

Walking into Traverse International Airport was to walk back in time. The one-story terminal was small and looked as though it could have been the setting for an old black and white film. There was a small waiting room, two ticket counters, and a window wall with double doors leading outside to the tarmac. On the far side of the solitary runway sat two, old hangers — one for a coast guard search and rescue helicopter, the other for commuter jets. It was deemed 'international' only by virtue of its proximity to the Canadian border.

William Cameron MacCrarey had barely made it through the entrance when memories of a summer long ago came flooding back. He felt that all too familiar tightness in his chest and came to a stop. "I can't do this," he whispered.

Merrill, now several steps ahead of him, halted and turned around. "What is it, m'boy?"

"I...I was just remembering something...someone."

Merrill walked back to where Mac was standing. He gently placed his hand on Mac's shoulder, guiding him across the lobby and out onto the tarmac where the private jet was waiting.

"Please. Tell me about her, lad."

"Why do you assume it was a her?" Mac asked.

The Elder gave a chuckle and said, "Laddy, who else but a woman could pain a man's heart so?"

Mac nodded slowly. "Those are the first words out of your mouth I know for sure to be true, old man."

"Tell me about her, lad," said Merrill as he led his traveling companion up the steps into the plane's cabin. Merrill settled into an aisle seat and gestured for Mac to take the opposite one.

"I vacationed here for years," Mac began. "I flew in and out of this airport...I don't know how many times, but after that summer...coming here was never the same again."

"How so?" the Elder asked, pretending not to know.

"I flew in from New York — this was about four years ago — took a taxi to a friend's home where I have a 1968 Mustang stored in an old pole barn and drove into Traverse." He smiled sadly. "There's a narrow river that runs between downtown and the beach and empties into the bay. Beautiful blue-green water. Boaters weigh anchor just off shore in the summer time or moor along the river's boardwalk. Well, this day the Cherry Festival was going on downtown – carnival rides, game booths, food vendor stands. I can remember everything as if it happened yesterday. Not a cloud in the sky; hot and sticky; the clacking, throbbing sound of rides mixing with the screams and laughs of kids; the smell of caramel corn and cotton candy and elephant ears." He sighed. "Some days, you feel like life has you by the throat, but other days...other days you feel like life is the ripest, sweetest cherry you can imagine, waiting for you to pluck it from the tree. Well, that was one of those days, Merrill. I could have conquered the world."

Aye, Merrill thought to himself. Y'are closer to that than you think, lad.

"I noticed her – Genevieve, her name was Genevieve – with some friends at a game booth. Long hair, blue eyes, a copper sundress hugging her figure. I bought a couple fresh-squeezed lemonades, walked over, and handed her one." He paused, remembering.

The pilot stepped out of the cockpit to announce they'd be taking off momentarily, then grabbed the stair-door and pulled it up. The dull thump as it closed and the slight shudder of the cabin seemed to startle Mac back to the present. He looked around as if surprised he was on a plane. "What the hell am I doing here?" he grumbled. "I don't know you from Adam, for chrissakes. Forget this," and he started to get up.

Merrill gently took hold of his arm. "The first leg of our trip is a short flight, lad. I'll make a deal with you. I'll tell you about your family and me Clan, you tell me about Genevieve, and if you want to return to Traverse, so be it. I'll fly you back."

Mac hesitated, staring at the Elder. "This is nuts," he muttered, but slowly sat back down.

"Tell me about Genevieve and then I'll tell you me tale… and an incredible one it tis," Merrill smiled.

Mac sighed, gave a quick nod, and fastened his seatbelt. A few minutes later they were taxiing onto the runway.

"We walked and talked for hours," Mac began again, "had dinner, sat on the beach and watched the sun set…and I realized what love at first sight is." He turned and looked out the window. "It's meeting someone who makes you see how empty your life is."

Merrill nodded with a knowing smile. "Aye, laddy. That it is."

"We saw each other every day, went to movies together, had late-night drinks at beachside cafes, drove out to the wineries on the peninsula. From the moment she entered my life, I felt such…passion, such longing and…and hope." He sighed. "We dated for almost four years."

"Do you still love her?" Merrill asked, having already surmised the answer.

"Yes," Mac answered without hesitation, closing his eyes for a moment and running his fingers through his thick, wavy hair. "That was never the problem."

"Then what was?" the Elder asked, though he knew the answer.

A look of frustration and then anger crossed Mac's face. "Love wasn't enough. There was still an emptiness inside me. I'm not complete somehow…like I should have been something more, or…or done something else."

"Like what, laddy?"

Mac gave him an exasperated look. "I don't know. Written a novel, solved one of the mysteries of the ages, run for office, been a doctor. It's just that nothing quite seemed to fit, you know? I felt like my life had amounted to nothing and not even Genevieve could change that." He sighed again, his head falling into his open hands. "She must have sensed it and decided she wasn't enough…that she couldn't make me happy… like it was her responsibility or something." He shook his head, his face reflecting his guilt and sadness. "Eventually she started making excuses to spend time away, returned fewer and fewer of my calls…then one night she walked out of my life forever."

"We should have a smooth flight all the way to D.C., gentlemen," the Captain announced over the intercom. "Our total flight time should be one hour, 47 minutes."

"We're going to Washington?"

"We're going *home*, lad," answered Merrill.

"You're from Washington?" Mac asked incredulously.

Merrill chuckled. "No. My home. Your home, m'boy. *England.*"

"England," echoed Mac. "Yeah, right."

"You've been to London before. On business, I think."

Mac nodded, then caught himself. "Wait a minute. How do you –?"

"We've always kept an eye on you – and your brother, may he rest in peace – from a distance, of course. We had to let you make of yourself what you will, not what we might have wanted. You had to be free to develop your own convictions, make your own mistakes, develop your own sense of honor –"

"Why?"

"There's a greatness within you, Mac. You had to find that on your own…you still have to."

"I tried to kill myself," Mac rejoined. "There's no greatness in that. And if this 'we' you keep referring to chose to keep their distance, why are you here now?"

"Believe me, laddy, there were those who didn't want me to come. But, most did. They've a great deal of faith in you, as do I. Now it's me job to make sure you believe what I have to tell you." He nodded at the wet bar and unclicked his seat belt. "But, let's have a drink first, and you can tell me more about Genevieve."

2

Mac leaned against his 1968 red Mustang convertible in the rutted grassy driveway, looking up at the early evening sunlight as it fell through the leaves of maple and birch trees in a kinetic, kaleidoscopic wonder. Their intertwining branches formed a natural cavern of sorts above the driveway and century-old cottage. The screen door slammed against the wooden doorframe and Genevieve skipped down the steps. She was wearing a low-cut, knee-length black dress that accentuated every shapely curve of her figure, and her beautiful red hair cascaded about her shoulders.

"You look beautiful," Mac breathed, his words unintentionally conveying his awe and desire.

"Thank-you," she blushed, hugging him.

"I missed you," he said.

"We just saw each other last night," she giggled.

"Just? It feels like ages ago," he smiled, opening the car door for her and staring at her firm, tanned legs as she got in.

"Are you going to be able to keep your eyes on the road?" Genevieve teased.

Now it was Mac's turn to blush. "I'll try, but it'll be hard."

Genevieve giggled again. "I'm glad you like looking at me."

"That I do," Mac grinned and closed her door.

The half hour's drive to the Bower's Harbor Inn passed quickly by in enjoyable conversation and glances across Traverse Bay at the setting sun. Mac turned off the two-lane that ran along the west shore of Mission Point and into the semi-circular drive leading up to the old inn. After the valet drove off, the two of them stood there for a moment gazing out at the water as lightning bugs began to glow, crickets chirped, and ropes clapped in the breeze against the aluminum masts of sailboats anchored in the marina.

"It's so beautiful," Genevieve sighed.

"Yes," Mac agreed, turning to look at her, "but not as beautiful as you."

She smiled coyly, took his arm, and led him towards the front door. Mac held it open for her and she brushed against him as she walked in. The sweet, musky scent of her perfume and the warmth of her body, the way she looked at him and his feelings of awe crystallized in that moment into a realization that, without reservation and with a passion he'd never known before, he truly, deeply loved her. So much could be theirs if they were willing to risk their hearts. Was he willing to risk his? Was it even fair to tell her how he felt, knowing that he was leaving in the morning?

"What are you thinking?" Genevieve asked with a curious grin. She and the hostess stood in the foyer looking at Mac who suddenly realized he was still standing in the doorway.

Closing the door and walking towards them, he said, "How perfect tonight is."

"Mmmm, good answer," the hostess said with a smile as she started for the dining room.

"Could we sit by the window, so we can watch the sunset?" Mac asked as they followed.

"I think I can arrange that," the hostess said over her shoulder.

Dinner was wonderful, the conversation stimulating. Over dessert and coffee, Genevieve caught Mac staring at her again with a look she could only describe as amazement.

"Now what are you thinking?" she asked playfully.

"Sorry," he said with a self-conscious smile.

Not for staring, though. He was sorry for not answering with his heart. He absently picked up his coffee cup and swirled its contents around. Regret was already welling up in his mind. Without taking his eyes off the swirling suffusion, he said, "Actually…I was thinking about how my heart races whenever I see you walking towards me. How I have to remind myself to breathe when I'm around you. How I've found myself believing in happy endings for the first time." He took her hand. "And I've found myself believing in love."

The smile left Genevieve's face. She pulled her hand away and turned to look out the window. Mac felt his chest tightening. He'd gone too far, hadn't he? Opened up too much, hoped for too much. "Maybe I should…ask for the check and…we should call it an evening?" he said, hoping he was wrong.

Still looking out the window, she nodded.

Mac's heart sank. He looked around, spotted the waitress and waved her over. Genevieve rose from the table, walked to the foyer, and out the front door. Mac waited for the black leather folder to arrive, and without looking inside threw a handful of bills on the table, stood, and followed Genevieve outside.

The night sky was crystal clear and the breeze from the bay was moist and warm as they walked to the Mustang. He opened the door for her and turned to walk around the car when she grabbed his arm.

"Mac, we've only known each other two weeks," she said. Mac guessed what was coming next. "We've had a wonderful time. We've shared so much with each other, but…but I haven't shared everything with you. I've done things in my past I wish I hadn't." She let go of his arm and looked out at the bay. "Love…so soon. I've never –" she sighed. "Part of me wishes we'd never met. It frightens me to feel the way I do. You're so kind and funny and smart…and I feel so comfortable and content when we're together." She turned to look at him again "And you have the most beautiful blue eyes. But, what you said to me inside, it…I –"

Mac stepped closer. "Say what you feel," he whispered. A breeze came up and gently blew the hair back over her shoulders as a tear rolled down her cheek. "Say what you feel, Genevieve. Please."

Her eyes fell. She shook her head and got into the car. Silently, Mac turned and walked around the Mustang. He got in and drove around the looping drive to the road, turned left, and headed south.

The trees between the road and the beach would, from time to time, thin out just enough to see the lights of Traverse lining the edge of the water at the far end of the bay like a string of pearls on black satin. The night remained full of un-requited feelings and thoughts unarticulated while soft music drifted out of the CD player. Genevieve turned to look at Mac and he noticed the faint light from a nearly full moon catching the tears on her cheeks.

Without a word, he pulled the Mustang onto the sandy shoulder of the road. Shifting into park, he turned to look at her and as he did she leaned towards him, a tear falling from the soft curve of her chin, her warm full lips parting slightly. In that moment, there were no more walls, no risks too great, no holding back. Mac gently kissed her and whispered, "I love you, Genevieve."

The tears came again, but this time with a warm smile. "I love you, too," she said.

He wrapped his arms around her and whispered again, "I love you, Genevieve. I'll always love you."

"How fortunate I was, how rare it is to find what I found…how much I've lost since she left," Mac said as if to himself. "I'll always love her."

"We should be landing at Washington's Dulles Interna-tional Airport in about twenty minutes," the pilot announced over the intercom. "Please fasten your seat belts, gentlemen."

"So, why D.C.?" Mac asked, glad to change the subject.

"We have someone to visit," Merrill said, none too happily. "You mentioned she'd done things she wished she hadn't. What did she mean?"

Mac raised an eye brow. "A short answer wouldn't evoke the empathy she deserves. People tend to judge others too quickly. And the long explanation is, well, long."

Merrill glanced around the plane's cabin with a wry grin. "I'm not going anywhere you're not."

Mac smiled. "Alright, then. But, don't tell me I didn't warn you." After gathering his thoughts for a moment, he began, "Genevieve's family emigrated from Quebec to Detroit in the 70's so her old man could get a job in the plants. He was a decent man, though emotionally absent, and her mother who worked at Henry Ford Hospital as a nurse was just this side of a saint. As a child, Genevieve did well in school, made lots of friends, and was the prettiest girl in class. In middle school, she was the sun to the boys' planets. She was beginning her journey into womanhood and could have become anything she wanted to." A look of bitterness crossed his face. "Then her charmed life became a nightmare. Genevieve's mother was diagnosed with cancer and passed away less than a year later, leaving her father to find solace in a bottle. He lost his job, they lost their house, and practically overnight Genevieve found herself in a new school with no friends and no family other than a father who attended late night mass at the local watering hole. She fell in with the wrong crowd, started smoking weed and drinking as an escape, got taken advantage of by boys, started skipping classes and let her grades slip. She dropped out of high school, ran away from home…and met a man named Boothe who gave her a job at a gentlemen's club on Eight Mile, never asking how old she was. More drugs, more booze, a bastard like Boothe for a boss and one morning she woke up in a motel room with a complete stranger and no recollection of how she'd gotten there. She slipped out of bed trying not to wake him, but before she made it to the door he sat up and asked, 'What do I owe you for the –?' Well, you get the picture. She burst into tears, ran out, and spent the rest of the morning in her apartment shower crying. That day Genevieve took a good long look at her life and vowed that she was going to change it. Within a year, she was living in Traverse, enrolled in a GED program, and waitressing at a little place downtown. Eventually, she attended Northwestern, earned bachelor's degrees in psychology and sociology, and got a job with the Grand Traverse County Department of Social Services. A decade later, she was standing at a carnival booth during Cherry Festival wearing a copper sun dress…and I fell in love with her."

The two of them walked up to a typically tacky airport saloon called the Hangerover Bar and Grill. Just outside stood a man looking first one way, then the other, wearing mirrored aviator sunglasses, an earpiece, and a bad suit.

"Here we are, lad," Merrill announced as he strode past the secret serviceman.

Once inside, the Englishman stopped, looked around, and then headed for a table in the far corner where a familiar-looking, dark haired thirty-something man in a well-tailored suit and silk tie sat watching them approach, his fingers drumming on the table.

He stood before Merrill reached the table. "Mr. MaGeah," he began irritably. "I'm a busy man and I don't have time to drop everything and drive out of the City on a whim."

"Sit down, Senator," Merrill ordered as he took a chair. "This won't take long."

Hesitantly, the man obeyed.

That's why he looked so familiar, Mac realized. He'd been on the news several times in the past year or two. His name was Jack Abrams, Republican Senator from Virginia and Chair of the Senate Foreign Affairs Committee, a particularly influential position given that the Committee was solely responsible for doling out financial aid to foreign nations and non-governmental organizations – NGOs – all over the world. What's more, it recommended or denounced to the full Senate the President's nominees for all overseas appointments, including Ambassadorships to foreign nations.

Merrill introduced Abrams to Mac who extended his hand and began, "Nice to meet –"

"Look, Mr. MaGeah," Senator Abrams interrupted, "I'm only here out of respect for my grandfather."

Mac withdrew his hand.

"Your grandfather," Merrill said irritably, "has been, and continues to be, a good friend of me Clan. I met him a long time ago, when you were but a gleam in your mother's eye –"

"I don't care about your Clan," Abrams snapped as he stood again. "I think it's all pipedreams and fairy tales. I came here, I met you, and having fulfilled my grandfather's wishes I now have more pressing business to attend to."

"Your grandfather asked you to do something else, did he not?" Merrill said impatiently.

With unmasked frustration, Abrams replied, "Yes…but he's an old man and I'm sure he must've been mistaken."

"Has the President nominated someone else?"

"No, but –"

"Is the position still open, Senator?"

The Senator hesitated. "Yes, but –"

"Not anymore." Now it was Merrill's turn to stand. Grabbing his coat, he pulled out an envelope and handed it to

Abrams. "Here is his background and you've officially met your new candidate. Make the arrangements for the hearing." Glancing over at Mac, who was still sitting, he said, "Come along, lad." And with that, he abruptly turned to leave.

"Uh," Mac stammered as his travel companion walked away, "nice to meet you, sir." He stood and followed Merrill out into the concourse. Glancing back as they passed the Secret Service agent, he exclaimed, "Merrill, you just dissed a Senator of the United States of America!"

"He's rich and a politician. That doesn't make him special, only privileged at the expense of the citizenry. The sad history of the world is replete with the likes of him, lad."

"Did you mean the President of the United States?" Mac asked as they headed back towards the gates. "What's this Clan thing all about anyway? And what position are you a candidate for?"

"Not me. You."

"Me?" Mac replied in astonishment. "What position? Why?"

"You must learn about the past and let history open your mind to what lies ahead."

Mac wanted answers but realized with new respect that any man who treated a U.S. Senator like a spoiled child would get around to explaining things when he was damned good and ready.

They boarded the jet again and soon were taxiing out to the runway.

"Flight time to New York City, 30 minutes, Mr. MaGeah," said the voice of the Captain.

"Now we're going to New York? How long's our layover there?"

"A day," Merrill answered. "We have one more thing to do before we leave for England."

Mac didn't bother asking what. "And if I choose to go home?"

"Then I'll send you home."

Mac turned to the window. "Alright. So, where are we staying?"

Merrill reached into his coat pocket, pulled out a crumpled scrap of paper and looked at it. "Is the Plaza a decent hotel?"

Mac chuckled. "Oh, yeah. And expensive."

"Not to worry, lad. You and I aren't paying for it."

"Who is?"

Merrill gave him a schoolteacher look.

"The same person who lent us this jet?"

"Aye," Merrill smiled as he leaned back in his seat. "Senator Abrams' grandfather," and he closed his eyes.

"No, no, no – you owe me a story."

"Tonight. Over dinner."

Luckey's sat at 57th Street and Sixth Avenue. Merrill was on his third beer, Mac his first.

"You ever had a microbrewery beer?" Mac commented. "Short's Brewery has an IPA –"

"That's sissy stuff! Wait 'til you throw back a stout with me lads in Mary's Pub back home," boasted Merrill, draining his glass and thudding it down on the table. "Quid pro quo time, laddy. You've told me about Genevieve and now I've an amazing story to tell you. It's rather a long one, though, so… let's get another pint, eh?" he said with a wink and a smile.

Mac chuckled and gladly motioned to the waiter, holding up two fingers and pointing to their empty glasses. Since his dinner companion became more animated with each glass he downed, it promised to be an interesting story, if for no other reason than to watch him tell it.

"The importance of history cannot be overstated," Merrill began with the gusto of a man fully in his element. "Nationalities, politics, geography, sociology, war, religion, world economics, even art and science can be truly understood only when illuminated by the light of the past. Edward Gibbon wrote that history is a register of the crimes, follies, and misfortunes of humankind. David McCullough said that history is about life, human nature, our failings or noblest achievements, cause and effect. When we learn about history, we discover what choices we have today, what works and what doesn't. With knowledge of the past, we can alter the future. So, I ask for your patience, lad, as I tell you about your family's past and its imprint on history. We won't get through the whole story tonight but get through it we will." The Englishman sat back, reflected for a moment, and said, "We'll start with ancient Greece."

"Greece? I'm Greek?"

"No, y'are not Greek," Merrill said with feigned exasperation. "But, to appreciate the world your ancestors arose from, you first have to know what created it. I want you to understand who you are, which is to say who you came from, why y'are so important to me Clan and its friends, why we sent you to Michigan and Harvard —"

"Whoa, whoa, whoa! Hold on!" Mac said. "*You* sent me those letters, paid for my tuition, and got me my job at the firm?"

Merrill shook his head. "No, not me. But, you'll meet who did…very soon."

"Who? When?" Mac pressed as the waiter approached.

"Our Keeper. Tomorrow," Merrill answered, snatching the pints off the waiter's tray.

Mac closed his eyes, leaned forward on his elbows and rubbed his temples. "What's a Keeper?"

"The man who keeps what needs keeping, mate!" Merrill quipped and broke into a hearty laugh.

"Look, I just met you this morning," said Mac, pointing his finger at the Elder. "I've done what you asked and flown half way across the country, now stop evading my questions and start answering –"

"You," interrupted Merrill with a pointing finger of his own, "shall have your answers tomorrow, but do not expect to find comfort in them. For now, I ask that you simply listen!"

Mac dropped his hand to the table with a thump and stared at the Englishman. Finally, he let out something between a laugh and a grunt. "Fine," he conceded, reaching for his glass. "Go ahead."

Merrill lifted his pint as well, took a gulp, and launched into his dissertation. "Ancient Greece was poor in natural resources and surrounded on three sides by water –" He let out a loud belch. "– the Mediterranean, the Aegean, and the Ionian Seas. Thus, she depended heavily on trade and her people were an adventuresome lot. They settled colonies as far east as the Black Sea and as far west as Iberia – modern day Spain. Each colony was a separate city-state." He took another swig of stout and wiped his mouth on the sleeve of his jacket. "The polis – the Greek city-state – was the peoples' church, school, and social structure. Its citizens considered themselves sovereign and chose as their government the truest democracy the world has ever known. One person, one vote. The choosing of officials to pass laws and jurors to pass judgment was by lot, with the poor and rich included alike. Such practices were unheard of in the world prior to the Greeks, as was their encouragement of free thought. Momentous accomplishments and unrivaled intellectualism flourished within her empire, allowing her people to take the first step away from gods and fate and towards humanity and science. Freedom of speech, a supposedly novel idea enshrined in your Bill of Rights, was the right of every Greek citizen. Democritus of Abdera developed the hypothesis that matter was composed of tiny particles he called atoms. Socrates believed in the existence of a soul hindered by the body in life but free in death to seek and find the one truth –" and on and on his exposition went.

He lifted his seventh glass. "Eventually, the Greek world was subsumed by the Roman Empire, and after she fell, most of Greece's and Rome's intellectual advancements were lost for a millennium. Imagine if we *hadn't* lost all that time, laddy. We'd be far more forward-thinking then we are now." He took a healthy swig of his Guinness. "Let's explore what led to Rome's fall." One more gulp and his glass was empty. "After we get another pint, eh?" Spotting the waiter across the restaurant, Merrill flailed his arms wildly to attract the young man's – and everyone else's – attention. He held up his empty glass, the waiter nodded with an amused grin, and the Elder dropped it on the table. Mac caught it on the bounce. "Early Rome was governed by a monarchy that was advised by a council of the wealthy called the Senate. The Senators selected successor kings, who in turn were subject to approval by the Assembly of Clans, a legislative body of the commoners. Eventually, to cripple the possibility of tyranny, the monarchy was eliminated altogether, and the Senate and Assembly ruled the Empire for two centuries, spreading the blessings of peace, prosperity, and intellectualism throughout the ancient world."

"Spreading the blessings?" Mac said sardonically. "You mean they conquered the ancient world and subjected its people?"

Merrill gave an innocent shrug. "But, *what* did they actually conquer? Survival-of-the-fittest barbarianism? Tribal anarchy? Monarchical tyranny? Everyone within the arms of the Empire enjoyed the benefits of Greek and Roman culture."

"Even Judea?" Mac said. "The Bible doesn't exactly give a glowing review of Roman occupation."

"Judea was part of Alexander the Great's empire from 332 BC on. His successors brought Hellenism to the Middle East until Rome conquered what remained of Alexander's empire in 63 BC. The Jews were a proud and stubborn monotheistic people occupied by a polytheistic empire. So, yes, they were an unhappy lot. They would have been unhappy under *anyone's* rule if they didn't believe in the God of Moses." Merrill held up a hand to forestall Mac's counter argument. "No, Rome wasn't perfect, but her civilizing influence made the conquered lands who *accepted* her better off." He leaned back and again drained his glass. "Julius Caesar became the first Roman General to cross the English Channel to invade Britain in 51 BC. Did you know that?"

Mac shook his head.

"He conquered the barbaroi from the Alps to Britain before returning –"

"Barboroi?" Mac interrupted. "The etymology of barbarian?"

"Aye. It was a word used to describe the peoples beyond Roman control, outside of the empire in other words. The word barbarian was never meant to be derogatory, just a relative statement reflecting geography and governance. So, Caesar turned his forces on his beloved Rome to purge her of corruption and restore her glory. He vanquished General Pompey, who'd been hired by the Senate to fight on their behalf, and declared himself father of his country, Imperator, Consul, and Pontifex Maximus."

The waiter dropped off two more stouts.

"Pontifex Maximus?" Mac said curiously. "The Pope?"

Merrill nodded and tipped his pint. "The Emperors were the political *and* spiritual leaders of Rome. Her rituals and regalia survive to this day, enshrined forever in the Roman Catholic Church and the office of the Pope." He gave a loud belch. "Under Caesar, Rome's conquered lands were united into a single commonwealth and copious reforms were instigated. But, alas, as immortalized by William Shakespeare, Caesar was assassinated in 44 BC. His Empire stretched 3000 miles from Iberia in the west to Persia in the east, and 2000 miles from the Sahara to England. His successor, Octavian Augustus, halted Rome's expansion and appointed autonomous governors to the provinces. He made taxation more equitable with a census, sent inspectors to watch over the tax collectors, respected provincial institutions, strengthened the Empire's economy, and allowed the barbaroi to become Roman citizens." Merrill nodded again and gulped down more stout. "Rome's stoic legal system granted Roman citizens many of the rights we have, or strive to have, today. For example, a person's color or religion was irrelevant and interracial marriage was legal and widespread."

"Stoic?" Mac said.

"Aye. Stoic —" he downed the last of his pint, "— as in Stoicism. A philosophy originating with Zeno of Athens who believed that living a life in harmony with nature and striving toward virtue, duty, and the natural laws of right and reason — known as justitia — should be one's lifelong goal."

"The etymology of justice," Mac noted.

The dinner plates had long since been carted away, the restaurant was nearly empty, and though his storytelling was unwavering, the rest of him was obviously drunk.

"Hey, old man, why don't we walk back to the Plaza? We'll get some fresh air, maybe some coffee –"

"I'm *fine*, lad. Now, where was I? Ah! Augustus." He looked about for the waiter. "Augustus –" he repeated absently as his head swiveled one way and then the other.

"Merrill, one more Guinness and I'll have to *carry* you back to the Plaza. Let's go." Mac stood up and started around the table.

"Oy!" Merrill bellowed. "I can drink more than *ten* men and still have the what for to make a snot-nose wee lad like you show his elder some *respect.*" He pushed his chair back from the table to stand but instead of sliding it tipped backwards, too far backwards –

His arms started swinging to regain his balance but to no avail. The chair fell backwards with a loud thump. Dazed and embarrassed, Merrill laid there staring up at the ceiling. After a moment, he said quietly, "Mac."

"Yes, sir?" he replied, feigning respect.

"We're going."

"If you insist."

"I do. Now help me up, lad."

Suppressing a smile, Mac helped the Elder to his feet and after paying the bill, they stepped out into the cold New York night. They walked up to Central Park South and turned right.

"So, Merrill," Mac asked, making conversation, "how do you know so much about history?"

The Englishman stopped, straightened himself up to his full height and replied with as much pretentiousness as he could muster under the circumstances, "I was a professor of history for 28 years, m'boy."

Mac raised an eyebrow. "Impressive," he said and meant it. "Where did you teach?"

"Cambridge University in England," he answered with obvious pride. "And if you'd pursued your PhD at Cambridge as the Keeper hoped, you and I would have met years ago."

"Ah, well," Mac grinned, "my loss."

"And a great loss at that!"

Without exchanging another word, the two tired men walked the last few blocks to the Plaza, climbed the front steps, and stumbled through the revolving door. After pouring Merrill into his room, Mac walked down the hall, opened the door to his own room, and crossed over to the window in the darkness. Looking out, he noticed the way the lights of the city framed Central Park and recalled driving along the shore of Mission Point – the Mustang's top was down, the warm wind blew Genevieve's hair about her shoulders, Miles Davis was playing on the stereo, and the lights of Traverse lined the edge of the Bay like a string of pearls.

As the new day began, Mac wondered what it would bring. To his surprise, he looked forward to finding out. Maybe this was living life, he thought…simply having something to look forward to.

Seven a.m. and the phone in his room was ringing.

Mac picked up the receiver. "What?" he mumbled.

"Get your backside out of bed, lad," Merrill exclaimed, "and meet me in Rumplemeyer's."

"Aren't you hungover, old man?"

"Why would I be hung over?" he said innocently. "Now, get a move on."

"Where are we going?" Mac yawned.

"The United Nations."

"The *what?* Why?"

"To prepare you for the position y'are going to take."

"What —"

Merrill cut him off. "Rumplemeyer's, fifteen minutes," and he hung up.

"Why didn't I just go home?" Mac muttered. But then unbidden thoughts of returning to his condo where he nearly ended his life flitted through his mind. He forced out a breath as if punched and grumbled, "Just one more day and —" another punch, "— well, maybe two days."

After a quick repast and light conversation, they stepped once again onto Central Park South. Mac looked across at the snow-dusted park sparkling in the mid-winter sun. He smiled to himself and started for the curb to hail a cab. Merrill grabbed his arm.

"Our ride's already here, lad," and he nodded towards a uniformed chauffeur holding the door open to a late model black Lincoln limousine.

"Compliments of Michael Abrams, Mr. MaGeah," the man said cheerfully to Merrill as he and Mac approached. "He instructed me to tell you his grandson will make the arrangements as you requested."

"Thank Michael for me, Charles," Merrill replied as he bent down to get into the car. "To the United Nations campus, if you'd be so kind."

Charles turned into traffic and headed east across town. Turning onto First Avenue, he asked, "Which building, Mr. MaGeah?"

"The General Assembly building, my good man," he replied, clearly enjoying the VIP treatment.

Twenty minutes later, their car came to a stop beside a large, boxy white structure along the East River with the flags of nearly two hundred nations flying atop a long row of flagpoles.

"When shall I pick you up, sir?" Charles asked as he held the car door open.

Stepping out onto the sidewalk, Merrill replied, "In an hour, if you would please."

"I'll meet you back here then, Mr. MaGeah."

Merrill gave a nod and started across the plaza of flags. He looked up at the clear blue sky and out at the boats in the East River and then at double-decker Queensboro Bridge. "Ah, what a *glorious* day," he said as they passed a sculpture of a pistol with its barrel tied in a knot.

Entering the boxy white building, they purchased two tour tickets and strolled about the large lobby reading the kiosks and displays promoting the UN's special events and missions. Soon, their guide, Chiang Hwa, gathered the tour group together, introduced herself, and gave a brief speech about the United Nations.

"Issues affecting every aspect of life on this planet are addressed by the United Nations," the attractive twenty-something Chinese woman began in flawless American English, "the environment, nuclear and chemical weapons monitoring, arms trade, monetary policy, the global economy, human rights, international law, world population, health, space exploration, and more. Although the UN is not officially a world government, it can be thought of as a 'world parliament' since its actions reflect the concerns of the international community and carry the moral weight of world opinion. Now, if you will please follow me."

Their first stop was a gallery of wall hangings and display cases. Hwa discussed each one in turn as the huddled group moved slowly down the row. She then led them in and out of the various Council Chambers, reciting facts and figures in a well-rehearsed but friendly style.

"The land on which the United Nations headquarters stands was a gift from John D. Rockefeller in the late 1940s. The campus consists of four main buildings – the General Assembly building, which you are now in, the 39-story glass and marble Secretariat Building where the ambassadors have their offices, the interconnecting Conference Building, and the Dag Hammarskjold Library. The land is considered international territory and belongs to all the member nations of the UN. Together, these nations have pledged to promote world peace, security, self-determination, equal rights, and economic and social well-being for everyone.

"At the end of World War Two, fifty-one countries signed the United Nations charter in San Francisco. Today, there are 193 member nations. Over 3,000 delegates are sent to New York for the annual sessions of the General Assembly, and 16,000 international staff members work in the headquarters and satellite offices around the world, carrying out the day-to-day directives of the various Councils. Although there are as many languages as there are nations in the world, only six official languages are spoken at the UN – Arabic, Chinese, English, French, Russian, and Spanish." Hwa led the group towards a bank of elevators at the end of the gallery. "The United Nations is made up of six main organs – the General Assembly, the Security Council, the Trusteeship Council, the Economic and Social Council, the Secretariat, and the International Court of Justice. All sit in New York, except for the Court of Justice which resides in The Hague, Netherlands. Also known as the World Court, it is composed of fifteen judges who preside over cases brought to them by member nations in accordance with international law.

"Heading the Secretariat is the Secretary-General, currently René Boujeau of Canada. His role is to serve as the international representative of the United Nations, report to the General Assembly, and bring matters before the Security Council, whose mandate is to maintain peace and security around the world. Of the Security Council's fifteen members, five are permanent – China, France, Russia, the UK, and the United States. The other ten members are elected by the General Assembly and rotate through two-year terms. The Security Council is the only UN body whose decisions must be fulfilled by the member nations under the terms of the Charter. It is in permanent session 24-hours a day, 365 days a year. It can recommend new members to the General Assembly; impose economic and diplomatic sanctions on offending countries; or call on nations to employ 'any means necessary' to force the cessation of hostilities between warring nations or peoples. Such means, however, are almost never used and instead the UN's actions are considered peace*keeping*. Member nations volunteer their soldiers as peacekeepers to enforce a cease-fire once all sides to the conflict have agreed. In 1988, the United Nations was awarded the Nobel Peace Prize in recognition of its contribution to world peace since its formation 40 years earlier."

Hwa reached the elevators and pressed a button marked 'B.' The door slid open and she led everyone inside.

"The Trusteeship Council was responsible for transitioning former colonies and territories to independent nations. Over eighty former colonies have attained self-determination and nearly 750 million people have gained their independence with the Council's assistance. The last trust territory was Palau and in 1994, the Trusteeship Council suspended its operations.

"The Economic and Social Council promotes what its name implies. It is responsible for UNICEF, the World Health

Organization, and the UN High Commissioner for Refugees. Nearly eighty percent of the UN's resources are devoted to the Economic and Social Council's concerns."

The door slid open and they walked out onto a balcony overlooking the General Assembly chamber.

"The General Assembly is the main body of the UN and meets in this room. Every member nation is represented, and each has a single vote, regardless of size, wealth, or status. Each rotates their position on the floor of the chamber once a year, with the first seat being drawn at random. The chamber is five stories tall and forms a semi-circle around a main stage. On either side of the chamber above the main floor are four stories of glassed-in rooms for interpreters who relay the official conversations of speakers to their delegates on the floor.

"Once a year, according to their size and affluence, the member states are asked to pay for the UN's operating costs. Compared to the GDPs of almost every country in the world, the UN's operating costs are quite inconsequential. And yet every year as many as 100 member nations, including the United States, do not pay their full share.

"Member states are also assessed for the costs of worldwide peacekeeping actions in places like the Congo, Cyprus, Haiti, and Lebanon. There are 14 peacekeeping operations currently underway and more than half of their operating costs remain unpaid by UN members. Therefore, the burden of paying for troops and their supplies falls on the nations who volunteered their troops in the first place." Hwa turned back towards the elevators, beckoning her charges to follow. "Clearly, if this trend continues, the UN's peacekeeping capability will be jeopardized." She pressed the down button. "I would be pleased to answer any of your questions while we make our way back to the main lobby."

After returning to the mezzanine, she bowed slightly, said her farewell, and released her tourists into a maze of shops leading back to the lobby. People of every ethnic persuasion imaginable milled about the souvenir stands, the UN post office, the bookstore, and the coffee shop. Mac grabbed a cappuccino and Merrill a tea.

"Now we've a flight to catch, lad. We're going home!"

In his stately office atop the Secretariat Building, Under Secretary-General Gerhardt Schoen stared at the London Heathrow flight log and contemplated its significance. Why had Michael Abrams made his private jet available to the Clan? What was so damned important about the little Lake Michigan town they flew to? Why had the Clan Elder just visited the General Assembly Building? And who was that man with him?

Getting up from behind his desk, he walked to the window overlooking the East River. The faint reflection in the glass revealed a trim, 47-year-old man with short-cropped blonde, almost white hair, pale blue-gray eyes, and the faint remnants of a scar running down the left cheek of his rectangular face. "Could he be the last one?" he wondered aloud in German as he watched a cargo freighter heading north. His pulse quickened at the mere thought of it. "The last one," he hissed. Just one more…*one more* and the bloodline, the heresy, the *evil* would be erased forever.

The ringing of his desk phone interrupted his reverie. Schoen looked at the display and noticed it was the private encrypted line. He instinctively snapped to attention despite being alone in his office, and picked up the receiver.

"Mein Herr," he said into the receiver.

"Have we a new associate in Cyprus?" Secretary-General Rene Boujeau asked. He was calling from his office upstairs, sitting behind an ornate desk covered with reports, newspaper clippings, a half-eaten sandwich on a china plate and a teacup. It never even crossed his mind to walk downstairs and see Schoen. Underlings visited him, not the other way around. "The island's strategic location is key to our plans."

"We will, mein Herr," Schoen assured him. "Soon."

Boujeau's cold, professional demeanor in combination with his graying black hair, six-foot seven frame, and dark intense eyes granted him an air of intimidation – a characteristic he used to his advantage. "Who have you chosen?" he said impatiently.

"Pompous Zeda, mein Herr."

"Fine. Make a deal with him. Now."

"Ja, mein Herr," he assured his boss. "Mein Herr, I believe –"

"And what of our assets?" Boujeau interrupted without apology.

"On schedule. Perhaps five more years, maybe less, and we shall surpass a trillion Euros in weaponry, mein Herr."

"Their distribution?"

"General Mendenberg is staging our arms in the most advantageous of venues within the countries our puppets control."

"I expected no less, Gerhardt," replied Boujeau.

"Mein Herr, Michael Abrams let one of the Elders use his private jet and –"

"Oh, Gerhardt," the Secretary-General replied with a bored shake of his head, "this Clan business is of no consequence. Why do you concern yourself with it so?"

To Schoen, nothing in the world was of greater concern. "Mein Herr, the Elder was here. Today! And he had someone with him. A man who, who could be the last one. We *must* find out."

Boujeau reached for his teacup. "It is of no consequence," he repeated. "But," he sighed, "if you wish to pursue this obsession, my friend, then you may do so…but don't let it interfere with our more important matters."

"Ja, mein Herr," Schoen promised with a glint in his eye and a click of his heels.

"Now, give me Cyprus!" ordered the Secretary-General and unceremoniously hung up.

The Under Secretary-General set the receiver down and pushed the intercom button for his administrative assistant, "Get me on a flight to Nicosia. Now."

They arrived at LaGuardia shortly after noon. As they walked down the gangway towards the waiting British Airways 747, Merrill's countenance grew ever brighter.

"Great Britain," he beamed. "That's where all your questions will be answered, lad."

They walked through the cabin door and found their seats in First Class.

"Did you know that Britain was part of the Roman Empire for four centuries?" the prideful Elder asked as he stowed his travel bag and took his seat.

Stowing his own bag, Mac replied distractedly, "Mmmm, long time."

"The poet Claudian wrote that Rome took the conquered to her bosom, turning her subjects to citizens by the bond of affection. Tribal warfare, never-ending battles, sacrifices to gods, brutish kingdoms rising and falling — such were the barbaroi's fate until Rome brought them civilization, stability, and prosperity. That's how it was for the Britons, whose lives and thoughts became one with the Empire. To be a Briton was to be a Roman. Many even bore Roman names and each was as much a citizen of the Empire as they would have been in Africa or Palestine or even Rome." The stewardess asked if they'd like a beverage – a beer for Merrill, coffee for Mac. "But, alas, in 410 AD, or CE for Common Era as they say today, the Empire suffered its greatest defeat in 800 years – the Sack of Rome. To defend her, the legions defending Britain were sent to the mainland. Emperor Honorius granted Britain the powers of federation, and never again would she be part of the Empire. Precious little survived to tell us about the next century and a half. Much of what was written about it came from the pen of just one man – a priest named Gildas of Clyde. He said families began changing their Latin names to ones with a more native origin or spelling. There was a nobleman named Vitalinus, for instance, who became known as Vortigern. It was he who convened a Council to deal with the attacks along Britain's northern and western frontiers which had begun after the Roman legions left. The Council decided to hire Saxon mercenaries under the command of a man named Hengest to fight along the frontiers. He and Vortigern together achieved great victories, and after Vortigern's daughter was married off to the Irish King Loegaire, and an acceptable border arrangement was agreed to by the Scottish King Cunneda, peace along the old Roman frontiers was secured.

"Yet, life did not return to the old ways. You see, the Saxons refused to return home. Instead, they settled in the southeastern lowlands and over the next generation grew in number and power. Finally, in 442, Hengest rose up against Vortigern and the Council. His Saxons took whatever they wanted; whole towns fell to them; trade and prosperity waned; fear and resentment swept the land. So, the Council summoned

Hengest and his warlords to meet, unarmed, to draft a treaty of co-existence. But, when the elders of the Council arrived, Hengest's soldiers ambushed and killed them. Some three hundred elders of Britain died that day, and with them nearly all memory of the glory of Rome. The following decades were darkened to historical record, yet out of the darkness arose the legend of a man and his glorious realm that's captured the hearts and minds of every generation since. Me Clan, the Clan Camulodunum, has survived for 1,500 years for one purpose – to someday fulfill the promise of that legend. And that day has finally arrived."

Merrill leaned forward, looked into Mac's eyes, and said, "A wee bit mysterious, eh lad?" then broke into a hearty laugh.

"What legend?" Mac asked in frustration. "What promise?"

Merrill refused to say anymore. "Me Keeper will tell you the rest of the story."

So, they spent the rest of the flight talking about the UN and its missions, swapping stories of their travels, discussing books they'd read, and commenting on the various political happenings in Washington and abroad.

Early that evening they arrived at Heathrow, and after clearing customs, hailed a cab to Victoria Station. From there, they boarded the number 10 train heading west, and shortly after midnight, stepped out onto a dark and empty station platform in Bath. Deciding they needed the fresh air and exercise, they walked the four kilometers to an out-of-the-way inn on the edge of town to settle in for the night.

Mac fell asleep as soon as his head hit the pillow. But dreams of long ago battles and bloody victories in lands he'd never been to haunted his sleep. As disturbing as they were, though, they possessed a strange hopefulness.

At five A.M. a knock sounded at the door.

"Doesn't that man sleep?" Mac grumbled, pulling the sheets back and stumbling across the room. He pulled open the door to find Merrill standing there wide-awake and smiling, dressed in traveling clothes.

"A grand day we have before us, lad, a grand day indeed! Did you sleep well?"

"Go away," snapped Mac, swinging the door closed. "It'll still be grand in a few hours."

Merrill's stout arm caught the door and pushed it open. "The sun'll be rising soon and there's something I want you to see," he said. "The truth lies not far off, and the day cradles wonders in her arms for you!"

"The truth," Mac mumbled sardonically. "Fine," he sighed. "Give me a few minutes. I'll meet you downstairs."

"That's a good lad," smiled the Elder and pulled the door closed. As he walked down the hall he said to himself, "Besides, your dreams were keeping you from a sound sleep."

The night still held firm, though the dawn was mounting its charge, as William Cameron MacCrarey and Merrill MaGeah walked alone through the chilly, misty streets of Bath. Stopping at a bakery that was just opening for the day, they each bought a cup of tea and a scone. Soon, the centuries-old shops and cottages gave way to open fields and groves of trees. They turned north onto a country lane that soon faded into a footpath twisting up into the hills.

"We've a bit of a walk ahead of us, lad, so if you don't mind, I'll continue me history lesson."

"Fine," Mac said with a yawn, glad to not have to hold up his end of a conversation.

Merrill took a sip of his tea and resumed where he'd left off at Luckey's. "After the elders were betrayed by Hengest, a long shadow fell over Britain. For nearly a generation, the Britons lived in constant fear of Saxon warlords ruling by the sword, but eventually a resistance movement took hold. Under the leadership of Ambrosius Aurelianus, the Britons slowly pounded the Saxon army into a stalemate. Their final battle took place at Mons Badonnicus, and there the fate of Britain was decided once and for all.

"But, it was not Ambrosius who led the English that day, for he'd died in battle some time before. No, the man who commanded the cavalry *that* day was a warrior of peasant birth and Roman name. Ambrosius had chosen him to be his second-in-command, and he so respected Ambrosius that after his death, this great man refused every promotion and title and wished simply to be called the Second. He possessed a quality of character rare in those days and even more so today. He was decisive yet thoughtful, fair and humble, generous to all, fearless in battle yet reticent to take another life, and loved by soldiers and citizens like." Merrill looked over at Mac and said, "Remember, lad, a ruler can command minds and hearts only by earning respect and returning it in equal measure." He pointed away from the path they'd been following. "This way," he said, and traipsed off into the tall, dew-dampened field grass.

Mac followed behind his storyteller and noticed as the sky grew lighter that they were heading towards a massive hill. The grade became increasingly steep and the hike more arduous, but it did little to hinder Merrill's recounting of the Second's deeds.

"The battle of Mons Badonnicus took place in 470 CE. The Britons were mostly cavalry and they were greatly outnumbered by the Saxon foot soldiers. To even the odds, the Second led his men to Mons Baddonicus –" and just as he said the name, they reached the crest of the hill they'd been climbing, "– Baden Hill!"

The top of the hill was broad and flat – a treeless meadow of tall gently waving grass, framed by the golden-red hues of dawn. With the eagerness of a schoolboy, Merrill led Mac to the southern edge of the field and pointed to the valley below. "Oesc and his infantry camped right down there. Knowing they were at a strategic disadvantage, they chose to lay siege to the hill instead of attacking the high ground and taking heavy losses. On the ninth night of the seige, a heavy fog rolled in and blanketed the valley and surrounding hills. When the blood-red dawn broke and the stars began to fade, the Second and his men looked out beyond their meadow and saw nothing but billowy white clouds! In that moment, the Second realized that by the fates, God's good graces, or merely nature's happenstance, their chance at victory was at hand. All they had to do was take it, and war with the Saxons would finally end."

Now Merrill grabbed Mac's arm and hurried off to the north edge of the meadow.

"At once, the Second ordered his men to prepare for battle. When the sun rose above the clouds, he gave the war cry! On the lead horse, he led the charge. In two columns, side by side, his cavalry plunged down Mons Baddonicus headlong into the swirling mist. Like apparitions of the Reaper himself, the Second's men appeared out of the ghostly haze wielding their freshly sharpened swords. Thundering hooves and the horsemen's battle cries sent Oesc and his men scattering in fear! Driving straight through to the far side of the camp, the two columns of cavalry separated, one turning east, the other west. Flanking the fleeing Saxons in both directions, the cavalrymen deftly herded their foe around Mons Baddonicus to a deep hollow on the far side –" Reaching the edge of the meadow, Merrill pointed at a marshy bowl-shaped depression far below. After taking a moment to catch his breath, he said excitedly, "– there! The Saxons were huddled there en masse, surrounded by the Britons. Then, all grew eerily quiet. The infantrymen stood silently waiting. The horsemen, their blades at the ready, sat stock still watching over their enemy, awaiting orders.

"The Second understood that murder or mercy, death or dishonor, was but a command away. His actions or inactions would color the future of his island and the peace to come, so he urged his horse forward and descended into the hollow. 'Oesc of Kent!' he called out. 'Come forward and hear me!' Barely had the words left his lips than a massive brute with long blonde, almost white hair charged out of the mass of infantrymen at full tilt! Oesc's gray-blue eyes were wild with bloodlust, his face crimson with rage, and his hodgepodge of animal skins matted with filth and blood. Raising his sword, the warlord cried, 'Attack and honor your fathers!' But none of the soldiers dared move an inch for fear of being sent straight to Valhalla by the horsemen.

"The Second turned his horse slightly to the left, the sword in his right-hand dangling at his side. The warlord's blade slashed through the air and just before it struck, the Second gripped his sword's handle with all his might and swung it up in one, swift flowing arc! It met Oesc's with a thunderous clang, the force of its blow twisting the warlord's torso away from the Second. Bringing his sword around, the Second struck the Saxon hard on the back with the blade's flat side and sent him sprawling to the ground, cursing with fury.

"With a flick of his reins, the Second sidled over and placed the tip of his sword on Oesc's chest. 'Mercy shall be granted you and your warriors!' the Second proclaimed for all to hear. 'You shall be free men in the lands of my choosing! Surrender, and my promises shall be as true as the steel now laid upon your breast!'

"Oesc looked about at the beseeching faces of his soldiers, who moments ago had defied his order to attack, and realized he had but two choices – an honorable surrender or a noble death. Admitting to himself that he was hardly eager to see the great halls of Valhalla, he grudgingly accepted the Second's terms.

"And in that moment, three generations of war ended. Tears filled the Second's eyes as his cavalrymen cheered and began chanting his name – 'Artorius! Artorius! Artorius! –' A new age of peace and prosperity for Britain began that day… and would create a legend the world still dreams of."

Merrill turned to look at Mac with an expression that could only be described as overwhelming hope. "Time to head back, lad," he said with a proud smile. "There are those who await you."

Merrill nudged his fellow traveler with an elbow. "We'll be pulling into the station soon, laddy."

Mac, who'd nodded off shortly after leaving Bath, yawned and peered out at the passing countryside and pale blue sky.

"From there we drive to Camleton," said the Elder.

"What's in Camleton?"

"Me Clan, mate," Merrill replied happily, "me Clan Camulodunum!"

"Camulodunum," Mac repeated groggily. "Camleton."

"Aye. Many British towns were founded by the Romans but now go by English names. Salisbury was once called Sarum, for instance. London was called Londinium. Camleton was Camulodunum. In Roman times, Camulodunum was a provincial civitas governing the agricultural lands all along Hadrian's Wall. From the Irish Sea in the west to the North Sea in the east."

Still trying to shake off his sleep, Mac nodded vacantly. "So, this…Clan Camulodunum…what is it?"

"It's a Clan of many families, all descended from those who fought with the Second at Baden Hill."

That woke Mac up. "Really? You've tracked the genealogy of – how many families?"

"More than a thousand," Merrill answered.

"You've tracked the genealogy of more than a *thousand* families for 1500 years?"

"Aye," Merrill replied with smug matter-of-factness, "including yours."

"Mine? I'm –?"

"You are a descendent of a man who fought at Baden Hill."

"Whoa," Mac breathed.

"In fact," Merrill grinned, "y'are the descendent of the Second."

Mac was dumbstruck. He couldn't believe what he was hearing!

"And after Mons Baddonicus, the Second took the English name of…ah, but that's a story the Keeper wishes to tell," said Merrill with a mischievous smile.

The train pulled into the station and they were first onto the platform. Weary travelers crossed through the long, narrow terminal and out to the bustling sidewalk beyond. Merrill scanned the cars and cabs crowding the curb until his eyes fell upon a young woman standing beside a beat up old Astin Martin. Amused, he asked with a jovial laugh, "So, laddy, can you tell who's here to pick us up?"

Mac played along – there were businessmen coming and going, a handful of families greeting loved ones and guiding them to waiting cars, two lovers kissing and hurrying off to a cab, porters luggage from handcarts…and a very young woman staring at him! She had long mousy hair, pretty hazel eyes, and very pale skin. She was comely in a plain-sort-of-way, wearing a knee-length green and black plaid woolen dress, black stockings, a dark green jacket with the Queens College crest of red and white eagles on the front…and an expression of disbelieving awe.

Pointing, he said wryly, "I'll take a wild guess and say her?"

"Y'are a *genius,* lad," Merrill mocked. "Now, grab the bags and let's go. Time's wasting."

As they walked over to her, she stood perfectly still, her wide eyes fixed on the American.

"This is Clarice Ambrose," Merrill said as they approached. "She's the newest member of me Clan. Say hello, Clarice."

She didn't say a word. Merrill chuckled. "When y'are sixteen and a descendant, you become a member. About half of the surviving families live in Great Britain. The rest live all over the world."

"Surviving?" asked Mac, all too aware that Clarice was still staring at him.

"The families are a proud lot with a strong sense of honor and duty to their countries. Many have gone off to war over the centuries and not returned. The Great Wars with Germany sadly ended several family lines." Turning to Clarice, he said, "Put our bags in the car, dear."

She seemed to register Merrill's presence for the first time as her eyes flitted his way, but then resumed staring at Mac. With a little nod, she reached for the bags.

"*I'll* get the bags, Clarice," Mac insisted, giving the Elder a reproachful look. "Not very chivalrous of you, old man." He reached down but Clarice snatched up the bags and hurried around the car.

"Too slow, *young* man," Merrill laughed.

"Why was she staring at me like that?" Mac asked. "She doesn't even know who I am."

"That wee lass knows more about who you are than *you* do, laddy."

"Not likely."

"You'll see," chortled the Elder as Clarice opened the car doors for them. "To the gathering, my dear!"

After her guests climbed in, the newest Clansperson slid in behind the wheel, put the car in gear with a grind and a lurch, and sped off through the labyrinthine streets. In short order, the city was behind them and the English countryside was speeding by. An hour-and-a-half later, Clarice downshifted and turned onto a rutted old road that wound its way up into the hills of northern England. Eventually the little Astin Martin crested a ridge and whined and rattled its way down into a broad river valley. As they descended, Mac spied a clutch of buildings in the distance and wondered if that was where they were heading. Surrounding then were meadows, well-tended pastures, apple orchards, outcroppings of moss-covered rocks, farmhouses, and gnarled stands of hardwoods. All in all, the valley had a pleasant cast to it that bespoke of a long, gracious history.

Clarice found her way to a bumpy two-lane and sped north. After passing through a tiny village, she turned onto an old cart path and ambled into a wood of gnarled old trees. Bouncing along, they soon came upon a very old building with an eclectic array of cars, bicycles, and horse-drawn carriages parked willy-nilly around it.

Mac noted that three of the building's walls were made of field stones, and its doorway and windows were framed with rough-hewn beams. The fourth wall, oddly enough, appeared to be much older and made of kiln-fired bricks. It continued past the others perhaps two hundred feet into the woods and rose so high that the canopy of trees hid its crown. He was about to ask whether it had been part of an old cathedral or fortress when Clarice let out the clutch before shifting into neutral and stalled the Astin Martin with a teeth-rattling lurch.

"Someone needs to teach her how to drive a stick," Mac said under his breath as he climbed out of the back seat.

"Wait here until I call for you," Merrill told him and headed for the double doors of the building, Clarice in tow.

Mac stepped away from the car and strolled over to a nearby clearing. Gazing up at the sky and the surrounding hills, he judged they must have entered the valley from the south. He was wondering what it was about the ridges that didn't seem quite natural when the doors opened. The murmur of friendly conversations rolled out and quickly faded away. Mac turned to see Merrill standing on the stoop, addressing a crowd of people standing just inside the doorway.

"Thank you for coming back so soon after our last gathering. I know many of you traveled a long way to be here this afternoon but keep this in mind…you didn't just travel many miles," he smiled, "you traveled many centuries."

Soft laughter and a smattering of applause drifted out the doors of what Mac now guessed was an old hall.

"In recent generations," Merrill went on, "our families have rarely met a direct descendent of the Second. That alone would make this day important to us. But of even greater importance is what we are about to do. You brave souls have chosen this time in history to open the Clan to the world for the greater purpose we've always believed in. And for that, I'm proud of you," he said with a slight bow as he stepped aside.

"Families of the Clan, I give you the man we've placed our faith and hopes in – William Cameron MacCrarey!"

Everyone began to applaud. Mac just stood there staring back, slack-jawed and looking thunderstruck.

"Come, laddy!" Merrill called cheerfully.

The applause grew louder and voices beckoned. Reluctantly obliging, he awkwardly walked over to the stoop and stepped inside. Cool and dank, the vast hall had planked wood floors, rough-hewn timber beams, three walls of stone and one of brittle, cracked brick. No sooner had he entered than a cheer went up. As one, the Clansfolk – at least two hundred of them – surged forward to introduce themselves. Most shook his hand, others touched him as if to prove he was real, and some simply stood back and stared.

"Our hopes are with you," said a young man.

"You'll never know how much I hoped this day would come before I went on, dear," an elderly matron told him.

"The Clan will watch over you," a woman carrying a toddler promised.

"Alright, everyone! Alright. Let the Keeper through," Merrill called out. With that, the sea of Clansfolk parted. All eyes turned towards a tall, broad-shouldered man with long silvery-gray hair wearing a loose-fitting tan woolen sweater and worn brown corduroys. He stood facing a broad hearth at the far end of the great room warming his hands over a fire. Slowly, he turned to face Mac and at once a pleased smile crossed his weathered face. Mac couldn't help but smile in return. The Keeper appeared to be in his seventies, with bright blue eyes that exuded authority, yet revealed an empathy and kindness that put one instantly at ease.

Merrill and the Keeper walked towards each other, meeting in the middle of the room in a warm embrace. "Welcome home, old friend," the Keeper smiled. "All went well?"

"Aye," Merrill replied. "Nothing we didn't anticipate."

The Keeper looked again at Mac and then around the room at his fellow Clansfolk. "Well," he proclaimed merrily, "let's make our distinguished guest feel welcomed!"

A rowdy cheer went up and again the Clansfolk gathered around their guest as Merrill and the Keeper sat down at one of the far tables to talk.

Eventually the salutations wound down and the women-folk turned their attention to dinner and catching up on family happenings. A wild boar and several large pots of soups and stews were hung over the fire to cook, their aromas filling the hall with a most delectable aroma. The menfolk readied the tables and benches for the feast, swapped stories, and smoked their pipes.

Mac sat down with a family from Brittany who'd taken the Chunnel train to England the day before just to meet him. Soon, Merrill and the Keeper joined them.

"Lad, this is me Clan's Keeper, Kyle Dunham."

"K.D.," Mac smiled. "You're the one who wrote me those letters."

"I am," Kyle said with a smile, but nodded to his Clansfolk whose collective attention had now turned to the Keeper. "But, *they* arranged for your education. They've taken an oath to look after the heirs, and it is a Keeper's duty to use his influence on their behalf."

Mac gave a thank-you nod to the gathering and asked, "What are you a Keeper of?"

A good-natured sort, Kyle said, "Of what needs keeping, of course," and the Clansfolk laughed. "I will tell you soon enough, Mac. But I imagine you'd like to know who your real parents were, yes?" Without awaiting a response, he went on, "Their names were Finn and Anna Lawton of Cymry, Wales.

They died in an automobile accident when you were a wee lad, just after your brother Clark was born. Anna was a Clan member and a descendant of the Second, like you. She was an only child and her parents were deceased, so we needed to find you another home. The MacCrarey's were related to the Clan by marriage and unable to have children of their own, so you were given to them and raised in Chicago."

"I have no living blood relatives, then?" Mac asked somberly.

"I'm afraid not, lad," Kyle replied. "Now that Clark is gone, you are the last of your family line. Only you survive as testimony to all who came before you. And if you'll permit me, I shall tell you the last and most important piece of the story Merrill's recounted during your travels."

Mac gave an absent nod.

"Your ancestor was given a Roman name at birth – Artorius – and his was the second generation to grow up in a post-Roman Britain. He and his peers watched helplessly as the world their grandparents took for granted slowly collapsed. They cringed and chafed against the injustice of Saxon rule. And they willingly followed Ambrosius into war.

"After the battle of Baden Hill, the Second placed his mantle of leadership in this valley. He and the men who had fought with him created what he dubbed the Council of Camulodunum." The Keeper swept his hand about the great hall. "The descendants of whom sit before you now."

Awed, Mac looked around at the clansfolk and saw in their smiling faces not just hope, but the sweep of time. "Are you a descendant as well, Kyle?" he asked, still taking in the faces of those around him.

"Aye. Of the Council's first Keeper, Artorius' advisor and archivist – an aged historian born when our land was still Roman."

"Archivist," Mac repeated.

Kyle nodded. "He preserved the records of Artorius' governance. Written in Gaelic and Latin, they remain to this day in the Clan's possession…and *that* is what I am keeper of," he smiled.

"May I read them?" Mac asked hopefully. "Have they been translated?"

"Of course, but they're less a biography of Artorius than a reflection of the world he helped create – a listing of his deeds, the laws he passed, the actions he took to forestall the coming of the Dark Ages to the British Isles."

"Did Artorius restore the island's Roman form of governance, its social structures and its economy?"

"No, that would have been too difficult after Hengest's slaughter of the Elders. Too many of the old ways died with them, you see. No, Artorius had to create an entirely new world."

"What form of governance did he choose, then, a monarchy? Did he declare himself king?"

A few of the Clansfolk chuckled at this.

"No," said Kyle, "though later generations thought of him as a king."

Several more of the Clansfolk snickered.

Slightly embarrassed, Mac glanced around and asked, "What's so funny?"

"Well," the Keeper grinned, "I guess it's best to tell you now. You see, after Baden Hill, the Britons gave up their Roman names and took Gaelicized ones. The Second was Artorius, and Artorius became –" He raised his hands and all eyes turned to Mac.

A sudden awareness came to him in a rush of exhilaration and dread. The name of a man who, until this moment, had been little more than a fairy tale, echoed across the centuries. In a voice barely above a whisper, he breathed, "Arthur."

Amidst the warm smiles and gentle applause of his Clansfolk, the Keeper exclaimed, "You are he. The legend alive in our presence! Arthur's last living descendent."

Mac's heart pounded and his hands shook. "You're saying King Arthur was as real as you or I? Knights and dragons and Merlin the Magician and all that fairy tale stuff?"

To that, there was much good-natured laughing.

"Well, I'm not so sure about dragons and magicians," Kyle chuckled, "but Arthur was real enough."

Several of the Clanswomen excused themselves to begin serving dinner. Two of the men went with them to tap the kegs of ale.

"Are not most fairy tales distorted legends of real people and events?" said Merrill. "Stories of Arthur were handed down by word of mouth for generations, gradually evolving into mythical legends. Seven centuries after Arthur's death, Geoffrey of Monmouth committed the legend to paper, making Arthur and his chivalrous knights everything the lords of Geoffrey's time were not. Later, Malory gave them suits of armor, and Tennyson blessed them with Victorian ideals. If it were not for the Clan, the true wonder of that glorious age would have been lost forever. Seventy-five generations have preserved the truth about the real Arthur for one reason – the world's people need *hope*. Hope that prejudice, ignorance, intolerance, greed, inequality, and oppression shall be ended once and for all by the strength and wisdom of a selfless leader. They dream of a new Camelot."

The Keeper put his hand on Mac's shoulder. "Within you lies a greatness the world has rarely seen. You will find that there is contentment in that, but with such a blessing comes great responsibility. You must set your mind and deeds on fulfilling the promise of your bloodline, and the hopes of those who dream of a better world."

There was so much to absorb – the enormity of it all, the awesome realization of what he was and the burden suddenly placed on him – that all Mac could do was sit in stunned silence.

Merrill, who'd been carefully observing Mac's reaction, nodded to the platters of aromatic delights being set upon the tables and said, "Shall we partake now of the wonderful feast that's been prepared for us?" Enthusiastic "Ayes!" and "Here, here's!" answered him, and the hall soon filled with the pleasing sounds of contented conversations and joviality mingled with the clinking of dishes, glasses, and silverware.

"King Arthur. I must be going nuts," Mac said to himself as Clarice walked up with a plate of food. "Oh, uh, thank-you," he said, with a quick smile, and with a blush she hurried off. He set the plate down and pushed it away as Merrill sat down. "Am I crazy or are all of you crazy?"

Merrill laughed. "Eat. You need to stay sharp. You'll be reading all day tomorrow."

"The Keeper's records?" Mac asked.

"Aye," The Elder nodded. "Within them await your final answers."

The hour was late and one by one the Clansfolk gathered up their belongings, said their good-byes, and left for home. Before Kyle departed, he made Mac promise to meet him back here at eight o'clock the next morning.

"Will y'be sleeping atop one of the tables tonight, laddy?" Merrill quipped as he grabbed his coat and lifted a rusty old lantern off its hook.

Holding the lantern up to light their way, he led Mac down a stone path and into the woods. Not far along, the brush cleared away and a canopy of weeping willow branches formed a living cavern around a small, white cottage. Merrill produced an old skeleton key and unlocked the front door. Inside was a single room with a tiny kitchen, a rustic table and four chairs, an old four-poster feather bed, and a couch in front of a fireplace. On the yellowing plaster walls hung colorful English landscapes by some of England's most renowned painters.

"Loo's out back," Merrill said with a yawn. "Take the bed. I'll sleep on the couch." And without another word, he blew out the lantern.

3

"For I dipt into the future, far as human eye could see,
Saw the vision of the world,
and all the wonder that would be."

— Alfred Lord Tennyson

William Cameron MacCrarey, distant son of Arthur, awoke with a start.

"What was that?" he said, straining to hear the far-off sounds of his dream. Men's yells and hoof beats…clanging swords and screams…

He tried to calm himself. "Just a dream," he whispered, sitting up. "Just a dream." For a moment, he wondered where he was. Then, the events of the prior evening came rushing back. "Oh," he moaned and fell back onto the bed.

A bubbling hiss came from the kitchen and he caught the delectable aroma of percolating coffee. "Merrill?" he called, glancing over to see an empty couch. Rolling out of bed, he threw on some clothes, ran his fingers through his hair, and walked over to the cupboard to find a cup.

The morning air was crisp and frost covered the tree branches. The sky was clear and pale blue, a gentle breeze carried the first scent of spring, and a distant solitary car was coming up the valley. He smiled and walked up the stone path to the welcoming old hall, sipping from his steaming mug as he went.

Merrill opened the double doors and called, "I see you found the coffee all right, lad." In both his hands was cradled a cup of tea.

"Aye," Mac answered.

"And how do you feel this fine day?"

"I feel…alive," Mac said with a grin, taking another sip of his coffee. "So, now what?"

The whir and chug of a straining engine announced the arrival of Clarice's Astin Martin.

"The Keeper wishes to show you what he keeps," Merrill smiled as the car bounced up the path, gave a grinding lurch, and stalled dead.

"I really need to show her how to drive a stick," Mac muttered.

The Keeper extricated himself from the passenger seat with a cheery salutation. "Top o' the morning, lads," he said, struggling with two bulky old leather valises.

"May I help?" Mac offered, walking over.

"This is me job, lad, but thank you kindly." Kyle closed the door with a foot and started for the hall.

Inside, he laid the valises on a table and Merrill opened the shudders to let in the morning sun. "These are the Keeper's charges, lad," Kyle proclaimed proudly. "Well, translated copies of them, anyway. The originals have to be kept in an environmentally controlled vault to keep them from deteriorating."

Kyle opened one of the valises, took out a leather-bound binder, and flipped it open. The pages were yellowed toward the edges, looking brittle to the touch, and the words appeared to have been typed on an old Smith-Corona. The lines of text didn't seem to form paragraphs as much as they formed stanzas like a poem, cascading down the page, and to the right of each was a date.

"Have a seat, heir of Arthur," Merrill told him.

"Learn…imagine…dream," said Kyle, his hand on Mac's shoulder. "We'll be back with brunch in a little while."

Mac gave a half-smile, sat down, and with another sip of coffee scanned the first page as the two Elders turned for the door. The sound of a latch, the creaking of hinges, the echoing thud of the door as it closed, and a moment later Clarice's Astin Martin whirred and chugged its way down the road.

The binder was like a ship's log, he discovered – acts and facts, hundreds of them strung together in chronological order, weaving a tapestry of one man's tremendous influence on a land and its grateful citizens. Nothing about it was mystical or magical. No fairy tale characters or sorcerers. Instead, a pleasant, peaceful world came to life through a meticulous tallying of details – an island existing in a happy, carefree bubble of time when anything could be dreamed of and made real.

The first entries came soon after the battle of Baden Hill when, true to his word, Arthur granted the Saxons title to the areas now called Sussex, Kent, and Norfolk. In return, they gave him their absolute loyalty and never again rose up during his lifetime. The Council of Camulodunum was formed in 471 AD, and in 472 Arthur married the daughter of one of his generals. Her name was Gwyneth of Arymem and over the next seven years she gave birth to five children – their two sons, Amyth and Patrick, and three daughters, Mallora, Ellyn, and Gythea. All were well-respected by the people and carried the beliefs and convictions of their parents forward into the next generation of Britons.

Arthur was not a divine presence on Earth or an elitist who believed in his superiority. He was not the latest King of a royal bloodline, nor did he establish a new aristocracy. He and the Council of Camulodunum handed the people the reins of power and created a nation the likes of which had never existed…and of which the world still dreams. Its style of Platonic democracy allowed men and women 16 and older to participate in the governance of the land. A House of the People was created as a counter-balance to the Council of families. All were equal in the eyes of the law, and in practice. Slavery was abolished. Economic and civil justice was granted to all people. No distinction of class was allowed. Mercenaries were forbidden. An independent judiciary was created. A progressive tax was levied. The consolidation of wealth was moderated. The old Roman roads, forums, baths, and aqueducts were re-built. Believers of the ancient anthropomorphic nature religions and followers of the burgeoning Catholic Church were granted freedom of worship alike. The Council gave preference to no religion, and temples and churches were subject to the same laws and taxes as the people. The arts, philosophy, and sciences flourished. Respected professors from all over Europe visited England. Tremendous advances in education were made. Illiteracy was nearly eradicated. A university for the intellectually gifted was established. And its graduates were often elected to the House, further advancing the remarkable world Arthur had founded.

His leadership spanned the 45 years between 470 and 515 CE. He was 75 when he died in his sleep. Stories of his accomplishments ascended to the realm of legend on the mainland of Europe, across which the shadow of the Dark Ages had begun to fall. Britain seemed a land of mystical powers, a place no one ever came back from, a heaven on the edge of the mortal world.

Thus, was born the legend of Camelot.

Its mere existence, though, created an inequity. Stories of her glory twisted into dark desires among the mainlanders. Within the lifetime of Arthur's grandchildren, war with the mainlanders returned with a vengeance, extinguishing the shining light of Camelot and allowing the Dark Ages to cast its pall. As time passed, the true glory of what Arthur had accomplished became a distorted fantasy of some faraway place and time.

Mac read the entire day, breaking only to partake in the brunch Kyle and Merrill had brought from town, and to run to the cottage for more coffee. Now as dusk was settling across the valley, he heard the whir and chug of Clarice's Astin Martin coming up the road.

"There she is now," Kyle said as he got up from the table. He and Merrill were sitting apart from Mac, debating world events, arguing politics, conversing over old books, and gossiping about the families like two old women.

"Hungry, lad?" Merrill asked, watching the Astin Martin through the window.

"Aye," Mac answered, leaning back in his chair and stretching.

"We've a fine dinner of English cuisine awaiting us down at Mary's pub," Merrill announced.

"Fine English cuisine, huh?" Mac smirked. "Isn't that a bit of an oxymoron?"

"My, aren't *we* amusing today," Merrill retorted.

Still grinning, Mac grabbed his coat and followed the Elders outside.

"How far along are you?" the Keeper asked.

"Third of the way through the second binder. Fascinating reading. What an amazing world Arthur and his Council created."

"Indeed. You must understand, though, that a great nation can only exist if the beliefs of her people are equally great," Kyle noted as they got into the car. "America could not have survived with its Constitution for two and a half centuries if it wasn't a just and noble document, or if her people had chosen not to believe in it anymore."

"Of course, most of your founding fathers were descended from Britons, so the 700 years – from William of Normandy to Cromwell – of evolving English law and parliamentary government was in their blood," boasted Merrill. "Well, what's say we throw back a few pints and tell a few tall tales with the lads down at the pub? Mary has her pot roast on the stove for us."

"What's that?" Mac asked warily.

"Boiled beef with carrots, potatoes, and cabbage," Merrill answered enthusiastically.

"Yum," Mac muttered.

"To Mary's, my good lady," exclaimed the Elder, and with a giggle and a lurch they were off.

During dinner, Kyle was eloquent and wise. Mac was inquisitive and upbeat. Merrill was enthusiastic and entertaining.

"Another pint, lass!" Merrill called to Mary.

Kyle quietly rubbed his chin, contemplating the exchange of ideas that had continued through dinner. "No, old friend. Let's go for a walk."

"I'm worried about your drinking, old man," Mac smiled as he stood.

"I'm touched," Merrill drolled.

"What you read, Mac, is not the past but the future," Kyle reflected aloud, standing up and reaching for his coat. "You are the bridge between them, the change and hope the Clan has for tomorrow. But, know that great change is not determined by the will and understanding of one or two individuals. It's brought about by the sum of individual decisions made by all men and women, separately and together – to fight or flee, to obey or disobey, to rage or be quiet." He placed two twenty-pound notes on the table.

"You outdid yourself tonight, love," Merrill called to Mary as they headed for the door.

"Anything for our last heir," she called back as her last guests walked out.

Kyle's breath swirled about his head as they walked. "Without faith that one's system of government works, anarchy must prevail, perhaps not right away, but not far off either. Every revolution, passive or bloody, is born of economic and social injustice. And every great nation will fall for one simple reason – the people will lose faith in their government's ability to ensure justice and freedom, civil liberties and equitable prosperity."

The sky above was crystal clear and the swath of the Milky Way stretched from one side of the valley to the other.

"Merrill," Kyle said, walking down the dimly lit street of the tiny hamlet, "tell the lad why we chose the Deputy U.S. Ambassadorship."

"Aye, Keeper. First, laddy, you must keep in mind that during its 1,500 years, the Clan has *never* placed the mantle of statesmanship on an heir of Arthur. Either the heir wasn't right for the times, or the times weren't right for the heir. But Arthur's blood truly courses through your veins, and I believe you will wear the mantle lightly…and use it wisely."

Mac gave an acknowledging but anxious nod. "But why the United Nations?"

"The UN is arguably the noblest enterprise of the twentieth century, but it's hampered by its own Charter and the politics of the Security Council. It can become so much more than it is now, if freed to do so and led by a wise leader."

"A wise leader, you say," said Mac, "but the Deputy U.S. Ambassador sounds more like a glorified gofer."

Merrill shook his head. "On the contrary, lad, it's the ideal position. You'd be in the thick of it, yet out of the spotlight. You'd be afforded the greatest room to act without being a political target."

"The world has come to a unique point in time," Kyle observed, "so rare as to be almost unimaginable. Our world parallels Arthur's in a myriad of ways…and the parallel our world needs most of all is you."

"I'm no Arthur," Mac insisted. "I nearly *killed* myself, for chrissakes."

"Because you felt profoundly lost. You desperately needed something in your life, something of great importance. Arthur was calling out to you, but you couldn't hear him. He laid a path for you to follow, but you couldn't see it. Now I have opened your mind and your heart and your eyes, and I ask that you follow him now…and trust in us."

"Of course," allowed Merrill, "you're still free to return home."

"What have I there?" Mac said. "A bottle of gin and a bottle of pills?" He sighed. "But, if I join the UN, could I really do something important?"

Kyle looked at him with a curious smile. "You know, lad, I hadn't noticed before…but you even *look* like Arthur."

Mac gave a dismissive wave of his hand. "You can't possibly know such a thing."

The Keeper chuckled. "Aye…I can…I've seen him."

"You – oh, I see. There's a painting of him, or something. Hidden away in your environmentally controlled vault. Right?"

Kyle smiled and shook his head. "When a family member comes of age, a ceremony is held beside his sarcophagus. The lid is removed and the newest member swears his or her loyalty to Arthur and his ideals."

"Holy – ! Where's his tomb?"

"Very near," answered Kyle, "and you shall see it. Quite soon." He nodded ahead. "Shall we stop for a spot of tea?"

The only other shop in town with its lights on was a tiny café. Outside its large, plate glass window sat a café table and four chairs.

Mac held open the café's door and said, "Age before beauty."

"Wisdom before all," Merrill rejoined with a grin and passed through. "Three teas and three scones, Mildred, if you'd be so kind," he said with a wink for the plump, kindly-looking matron behind the counter.

"Righto, Merrill, dearie," she smiled coyly.

Mac gave Kyle an amused look. The Keeper rolled his eyes and whispered, "The longest flirtation in recorded history."

"Earl Grey, Darjeeling, and Imperial," Merrill decided, looking at the day's chalkboard menu. "We'll sit outside. Join us if you can, love."

"I just might do that," she answered, pouring the teas, her cheeks flushing.

Mac could only speculate whether the blush was more from the steam or Merrill's invitation. Once outside and settled into the wrought iron café chairs, he asked, "You say our world parallels Arthur's, but aren't the parallels just coincidences?"

"Yes and no," said Merrill. "History repeats itself time and again. Acts and follies lead us to a point in time, acts and follies lead us away from it. Through the eyes of history, we have the luxury of seeing both the before and the after together. So, when the before happens, we can – if we're wise – construct the after.

"Let me give you a few examples of the before we face now. During Arthur's lifetime, Rome began its decent. As it did, provincialism took hold at the fringes. The once-united empire splintered into hundreds of independent principalities. The parallel to today is exemplified by what happened after World War Two – the world splintered into more independent nations as colonialism collapsed. Rome broke into ethnically and religiously-related kingdoms, and our world did the same – even more so after the Cold War ended, and former Soviet states broke away.

"Another before and parallel – the independent states birthed in the ruins of the Empire squabbled and fought for centuries. Prior to World War Two, the governments of Europe ruled four-fifths of the earth's population. As de-colonization occurred, and the Soviet Union fell, ever smaller countries of peoples formed. They tended to look and think alike, often suffering from nationalism, religious arrogance, provincialism, and xenophobia. Once again war among neighbors, ethnic clans, and religious sects broke out.

"Another before and parallel – terrorism. Example – during Rome's occupation, the Jews committed acts of terrorism against the State. The most fanatical were known as Sicarii. At public gatherings, they would come up behind their prey, stab them with a dagger called a sicae, and fade back into the crowd to escape. Today, Muslims view Jews as occupiers, but *their* sicae are guns and suicide bombers."

On and on went Merrill's litany of befores and parallels, ending with, "– and the more Arthur's world flourished, the more the people of Europe viewed Britain as a heaven on the edge of the mortal world. Though equity reigned within, Britain's very existence created inequity without. So, too, can we see this today. As Arthur's Britain was to Europe of the Dark Ages, America is to Central and South America. The EU is to Africa and Eurasia. The peoples in less advanced nations are becoming increasingly frustrated. Their bitterness is being channeled into extremism. Such is human nature, and the nature of inequity, a truth Britain discovered too late. If Camulodunum had spread to *all* the lands abandoned by the falling Roman Empire, the thousand-year long Dark Ages would have been avoided."

"I understand your parallels," Mac said respectfully, "but —"

"But the parallels in and of themselves are meaningless. Yes, lad. But, it's what you can do to take *advantage* of them that matters. It's what we learned from the past that we can apply to tomorrow. Computers, the Internet, wireless communications, international media outlets, 24-hour cable, satellite television, radio, and social media — everyone is closer than ever. Massive changes can happen in a heartbeat. Individuals on opposite sides of the globe can communicate with each other in real-time whenever they want. Social and news media enables us to know and influence what's happening almost as it happens — the Arab Spring a case in point. Never has the world been able to affect, and be affected by, events and peoples this thoroughly and quickly.

"Now, what we call democracies today are typically republics — politicians represent the people in the halls of government. The power to govern, therefore, is concentrated in the hands of a few. But, if every person regardless of where they live, the color of their skin, the ethnicity of their ancestors, or the religion they practice had access to the Internet or an iPhone, they could take part in real-time, Greek civitas-style democratic governance. Suppose that on a Friday afternoon Congress introduces a bill. They post it on the Internet, hyperlinks are embedded in the bill's text to websites providing unbiased background and context, social and news media expound on its virtues or vices, the citizenry casts a well-informed yea or nay, and on Monday the results are sent to elected representatives who cast their official votes.

"Let's take it to the next level. What do elected governments do for their people? They pass budgets, conduct international diplomacy, provide for the common defense, bolster the economy, build and maintain infrastructure, educate and train the young, and redistribute wealth to help those in need at home and abroad. With electronic voting, well-informed individuals could do all that – vote on a budget, pass domestic programs, declare war, respond to natural disasters, contract for goods and services, send troops and aid workers overseas, decide on trade policies and sanctions, et cetera, et cetera."

"Assuming the citizenry really does inform itself," Mac commented, "in an unbiased way.

"Aye. Then politicians would become little more than clerks, and capitols like Washington city-sized museums of history.

"And why are there capitols? Because sovereign nations exist. Why are there sovereign nations? Because people with common heredity and belief systems decided to isolate themselves from others. The longer they remain isolated, the more different they'll become from the nations around them. The more different people become, the more likely they'll end up in a conflict of some kind. But, today we have technologies and communications to *de*-isolate people – to break down barriers, to help them see our commonalities not just differences, to expose the pointlessness of isolationism and nationalism. If we could empower everyone to become well-informed and take responsibility for self-governance, and if everyone was connected real-time verbally and visually, then couldn't issues be decided globally? And what if a common language was spoken, a common currency created, inequities in economies eliminated, social programs to help the downtrodden global in scale, freedoms of religion and press commonplace, household income disparities far less dramatic. Then, nations would become more inter-dependent and conflicts between them would become unthinkable. War would be relegated to history books, standing armies would become superfluous, borders would be dissolved —"

Mac was nodding with understanding. "And sovereign nation-states would no longer be needed."

"And a single, worldwide government could come to pass…a *novum orbis regium*. And what international organization stands the best chance of creating such a government?"

"The United Nations," Mac smiled.

"The United Nations," said a self-satisfied Merrill, folding his hands contentedly across his ample belly.

"A *novum orbis regium*," pondered Mac. "Maybe even a single race of people could evolve. A smart, noble, kind, generous, and robust race of golden people with golden souls."

Kyle smiled. "Wouldn't that be something, eh?"

Mac woke again to a brewing pot of coffee. A plate of bangers and biscuits sat upon the kitchen counter with a note from Merrill saying he'd gone into town. Mac filled up his mug, grabbed the plate and a fork, and left for the hall.

Beams of sunlight poured through its windows, illuminating the dust hanging in the motionless air and creating the perfect light-fall for another enjoyable day of reading. A small, leather bound book sat next to the two binders.

"Thanks, Kyle," he whispered with a smile, setting his coffee and plate down.

He opened the second binder to where he'd left off the day before, took a bite of biscuit, and began reading. The hours passed quickly by and he was finishing the last page when Merrill walked in.

"Making good progress I see," the Elder said.

Mac nodded and closed the binder. "Sad how quickly Arthur's utopia fell apart after his death."

"Sad indeed, lad," he said as he sat down. "But is it not hopeful as well?"

Mac looked at him, reflecting for a moment. "Hopeful, for if a utopia existed once, then it could again?"

"Aye," Merrill smiled, "and isn't that what we all wish for?" He nodded at the small leather-bound book lying on the table. "Unfortunately, lad, we must now deal with something unpleasant. Look at the dates of births and deaths after 1914."

The book's cover read, *The Genealogy of Arthur's Descendants*. Mac picked it up with keen anticipation. The story of his family, his *real* family, was about to be revealed.

He flipped to the back of the book and leafed forward.

"Hmmm. My relatives seemed to die rather young, didn't they?"

Merrill nodded gravely.

"Because of the wars?"

"Not entirely, no. Your closest relatives were asked by the Elders not to enlist, though many did so anyway." He leaned forward. "The Clan has its friends, lad, but it also has its enemies. You must always be on guard."

Mac stared back in disbelief. "You mean, my relatives were…murdered?"

Merrill gave a grim nod.

"And my parents?"

As though the question were overdue, the Elder sighed. "Aye, lad."

"But, Clark…it was an accident, right? I was there."

Merrill was silent for a long moment. "Perhaps," he said finally. "Now, read. Come to the cottage when y'are done and we'll have supper with Kyle."

"Uh, yeah," Mac said absently. "Sure.

Merrill walked out and Mac sat there pondering why his family would be a threat to someone. Realizing he didn't know enough yet to answer that question, he took a deep breath, focused, and turned to the first page of the book. There was Arthur's name printed in big, bold letters. Under it in smaller print was '(440-515).' A line went across from his name to, 'Gwyneth of Arymem (449-521),' and from the center of that line a perpendicular one dropped down to the names, 'Amyth (473-525), Patrick (474-515), Mallora (476-539), Ellyn (477-519), and Gythea (479-540)' all in a row. Below them were the names of 15 grandchildren and below them the names of 28 great grandchildren. By the 1800s, the number of living descendants had reached nearly two-thousand.

Then, the number began dropping. Quickly.

Judging by the dates, the following generations of descendants often died before they married or had children. By the end of World War II, Arthur's bloodline had been decimated, and by the time his parents Finn Lawton and Anna Engels died, there were but two entries left in the book – his, William Cameron Lawton, and his brother's, Clark Robert Lawton.

Under Secretary-General Gerhardt Schoen was dressed in a black cotton Polo shirt, black pants, and black cap. Stepping inside the dimly lit bar, he removed his aviator glasses and looked around until he spied the unkempt, gaunt-looking, olive-skinned Pompous Zeda in his thread-bare fatigues staring back with intense black eyes from a dusty table in the darkest corner. Schoen grimly smiled to himself and started across the room. He relished his role as king-maker. He'd played it twenty-two times since he and René Boujeau secretly began their plan to bring about Der Viertes Reich – the Fourth Empire – as Schoen called it.

Zeda did not stand as Schoen approached. Instead, he kicked back a chair across the table from him, and gestured to it with a filthy hand. "Sit," he said in English.

Schoen despised him instinctively. He despised all of these simple-minded creatures. But, they were a means to an end, and the ends always justified the means. "In three months," he explained in passable Greek after he sat down, "a shipment of weapons – rifles, ammunition, sidearms, rocket launchers, uniforms, military vehicles – will be delivered to you aboard a ship called the *Shkhara*."

Zeda's eyes narrowed as he stared unblinkingly at Schoen. "I have little cash," he replied cagily.

Schoen handed him a slip of paper with an eleven-digit number handwritten on it. "That is an account number. You will pay the arms dealer from it. The remaining balance will belong to you."

Zeda glanced at the paper and then at Schoen. Stuffing the paper in his pocket, he hissed, "Why are you doing this? What do you want?"

Schoen leaned back in his chair. "I wish only for you to succeed in your quest to unite your homeland."

Zeda scoffed. "Bullshit"

"I want a well-armed nation led by a powerful soldier who owes me a favor," Schoen answered bluntly.

"What kind of favor?"

Schoen shrugged. "What difference does that make now? What matters is that you will be the supreme commander of your island…a very wealthy supreme commander. When the time comes for me to call in my favor, you will retire to a luxurious estate I know of in Brazil and live the rest of your days in hedonistic comfort. Is that not what we all wish for in the end?"

Not quite sure what hedonistic meant, Zeda debated whether to trust the pale German. "Anything else?"

"Oh, yes," Schoen answered darkly. "Your island is rich in copper, is it not?"

Zeda cautiously nodded.

"Once you are in control, you will simply arrange for all legitimate copper shipments to contain modest surpluses not reflected in the ships' manifests. The surpluses will be quietly offloaded at ports of my choosing and sold on the black market."

"That is all?" Zeda said, unphased.

"Do we have a deal?"

Zeda put his hand out. "Deal."

Schoen gave a contemptuously glance at the man's paw and pushed back his chair. "Three months. The *Shkhara*." He turned and walked out without another word between them.

Sleep did not come easy for him that night, nor did it stay long, but the morning was as glorious as the one before. Washing and getting dressed, he ventured outside with a coffee in one hand and his travel bag in the other.

His young admirer Clarice was waiting for him at the hall. Just the two of them would be going to the train station this morning. Merrill and Kyle had said their good-byes the night before.

"Ah! My chariot awaits," he said with a smile and a bow.

Clarice blushed and slipped into the Astin Martin.

Mac chuckled and slid into the passenger seat beside her. As they drove to Camleton, he spoke to her about the weather, the countryside, and other things of equal weight and importance. Not unexpectedly, it was a one-sided conversation. Until –

"Are you accepting the position?" Clarice asked timidly.

It was the first time he'd her voice and he turned to look at her. "Merrill and the Keeper are wondering the same thing. And judging from my family tree, if I take it, I may find myself in harm's way."

She said no more until they reached the station. Grabbing his bag from the trunk, she handed it to a porter and turned to face Mac. "Are you accepting the position?" she repeated, a bit more forcefully this time.

"Well," he sighed. "God knows I have no life to go back to. So, I might as well start a new one and try to live it as nobly as my ancestors did. And, I tried to throw my life away, so what difference does it make if I risk it now?"

Tears came to her eyes and she whispered the last lines of a poem written nine centuries ago. "'The trumpet sounds, the hooves resound. The righteous rise, the battle cries. But still he

sleeps, and mothers weep. Avalon awaits, great Arthur, awake.'"
She kissed him on the cheek. "Be careful," she said with a smile
and climbed into the Astin Martin. A moment later, she was
lost in the traffic.

"Until we meet again," he whispered.

Twelve hours later he touched down at Traverse International Airport. On his way through the terminal, he made a
call to Dr. Angela Fuentes.

The cab drove off as he opened the front door of his condo.
Walking into the living room, he saw that everything was just
as it was, right down to the bottle of gin and the empty pre-
scription vial sitting on the coffee table.

He'd dreaded this moment, and with good cause. The
reasons he'd tried to kill himself flited through his mind – the
self-loathing, the crushing disappointment, the loneliness –
and he felt like curling up in a ball on the floor.

But, then he thought of Merrill and Kyle, the United
Nations and the Clan. He took a step forward, then another
and still another, until he was outside on the deck staring at
the distant ice-covered bay. He wondered again who'd found
him that night.

Guess that's one more thing to talk with the good doctor
about tomorrow.

Patient files and psychology journals were strewn about Dr.
Angela Fuentes' desk. Opposite her in a comfortable dark
brown leather armchair sat her former patient.

"– and I'm leaving for New York in the morning. If I wasn't crazy before, I must be now," he chuckled.

Angela smiled. "You're not crazy. In fact, I'd say you're quite sane. And fortunate. You've found something to hold onto."

"Yes, I suppose so," he said. Then, he hesitated, uncomfortable bringing up the real reason for his visit. But, he took a deep breath and forged on. "Doc, there's something I never told you about the night I tried to kill myself. I don't know how else to describe it other than to say, I…I left. I left my condo and…went back in time. I was me, yet I was observing a younger me at the same time. I saw things that happened years ago, all the way back to my childhood."

Angela leaned forward in her chair, her brown eyes wide with excitement. "You're talking about a near-death experience!" she marveled, her face beaming. "Tell me – what was it like? How did you feel while it was happening? Tell me everything!"

"Well," Mac began awkwardly, "I felt sad at times…but it was comforting, too, in a way… even peaceful."

"How far back did you go?" she asked, having read case studies of NDEers experiencing full-life reviews.

"Clark's death," Mac replied, "and then pretty much straight through from there. What I noticed most was how interrelated events in my life were. Something happens and twenty years later something else is affected by it." He paused and ran his fingers through his hair. "What do you know about these, uh…what did you call 'em?"

"Near-death experiences," Angela repeated. "NDEs."

"Yeah. Are they –?" Mac began and hesitated again.

"A transition from earthly life to a spiritual one? A stairway to heaven?" Angela finished for him.

Mac nodded self-consciously. She sat back in her chair. "Science would say no. NDEs are a reflection, or perhaps a revelation, of human nature. Almost everyone who has an NDE as their bodies are shutting down says their senses are heightened beyond anything they've experienced before. They think more clearly, their consciousness is more expansive, they feel an intense connectedness with everything and everyone. I believe an NDE is an evolutionary response to a life and death situation. When our very survival is in question, our brain triggers something to enhance mental quickness, clarity, and recall."

"What about the feeling of observing myself – being me, yet seeing a younger me?"

"Stories abound of NDEers floating above or standing beside their bodies. Many recall quite accurately what was happening around them while they were having their out-of-body experience."

Mac paused, fidgeting in his chair. "Is it the soul leaving the body?"

Angela smiled. "So, here's the conundrum – did Man come from the soul, or did the soul come from Man?"

Mac thought about that for a moment before saying, "Is the soul a separate, immutable, undying entity, or –"

"Or did Man *invent* the soul. Yes," Angela nodded. "Is it more logical to say that there's a God and an afterlife, or that we all have brains that act in the same dramatic way under dire circumstances? There are ancient writings going back thousands of years describing NDEs – Jacob's dream of a ladder to heaven, for instance. Other accounts are found in Plato's Republic, North American Indian tales, Lithuanian folklore, the Tibetan Book of the Dead, even *Revelations*. Why there's even a painting in the Dalai Lama's temple of a man lying inert on the ground, eyes closed, while high above him the same man is hovering in mid-air, eyes open and arms stretched out before him like Superman."

"Then, man invented the soul to explain what he couldn't understand," Mac supposed.

Angela shrugged. "Who's to say for sure, but I would tend to agree with that. Death was much more present in people's lives a long time ago. Family members more often than not passed away at home. Your loved one is alive one moment and dead the next. They're warm and animated, then cold and stiff. What happened? Something must have left the body, right? And every so often, someone would experience what we now call an NDE. They returned after 'death' with a story of having left their bodies, or maybe re-living their past, and feeling at one with everything around them. So, people began to cling to the idea of surviving death. They came to believe that earthly life was merely a stepping stone to where the self or soul would transcend. They would finally leave behind the pain and sorrow of earthly life and see their loved ones again in paradise."

"They came to believe in heaven," Mac nodded in understanding. "But, science says what?"

"Well," Angela sighed. "They've duplicated NDEs by stimulating the temporal-parietal junction in the brains of test subjects, or by extreme and prolonged sensory-deprivation, or by creating intense external stimuli, or by injecting hallucinogenic drugs. Interesting story about the drugs – psychoactive plants, like peyote and cannabis, were used by ancient cultures to create transcendent states of being that in many ways mimicked NDEs. Fears and anxieties would fade away, they'd experience an intermixing of the past and present, they'd sense a suspension of time and an intense oneness with nature –"

"Huh. After I…came back, so to speak," Mac said, "I didn't feel so alone. I felt as though none of us really exist as individuals. We're all part of everything and everything is a part of us, you know? Not in some obscure metaphysical way, but in the sense that we…all of us, together…are the same. We're all part of a universal oneness."

"You've been given quite a gift, Mac, one that –" The phone on her desk rang and she picked up the receiver. "Dr. Fuentes," she said. Pause. "Give me a minute."

Mac stood as she laid the receiver down. "Come by the condo tonight, if you can," he told her. "I have some friends coming over for a little going away celebration."

"Mmmm, maybe," she equivocated. "I suppose we're not doctor and patient anymore."

"One other question, doc?" he asked, extending his hand to her.

But before he could ask, Angela smiled and said, "Sorry, I can't tell you."

"Doc, I'm sure it's in the police report and it's probably in your file on me. I have legal access to both now."

"You do," the good doctor replied, "but don't go looking for the name. Someday they'll come to you."

4

"The most beautiful emotion we can experience is the mysterious…the cradle of all true art and science. He to whom this emotion is a stranger, who can no longer wonder and stand rapt in awe, is as good as dead, a snuffed-out candle. The sense that behind anything that can be experienced there is something that our minds cannot grasp, whose beauty and sublimity reaches us only indirectly, this is religiousness. In this sense, and in this sense only, I am a devoutly religious man."

           – Albert Einstein

"For learning softeneth the heart and breedeth gentleness and charity."

           – Mark Twain

"Every preacher ought to be a philosopher…and every house of devotion a school of science."

           – Thomas Paine

The phone's ringing drew a heavy sigh. "Damned contractors," he muttered and thought of not answering. But, good soldier that he was, General Adolph Heinrich Mendenberg picked up the satellite phone and pressed Answer.

"Ja?" he asked impatiently.

"General," said an impatient Gerhardt Schoen, "I'm emailing you the details of another shipment of arms. This time to Cyprus."

"Mein Herr!" the General exclaimed as he stood and snapped to attention for a man 6,000 miles away.

"How did the diversion of phosphate exports turn out?" Schoen said.

"How good to hear from you," effused Mendenberg.

"The phosphate exports, General?" Schoen repeated irritably.

"One moment, Mein Herr," he replied, and opened a file on his PC. Scanning the rows of numbers in the electronic journal, he said, "A small shipment. Black market purchasers paid just under half a million Euros. But if we do as well on future shipments, then we should exceed fifty million by year end."

"Zehr gut. And our arms shipments to President Qadda?" he asked, referring to the military leader of Algeria he'd personally place in power ten years ago.

"On their way next week, mein Herr," Mendenberg replied, "that is, if the damned shipping contractors get everything to the *Shkhara* on schedule."

"Make sure they do," Schoen warned him. "Herr Boujeau has ordered us to increase our offensive weaponry to North Africa. Wire transfers to our Georgian arms dealer from my Swiss account will become more frequent. The *Shkhara* must sail round-the-clock from now on. The manifests will be sent to you 30 days in advance as usual. Understood?"

"Ja, Mein Herr."

"Gut," and the line went dead.

"Abrams residence."

"Gerald, this is Merrill. Please out the Senator on."

"One moment, sir."

After what seemed to Merrill an eternity, Gerald returned to the line. "I'm afraid the Senator is indisposed, sir, and is not taking calls."

Cursing, the Elder slammed the phone down and began dialing again. "Pompous bastard," he muttered.

Michael Abrams strolled along the mahogany-planked decks of his 47-foot cabin cruiser, the *Il Cigno*, anchored off the north shore of Key West. From the flying bridge, his friend and captain called down, "Phone, Mike!"

"I'll take it in the stateroom, Pete!" the former Senator called back, and headed below. A moment later, he picked up the receiver. "Abrams," he said, settling into a plush armchair.

"Michael!" barked Merrill. "Your bloody grandson is reneging on our agreement, just like I told you he would!"

The former Senator from Virginia chuckled and shook his head. "Merrill, my friend, don't worry about Jack. He's more than a bit full of himself, but the purse strings come back to me."

"He won't even take me damn calls!" blustered Merrill.

"It's only been a few days, old friend. Take a deep breath and trust me," Michael said with a smile. "He'll do what I tell him to, just like always."

Merrill gave a heavy sigh and said in a more conciliatory tone, "Kyle has a place of honor for you in the Keeper's history."

"Merrill," he laughed, "you're vinegar and sugar in a tea cup. I never know which I'll get next."

He heard Merrill's chuckle from across the sea and the two old friends talked of happier things. After they said their good-byes, Michael speed-dialed his grandson.

"Abrams residence."

"Gerald, Michael here. Please tell Jack I wish to speak with him."

"Of course, sir," Gerald replied and set the phone down again. A few moments later, Michael's grandson picked up.

"Grandfather," Jack Abrams said smugly. "How are the Keys?"

Ignoring the question and the smugness, the elder Abrams said firmly, "You're seeing to it that the President's nominee for Deputy U.S. Ambassador comes before your committee, right Jack?"

"Look, Grandfather, the person Senator Thomas and I picked, and Ambassador Tanner *wants*, is much more qualified *and* a major campaign contributor –"

"Get William Cameron MacCrarey before your committee, Jack, or I'll be using my fortune to back your opponent in the next election. Understood?"

The Senator knew very well that his grandfather never made threats. He made plans. Swallowing his pride yet again, he mustered what little sincerity he could and said, "I'm sure Mr. MacCrarey…could make a…decent Deputy Ambassador, sir."

"Prep him for the hearing, Jack. Good-bye."

No sooner had he heard the click of the line than the younger Abrams cursed and threw the phone across the room. "This is *my* life!" he yelled to no one. "*I'm* the Senator now, not that old fossil!" MacCrarey's a nobody. Grandfather's puppet. Hell, just because he made that donation to Princeton to get me through law school, and helped me become Senator…and gave me a job…and lets me live in his mansion…

His anger bubbled over again. "MacCrarey's going down in flames, old man!" he shouted. "And you can't do a damned thing about it!"

Mac opened his garage door. Washington, D.C. was fourteen hours and 900 miles away. Late winter. Jeep Grand Cherokee to the left; 1968 red convertible Mustang to the right. Which to take?

He slipped in behind the wheel of the Mustang.

Driving south along the ridge of the peninsula, he reached US-31 and turned right. Reaching M-72 in Acme, he headed east through rolling snow-covered hills to Grayling and picked up I-75 southbound. He pushed in the Bob Seger CD and turned up the volume.

"Woke last night to the sound of thunder. How far off I sat and wondered. Started hummin' a song from 1962! Ain't it funny how the night moves, when you just don't seem to have as much to lose! Strange how the night moves…"

Senator Jack Abrams wanted to meet before the confirmation hearings. The Senate Foreign Affairs Committee convened tomorrow, and Mac was one of several nominees who'd be appearing to answer questions.

Like a President who wants to appoint Supreme Court Justices and set the tone of future rulings, Senators want to appoint people of like mind, or at least of political advantage, to foster their personal agendas. Ambassadors to wealthy countries were quite valuable, but the Ambassador to the United Nations was pure gold. Mac was nominated for the Deputy

U.S. Ambassador to the UN, and would stand in for him during his absences. That made Mac pretty close to gold.

A U.S. Ambassador to the UN fills two roles – normal ambassadorial functions like any other UN Ambassador, and a permanent member of the UN Security Council. The Security Council can veto any action taken by the General Assembly, and the General Assembly must implement every resolution from the Security Council. The U.S. Ambassador, therefore, is a very powerful person, and Mac would be his second-in-command.

"I'll be the Second," Mac said to himself as he drove, "like Arthur was."

If I get approved, that is. Jack Abrams wasn't very keen on my nomination. Maybe he'll try to sabotage me. Hell, it would be easy enough. I have no political or diplomatic experience. And what if Abrams or the FBI digs up my ambulance records, or subpoena's Angela's case file on me? How could I defend my psychological soundness?

He shook his head and sighed. "What the hell am I doing?"

A clean-cut Aide in a Navy uniform looked up from his desk as Mac walked into the anteroom of Senator Abrams' office.

Wearing an expensive black business suit, black wingtips, white dress shirt, and a gold, red, and yellow Garcia tie, the man from Traverse cut quite an impressive figure.

The recently matriculated Annapolis man immediately stood. "Yes, sir?"

"I'm William Cameron MacCrarey. I have an appointment with the Senator," Mac said with a feigned I-do-this-sort-of-thing-everyday attitude.

"Yes, sir. One moment, sir."

Ensign York walked over to the Senator's office door and knocked.

"What is it?" came a distant and impatient reply.

The Aide opened the door and announced Mac's arrival.

"Well! Please show Mr. MacCrarey in," said the suddenly saccharin voice.

The Ensign turned and gestured for Mac.

"How's my old friend Merrill?" Jack asked, coming around his desk to meet Mac as he entered. They shook hands and Jack directed Mac to an armchair beside a coffee table with a tea serving and pastries. "By the way, do you go by William or Bill?" he said, sitting down in an identical chair on the other side of the table.

"Mac, actually. And Merrill's doing just fine, Senator. He, uh, sends his regards."

"Wonderful! Please give him my best when you see him next."

"I'm sure he'll want to hear everything you have to say."

"Yes. Right. Well, the Senate confirmation hearings start in an hour. I'm doing a big favor for my old friend Merrill, you know," he chuckled. "I don't want to disappoint him. Or you, Bill."

"Mac."

"Of course. So, no need to prep. Just routine questions from the Committee today."

Mac didn't believe him but said nothing.

"Procedurally, this is how it'll go," and the Senator explained that the Chair fields questions from Committee members, they'll ask about his background and experience, and then vote. All very simple. "That's it, Bill. How do you feel?"

"Mac. Fine."

"Right. Good." Abrams sat back, crossed his legs, and inquired casually, "How do you know my old friend Merrill, if you don't mind me asking?"

"No, I don't mind. Merrill and I just met a few days ago."

Abrams laughed. "You're kidding…right?"

"Nope," Mac answered, trying not to smile.

"Why would he ask my grandfather, I mean me, to nominate you to the UN if he hardly knows you?"

Mac stood up, "I suggest you ask your grandfather. If that's all, Senator –?"

"I…uh, yes," the Senator stammered, getting to his feet.

"Then I'll see you at the hearings," and Mac walked out of the office.

He arrived at the Senate Chamber a few minutes before the hearings were scheduled to begin. Stepping inside, he saw a few reporters and a handful of nominees in the first row. Several people Mac guessed were family members of the nominees sat here and there in the mostly empty gallery. In the front of the chamber was a raised semi-circular dais behind which the Senators sat. Several of them were milling about in front of the dais talking and laughing, including Jack Abrams.

Noticing Mac, Jack waved him over. "You're last today, Bill," he said in the same saccharin voice.

"His name is Mac," came a deep, confident voice. Mac turned to see an older and very familiar looking man walking down the center aisle towards them. His light tan suit and white hair accented his bronzed skin and bold blue eyes.

Jack Abrams' expression turned stone cold. "Grandfather," he forced out.

"Jack," the former Senator replied, handing his grandson a sheet of paper. "Go get the hearings started. I'll take care of Mr. MacCrarey."

"Yes, sir," the younger Abrams said resignedly and turned to rejoin his colleagues.

"Mr. Abrams, very nice to meet you," Mac said extending a hand. "Merrill and Kyle speak very highly of you."

"Call me Michael, please," he told him, shaking his hand warmly. "Merrill and Kyle are good men and it's been my pleasure to help the Clan whenever I can. Please sit with me, if you would be so kind."

Mac was taken aback by Michael's deference, especially given how he'd treated his own grandson. "Of course," Mac said, following the former Senator to a pair of seats near the back of the chamber.

Chairman Abrams rapped his gavel, asked everyone to stand for the invocation and pledge of allegiance, and called the first nominee. She was sworn in, asked to state her name, and told to take a seat at the table in front of the dais. Each Senator took a turn asking questions and when they had finished, Chairman Abrams called for a vote. Her unanimous confirmation was greeted with respectful applause from the gallery and the process repeated itself for the next nominee.

As the third confirmation came to a close, Michael leaned over to Mac, "When the opportunity presents itself, I want you to tell the Committee your real name and who you are. Jack knows about the Clan, but not your connection to it."

Mac looked at him as if he were crazy. "Who I am? You mean —" and his voice dropped to a whisper, "Arthur's descendant and all that?"

"That's exactly what I mean."

"But…won't they think I'm, you know…nuts?"

Michael laughed. "Of course, they will. Then, it'll be up to you and the Clan to prove it."

Mac closed his eyes. "What am I doing here?"

"You'll do fine," chuckled the elder Abrams. "Remember who you are."

"My fellow colleagues, esteemed members of the press, guests, and confirmees," Jack Abrams began with a photogenic smile and a nod to the confirmees, "it is my honor to formally nominate William Cameron MacCrarey for the position of Deputy United States Ambassador to the United Nations."

This was by far the most important nomination of the day, but still back-page news. Everyone sat up a little straighter and all eyes turned to Mac as he made his way to the front of the chamber and took a seat.

"It goes without saying that an appointment to the United Nations is extremely important to the United States," Abrams said in a tone void of all emotion as he read from the sheet of paper Michael had given him. "The Deputy will often be asked to fill the Ambassador's shoes and represent our great land before the nations of the world. He will be our voice, our ears, our conscience, and our vote on the Security Council. In his position, he will serve on several Committees and undertake numerous projects for both our Ambassador and the UN membership as a whole. I take great pride in presenting Mr. MacCrarey to the Committee, for in all the years I've followed this extraordinary man, he has exceeded my expectations at every turn. Rest assured that he will serve our nation and the world respectfully and honestly." Tossing the paper aside like a soiled rag, he gave Mac a smile that was anything but friendly. "Now, I'd like to give my colleagues the opportunity to ask him a few questions."

The first questions were softballs – what was his educational background, what work experience did he have, and so on. Soon, though, they graduated to more difficult ones – what did he think of so and so in this country or that, how would he handle such and such a situation.

A half-hour into the questioning, the chamber doors flew open and in rushed Ensign York. He hurried down the aisle and over to the desk of Senator Mitchell Thomas of Ohio. All present watched in rapt attention as the Senator's manicured hand covered the microphone and York passed him a file. As the young man whispered in Thomas' ear, a look of restrained disappointment and then anger crossed his face. Removing his hand, he announced with all the drama he could muster, "Ladies and gentlemen, some very disturbing information has just been brought to my attention."

Jack Abrams leaned back in his chair like the cat who caught the canary.

Thomas held up York's dossier, a FBI logo emblazoned on the cover. "Mr. MacCrarey. I have here discharge papers from a state hospital in a place called Traverse for a patient with your name…a patient who tried to commit suicide."

Surprised conversations broke out in the gallery and Abrams rapped his gavel on the desk. "Silence!" he barked, relishing his power and the press value of the moment.

"Is this true, Mr. MacCrarey? Did you try and take your own life, a life the Good Lord gave to you? Because if it is… then I must strongly object to your nomination on the grounds that you are morally unfit to serve as Deputy Ambassador."

Murmurs sounded from every corner and Abrams rapped his gavel again.

Mac turned to Michael for help, but the friend of the Clan simply smiled and gave an encouraging nod.

Mac turned back to the dais, took a deep breath, and said, "Senator…yes, it's true."

Gasps and excited conversations instantly filled the room. Reporters scribbled notes and cameras clicked. Jack banged his gavel on the desk and shouted, "Order!" as though he were a judge and the chamber was a courtroom.

"I spent a two-week observation period at the state hospital after I nearly OD-ed on painkillers and alcohol. But, I didn't try to end my life – my life tried to end me. I'd been living with feelings of crushing disappointment. I was incomplete. I should have been something more, or done something important with my life. Well," he smiled weakly, "this is that something important. I have been given the incredible opportunity to represent my country at the United Nations. And I will do that to the best of my ability."

He looked back at Michael who smiled and nodded again.

Mac cleared his throat. "I've also learned in recent days that I…I was not born William Cameron MacCrarey." Gasps of dismay, the hum of whispers, and the sharp rap of a gavel. "That surname belonged to the couple who raised me. My real last name, and that of my deceased brother, is Lawton. I am the last of that distinguished family…a blood line that goes back 1,500 years to one, extraordinary man…a Briton named Artorius, and known to the world as…Arthur."

This time the gallery filled with hushed conversations and condescending snickers. The reporters and Senators, Mac noted, seemed to be in hog heaven. Senator Thomas, his words dripping with incredulity, boomed, "You think you're King Arthur?"

Nonplussed, Mac answered, "I believe I'm *related* to the man *history* called King Arthur, Senator, and I found it rather hard to believe as well…at first."

The Senators were putting on their best media faces now. Thomas looked indignant and Jack Abrams looked positively euphoric.

"Mr. MacCrarey, I find this all highly unusual," declared a junior Senator from California, "and, frankly, I believe you are either delusional or a *liar.*"

"I am neither, Senator," Mac replied, "and in the absence of the facts, you have no basis for judging me to be either."

"Mr. MacCrarey, to be related to a fairy tale is *impossible*," accused Senator Thomas, "and to believe it for a moment raises serious doubts about your *sanity*. I could not *possibly* vote to confirm you as Deputy Ambassador now."

"It is the truth, Senator, and if I'm not mistaken the purpose of hearings like this is to get at the truth. Is that not so?"

Chairman Abrams spoke up with practiced indignation. "Of *course* it is, Mr. MacCrarey. I demand nothing less!"

"Well, then…I've shared with you the truth of my lineage, Senator."

"Can you *prove* it?" Jack challenged.

Without hesitation, Mac replied, "Yes. I can."

"That's absurd," Abrams said with a dismissive flourish of his gavel.

The Senator from Michigan held up a hand. "Hold on, Jack. Maybe we should give Mr. MacCrarey a chance to prove it."

"He says he's related to a character out of *book*, for crying out loud!"

"Let him try and prove it," insisted the Michigan Senator. He couldn't care less if Mac proved it or not, but he did want a prolonged hearing in the media spotlight.

"I agree," Thomas acquiesced, also realizing the PR bonanza suddenly afoot.

"What the –? But, this…that's –" faltered Abrams. Finally, he let out a long, frustrated sigh and slammed down his gavel. "These hearings will reconvene tomorrow morning at eleven." Pointing the gavel at Mac, Jack warned, "I expect you to have undeniable proof of who you claim to be. If not, this Committee will dismiss you out of hand. Do I make myself perfectly clear?"

"Perfectly," Mac stated coolly.

"Then we are adjourned."

The networks picked up the story and ran with it on their evening news. The next morning, every major paper carried the story below the fold on their front pages, and the morning talk shows were buzzing with it.

Schoen threw his coffee mug across his office, smashing it against the closed door. A moment later his startled secretary rushed in. "Are you all right, sir?" she asked urgently, glancing at the shards of glass strewn across the floor.

"Get out!" Schoen screamed, picking up a polished stone paperweight and heaving it at her.

With a shriek, she slammed the door behind her.

Hands shaking, the Under Secretary-General picked up the receiver and punched in Boujeau's private number. It took several rings, but finally his boss answered.

"Yes, Gerhardt?" said Boujeau.

"Mein Herr. William Cameron MacCrarey, the nominee for U.S. Deputy Ambassador, is *not* a MacCrarey!"

"What are you talking about?" said Boujeau with no small measure of exasperation.

"He's a *Lawton*."

Now the Under Secretary-General had his boss's attention. "Why does that name sound familiar?"

"It is for that family the Clan Camulodunum exists!"

"MacCrarey's nomination is tied to your Clan nonsense?"

The Secretary-General's continuing dismissal of the Clan grated on Schoen, but he forced out a, "Ja."

"Why would the Clan want one of their own in the General Assembly?"

Schoen knew damned well why. The Lawton's were direct descendants of Arthur. He'd never told his boss that, though. He simply said the Clan was a peacenik, socialist clique with important connections. "The Clan's trying to push their agenda by stealing a permanent seat on the Security Council. Their next ploy will be to kill Tanner and make it look like an accident, so MacCrarey can become Ambassador."

"That seems rather far-fetched, Gerhardt, but still…I don't like this."

"I can take care of him," Schoen said eagerly, his eyes flaring and the fingers on his free hand curling into claws.

"*No,* Gerhardt. We do not want any undue attention focused on us, not when we're so close. Watch and wait."

Schoen breathed out. "Ja, Herr Secretary-General," he answered resignedly

Mac stood in the doorway of the hearing chamber looking around in amazement. Beside him were Merrill MaGeah and Kyle Dunham who'd arrived in time for a late breakfast. What had been a nearly empty hearing room the day before was now standing room only. Kyle said to his companions, "I often wondered what the day would be like when the Clan's 1500 years of obscurity ended." He sighed and shook his head. "But, I never imagined it would be like this."

A TV talking head at the front of the chamber pointed at Mac and yelled, "There he is!"

A horde of reporters and photographers stampeded up the aisle shouting questions and clicking cameras. Kyle, Merrill, and Mac silently made their way to the front of the room. The Keeper carried with him the dusty old valises and set them on the table.

Chairman Abrams called the hearing to order and rapped his gavel. "All rise for the invocation and the pledge of allegiance."

Everyone bowed their heads as Mitchell Thomas began to speak. "Dear Father in Heaven, we humbly ask that you guide us with Your unerring wisdom as we represent You and our nation this morning. Ensure that our decisions are just in Your eyes and that we follow the teachings of Your Son in all our actions. Reveal to us Your wishes or reprimands for William Cameron MacCrarey, and allow us to judge him in accordance with Your will. Amen."

A chorus of "Amens" followed and everyone perfunctorily recited the pledge of allegiance. As they took their seats, Abrams leaned forward, glowering at Mac. "The floor is yours, Mr. MacCrarey…or Lawton or whoever you are. But let me warn you – I expect only the facts. Anything else and you will be dismissed posthaste. Am I clear?"

"Crystal," Mac replied.

"Then proceed," said the Senator.

"Let me begin by introducing two of my Clan elders – Kyle Dunham," gesturing to his right, "and Merrill MaGeah," gesturing to his left. "Kyle is my Clan's Keeper and I've asked him to explain our history."

Taking out one of the leather-bound binders and opening it to the first yellowing page, he began, "In the late fifth century, Anno Domini –"

An hour later, having told of Arthur's life, the Clan's mission, and Mac's lineage, Kyle closed, *The Genealogy of Arthur's Descendants*.

The Committee members, having listened to the Keeper in rapt silence, now let loose a cavalcade of questions. Unflustered, the Elder answered each in turn, often referring back to specific pages or events in the binders or genealogy. Try as he may, though, the tone of the Committee's questions and their body language hinted at lingering skepticism.

Still, Kyle's patience never faltered and his enthusiasm never waned.

Mac, on the other hand, became increasingly frustrated as the questions wore on.

After another hour of back and forth, the Chairman had had enough, and interrupted a question from the New Jersey Senator. "Mr. Dunham, my colleagues and I have been infinitely patient with you. Yet, I have neither heard nor seen *anything* that proves what Mr. MacCrarey said yesterday is true. At best, you've wasted our time and at *worst* you're a *liar* of monumental proportion! And you, Mr. MacCrarey, to believe this man shows questionable integrity and a blatant lack of good judgment, judgment that a Deputy Ambassador to the United Nations must have in abundance. Therefore, I have no choice but to move that you be dismissed from any further consideration. I also intend to investigate whether *charges* should be brought against *both* of you for lying under oath to an official body of the United States government!"

"I'll second the motion!" declared Thomas.

"All in favor?" said Abrams, raising his gavel.

But, before any "Ayes" could be voiced, Mac asked, "What *would* make you believe, Senator Abrams?"

Half the press was standing now, cameras and tape recorders in hand, while the other half sat on the edge of their seats scribbling furiously on note pads.

The Chairman froze, gavel still held high. "What would –? I wouldn't – All in favor say 'Aye!'"

"You're still after the *truth*, aren't you Senator?" challenged Mac.

Abrams swung the gavel towards Mac. "You insolent little –! The truth is *all* I demand. But so far, your Gofer hasn't given us anything but fairy tales."

"He is our *Keeper*," Mac said angrily, "and given the patience and respect he's shown your committee, he deserves yours in return."

A smattering of applause sounded from the gallery.

Abrams slammed his gavel down so hard he broke its head off. "Silence!" he screamed. "This mockery of my committee is over!"

The Senator from Michigan spoke up. "Jack, in the name of fairness, I suggest we hear Mr. MacCrarey out."

"Here, here," exclaimed the Senator from Massachusetts.

Abrams' face turned crimson. His moment was slipping away, but he couldn't risk being portrayed as a bully.

"Mr. MacCrarey," the Senator from California said with a careful balance of magnanimity and prudence, "you have the floor. I caution you, though…the patience of this Committee is wearing thin."

Mac gave a slight bow of his head and began evenly, "Just days ago, I was in the same position as you are now. I was being asked to believe something about myself that seemed impossible. But, they –" he said, pointing to Merrill and Kyle, "– convinced me that Arthur truly existed and his bloodline continued, unbroken, to this day. Yet," he added sincerely, "don't take my word for it. Or even theirs. Bring in a panel of experts. Send them to England to authenticate my claim. And reconvene this hearing in a week's time."

More than happy to keep the PR spotlight shining, the Senator from California quickly made a motion to do just that.

Another seconded it, and Abrams had no choice but to call a vote. It passed easily.

A three-professor panel was assembled, its members drawn from prestigious universities – Dr. Jonathon Joseph Kraeg, a Paleoanthropologist from Cambridge University; Dr. Jay Michener, a sociobiologist from Penn State; and Dr. Robert Ingersaul, an archaeologist from Yale. Three days after the hearing recessed, the Professors climbed out of a rented Range Rover in front of the old hall.

Through the open doorway stepped Merrill, Kyle, and Mac to greet their distinguished guests. Introductions were made all around, and Kyle welcomed the Professors inside. A few of the Clansfolk were busy with dinner preparations by the great hearth as the six of them sat down at one of the wooden tables.

"I trust you all know Latin?" Kyle asked, gesturing at the neatly arranged stacks of photocopies.

"Oh, yes," Dr. Kraeg said, and the others nodded. "Good. And Gaelic?"

"Not so much," chuckled Dr. Michener.

"These are copies of the original handwritten, post-Roman documents written in a mix of Latin and Gaelic. I can help you with the latter. In them you'll find a chronology of events depicting Artorius' creation of a free and united Britain."

"Thank-you, sir," said Dr. Michener. "Is there a historian familiar with this region of England we could talk to as well?"

The Keeper smiled. "I am the 40th Keeper, and 23 were my relatives. You shall find no one more familiar with Camulodunum than I. My family has had the honor of preserving our Clan's legacy, carrying on its purpose for being, and often keeping its existence a secret. First from the mainlanders, then from the Church, later from monarchs, and most recently from the Nazis. Too many believed the medieval fantasies of the Grail and Excalibur, and few have ever bothered to learn the truth."

"What truth is that?" asked Dr. Michener.

Kyle and Merrill told the Professors about Camulodunum, the history of the Clan, and its mission.

"The Clan has chosen now to place Arthur's last heir onto the world stage in hopes of bringing that one brief, shining moment to all nations." He gave a self-deprecating smile and added, "That shall be no small task, of course, but it's one that Mac and the Clan have sworn to pursue." Kyle gestured to the double doors. "Come!" he said and led the Professors outside.

Passing through the trees to a meadow, he halted. "Tomorrow, you and Merrill shall take the Range Rover and tour the Camulodunum's archaeological sites." With a wave of his hand, he asked, "Can you tell me what's unusual about the hills bordering our valley?"

The three professors looked up at the hills, but Mac spoke first. "There's something not natural about the ridges of these hills. They're different from the hills we drove through to get here, more…sharp, if you know what I mean. Like something's up there."

"Aye," Kyle smiled. "Not far from here is Hadrian's Wall, a stone and earthen barrier spanning the entire width of England. When it was first built, the wall was four meters wide and seven meters high. It was meant to keep the Scot clans at bay and mark the northern-most frontier of the Roman Empire. It had a walkway atop for guard patrols, forts to garrison Roman troops, and gates to allow traders, soldiers, and dignitaries to come and go." With a nod, he added, "Those aren't ridges, lads. They're the remains of ramparts like those of Hadrian's Wall. Our valley was formed some 20,000 years ago by glaciers pushing south from the Arctic. It's 60 kilometers long and 25 kilometers at its broadest. At Arthur's request, the valley was circumscribed by a 400-kilometer wall modeled after Hadrian's, but five times the length. Within its protection lay the province of Camulodunum - 14 towns, hundreds of family farms and orchards, a university, the Curia, and a quarter million citizens. There was even an old Roman circus where Arthur held something akin to the ancient Greek Olympics, which had been banned by Theodosius a century before."

He pointed to the ground beneath their feet. "We're standing over what once was Arthur's home. Keep that in the back of your mind and let's return to the hall."

Inside again, Kyle pointed at the old brick wall as he headed for the great hearth. "That is all that remains of the Curia – Arthur's Court and Council, his seat of government. For me Clansfolk, it's akin to the Western Wall in Jerusalem." Beckoning for the Professors, Merrill, and Mac to follow, he stepped into the tall arched brick hearth. After navigating around the cooking fire the Clanswomen were using to prepare dinner, he disappeared into the shadows beyond.

"What the –?" exclaimed Dr. Kraeg.

Merrill chuckled and followed the Keeper. A moment later, he too disappeared into he shadows.

"Well, when in Rome," Mac grinned and walked up to the hearth. Gingerly, he made his way around the cooking fire. Looking first left, then right he called over his shoulder, "There's a passageway back here. Come on!"

The others followed and soon they were trudging down a winding stone stairway into a large, vaulted underground chamber. It had been constructed of the same brick as the wall above. In the stanchions where torches once rested, electric lights glowed bright.

"These were the catacombs of Camulodunum," Merrill explained. "Many of our Clansfolk choose to be entombed here when they pass, just as their ancestors did."

Dr. Kraeg walked full circle around the perimeter of the chamber glancing down the numerous passageways. He did a double take and stopped in front of one. "Where's *that* one lead to?"

Not twenty feet in was a stainless-steel door with floor-to-ceiling windows on either side. Beyond was a well-lit, foyer-like room and another steel door.

"Looks like an airlock," Mac observed, standing beside the Professor.

"Very good, lad," Merrill said. "That is the Library."

"What kind of library?" Dr. Michener inquired.

Merrill cocked his head and grinned. "Why, *the* Library, of course. The greatest library in all of human history. The Library of Alexandria, founded by Alexander the Great himself in 330 B.C."

"You're *joking*," gasped Dr. Michener. "The Library of Alexandria disappeared *millennia* ago."

"To be precise," said Merrill, "the last remnants of it were destroyed by fire 1,700 years ago. But, the bulk of the library's collection had been secreted out of Alexandria two centuries before. A handful of scholars and the chief librarian feared for the library's safety and hired a Roman sea Captain to take the library's contents to the land furthest from the Emperor and the new Church. Under the cover of darkness and guided out to sea by the great lighthouse of Alexandria, the Captain set sail for Britannia."

"The library's contents," Kyle explained, "includes early Christian gospels that contradict later Church doctrine; holy books of pagan religions; histories of lost civilizations; maps and trade routes to great cities that had long since vanished;

ancient science, philosophy, and medicinal collections from across the known world."

"My God, Mr. Dunham," exclaimed Dr. Ingersaul. "Can we see them?"

"For the time being it shall remain off-limits," the Keeper replied firmly, and turned to the vaulted archway opposite the library. "Our purpose is to prove that Mac is the last living descendant of Arthur. If you will follow me –" and he disappeared into the darkened passageway beyond.

Without a word, Mac and the others did as they were asked, though Dr. Ingersaul longingly looked back at the airlock. Soon, they emerged into a brightly lit room, perfectly round, and circumscribed by Ionic columns supporting an elaborately carved stone cupola. The walls were made of white marble and in the center of a raised floor sat three sarcophagi bathed in bright, white light.

"We're underground," a puzzled Dr. Michener said looking up. "Where's the light coming from?"

"The Clan built what looks like an old fieldstone well directly above the burial chamber. It allows sunlight through the oculus at the top of the cupola."

"Why does that one look so much older than the two side-by-side ones?" asked Dr. Ingersaul, pointing at the yellow granite sarcophagus set to one side. On its lid was an exquisitely carved likeness of a young soldier.

"Because it is," Merrill replied reverently, "by nearly eight-hundred years."

"Who's in it?" Dr. Kraeg asked in amazement.

"That, doctor, is the Soma of Alexander the Great," Kyle proudly replied.

The professors gave a collective gasp of astonishment.

"But, that…he…no one knows *where* Alexander is buried," stammered Dr. Ingersaul. "He was entombed in Alexandria –"

"– in 330 BC," Merrill said, "after he died in battle at the age of 27. His mausoleum was near the Great Library, so he set sail out of the city with the books and the sea Captain."

Professors Ingersaul and Kraeg gravitated towards the Soma, but Dr. Michener reverently approached the two, side-by-side sarcophagi. They were made of the same white marble as the walls and floor. He leaned over the one to the right and read the inscription. Face beaming, he recited aloud, "'Hic Sileo Artorius, Primoris Quod Posterus Regnum Nostri Orbis!' 'Here Rests Arthur, First and Future King of Our World.'"

"My God," exclaimed Dr. Ingersaul, hurrying over. "Could it really be so?"

"Aye," said Merrill.

"And this one," said Kyle, pointing to the opposite sarcophagus, "contains Arthur's wife, Gwyneth."

"Genetic analysis…Carbon-14 dating," sputtered Dr. Michener. "If we could we get a skin or bone sample from his body, we could determine the age of his remains, his genetic haplogroup, and," hoisting a thumb at Mac, "whether he's a descendant."

"Of course, Doctor."

With his fingers, Mac slowly traced the engraved letters on Arthur's sarcophagus, viscerally sensing a connection with the great man within. The others turned to watch and slowly backed away. "May I see him?" Mac whispered deferentially.

Kyle gave a knowing smile and said, "Of, course, lad."

With a nod to Merrill, they left the room and returned a moment later with two sturdy oak beams, two meters long with long notches carved into them.

"If the three of you would be so kind," Merrill asked the professors.

Drs. Ingersaul and Kraeg took one of the beams, Merrill and Dr. Michener the other. Fitting the notches under the ends of the marble lid, the four men heaved and strained until they heard a deep "Whoomph!" like a cork pulled from an old jug. The lid slowly rose up and they carefully set it aside. Gathering around the sarcophagus, they looked down at the well-preserved remains of a man, average in size and proportion, dressed in a long white toga-like robe. His hands, fingers interlaced, rested atop his chest. To his left lay a sword, to his right a scroll of parchment.

Mac reached out and touched the sleeve of Arthur's tunic. "The sword he wielded in life to create peace…the parchment recording his deeds…the hands that held his bride and cradled his children –"

His voice trailed off and he looked up at Kyle. "Even if his blood *does* flow through my veins, how could I ever follow in his footsteps?"

Kyle placed his hand on Mac's shoulder. "Trust in yourself, as we do, and in time you'll discover what lies within you. For now, focus on your confirmation. Then –" he gave Merrill a smile.

"*Then,*" said the Elder, "we'll prepare you for what comes next."

The hearing chamber was again standing room only. The Senators called the three professors forward one by one. Dr. Michener was the last.

"And," he said, pointing at the wide-screen TV on the wall, "the DNA analysis coincides with Dr. Ingersaul's carbon-14 dating analysis. The inscription, 'Hic Sileo Artorius, Primoris Quod Posterus Regnum Nostri Orbis,' was carved between 400 and 500 CE, the same time period as the burial garments were from. There is no questioning the fact that he lived and died in the fifth century of the Common Era. The only question that remains, of course, is the man's true identity. Was he in fact…Arthur?

"As Dr. Kraeg testified, a man by the name of Artorius who later took the name Arthur, in fact existed and governed all of what is now known as England on the eve of Europe's collapse into the Dark Ages. The DNA sample of the man buried in the crypt and the DNA sample taken from Mr. MacCrarey, provides us with three facts. First, the man in the crypt was descended from an Anglo people living in the British Isles since 20,000 BC. Second, he and Mac have remarkably *little* variance at *all* from the original Anglo inhabitants. The parents of Mr. MacCrarey, and their parents before them, and so on and so forth for *thousands* of years have come from the same small haplogroup – that is to say, a genetically similar line of human beings. Third, and most importantly, Mr. MacCrarey's DNA is, unequivocally, of the same patrilineal line as the man entombed in the Curia."

A sense of excitement rippled through the gallery with a cheer here and applause there. Clicks from press photographer cameras and shouted questions from reporters competed with the insistent rap of Chairman Abram's gavel.

"DNA cannot tell us a man's name, nor what he accomplished in life. It can only tell us where his distant relatives came from and who he his descended from. In the end, a leap of faith is needed to believe the man entombed with Arthur's name truly is the legendary King Arthur. Nearly all legends have a kernel of truth hidden within them, and I believe we have found that truth here."

The chamber erupted into cheers and applause. Senator Thomas slumped down in his chair and Abrams rapped his gavel over and over until it broke again.

"I must say, Mr. MacCrarey," the Senator from California began respectfully, "that what we've heard today is nothing less than astounding. Never could I have imagined that in our day and age we'd be sitting here debating the reality of one of history's most noble, awe-inspiring men. I, for one," he continued, glancing around at his fellow senators and then at the cameras, "am convinced that King Arthur truly lived, and I am *equally* convinced that Mr. MacCrarey is his last descendant."

More cheers and applause.

The Senator from Michigan spoke up. "Mr. Chair, I agree with my colleague from California and I say we dispense with any further questions and call the vote."

"Call the vote!" the Senator from Iowa called.

"Here, here!" cried the Senator from Massachusetts.

Chairman Abrams leaned towards his microphone and said weakly, "Mr. MacCrarey, do you have any final words before I…call the vote?"

Mac nodded and stood. "Senators, I appreciate your patience and your willingness to allow these men," he gestured towards the professors, "to travel to England, do their research, and present their conclusions. I know this has been very unorthodox and I know you had ample reason to dismiss me out of hand.

"If I am confirmed, I promise to make my Clan and my country proud. During my time at the United Nations, I will conduct myself in a manner consistent with Arthur's ideals and pursue the vision he had for our world. This I swear to you, Senators," he turned and faced the audience, "and to you."

Applause filled the hearing room as Mac sat back down.

Head in hands, Abrams said, "All in favor of confirming William Cameron MacCrarey as Deputy U.S. Ambassador to the United Nations say 'Aye.'"

"Aye!" was the resounding reply from every Senator but two. Mitchell Thomas and Jack Abrams.

The audience stood and cheered.

The Senators hurried over to congratulate their new Deputy Ambassador as reporters and cameramen swarmed around them.

5

"Ye shall know the truth, and the truth shall make you free."

          – St. John

"The life that is unexamined is not worth living."

          – Socrates

"I see that I hold a sanctuary in their hearts, and
in the hearts of their descendants."

          – Charles Dickens

Gerhardt Schoen seethed as he watched the hearing live on TV.

"Arthur's vision for the world," he spat. All that he had feared was coming to pass. Again, he picked up the polished stone paperweight and was about to heave it at the screen when he noticed something curious. Why Abrams and Thomas? Why were they the only Senators still sitting? And why did the looks on their faces imply they hated MacCrarey almost as much as he did?

Whatever the reasons, their communal animosity could become useful. Relationships, however Machiavellian or nihilistic, were formed on the basis of mutuality. The Far Right in America understood that, and both Senators were Far Right.

Best to begin cultivating relationships.

U.S. Ambassador to the United Nations Jacob Tanner stepped out of the cab in front of an apartment building on 71st Street near Madison Avenue. He'd been there only once before and that had been nearly six years ago, just after his confirmation hearings. Before walking up to the building, he tossed a ten-dollar bill to the Bangladeshi driver through the open window as if tossing a bone to a rabid dog.

Inside the lobby, the African-American concierge in suit and tie asked, "Who are you here to see, sir?"

Tanner squinted at him, and in a purposefully intimidating voice said, "Secretary-General Boujeau. Hop to it, boy."

Forcing himself to smile, the gentleman with his care-worn face and short graying hair bowed slightly before picking up the house phone's receiver with a shaking hand. How he hated being treated like that, just because of the color of his skin. But he needed this job. His wife had just lost hers and his two boys were attending NYU.

A few minutes later, Tanner was being escorted into René Boujeau's sitting room.

"Would you care for coffee or tea, Mr. Ambassador?" the uniformed butler asked with a decidedly French accent.

"No," Tanner replied cautiously. "Where you from?"

"A small town outside of Paris, sir," the man answered cheerfully.

"French, huh?" he grunted and looked away. "Probably Catholic, too. My gramps landed at Normandy to *liberate* you

people. Now you just do what ever you *damn well* please —
don't listen to our President, vote against us on the Security
Council. No damn gratitude."

The Secretary-General walked in accompanied by Gerhardt
Schoen. "Jake, thank you for coming," he former said. "Sit
down, please," nodding towards one of the embroidered, nine-
teenth-century straight-backed chairs. "Tea, François," he said
to his man Friday, whose eyes had remained fixed on Tanner.

"François?" Boujeau repeated impatiently.

The butler turned to look at his boss. "Right away, sir,"
he replied, and stalked off with a final indignant glance at the
Ambassador.

"Damned frogs," muttered Tanner.

Schoen suppressed a grin. Boujeau ignored both of them.

"I assume you heard what happened at the confirmation
hearings today?"

"Sure the hell have," the Ambassador growled. "Is this guy
for real?"

"I assure you," Schoen replied gravely, "he is *very* real. And,
he will try to use his newfound popularity and political capital
to foster his Clan's agenda."

"That greenhorn? Shit, he won't see daylight. Don't worry."

"You will send him to Geneva," Schoen commanded.

"Geneva? Why –?"

"You will not assign him any duties. You will not contact
him without my approval. You will not send him on any missions. MacCrarey is to be completely isolated. Understood?"

A dozen questions ran through Tanner's mind. But like a
good soldier, he answered, "Understood."

"You are by far one of the best investments I've ever made,"
said Boujeau. "We both believe the United Nations is unnec-
essary, perhaps even dangerous."

"Abso-fuckin'-lutely," said Tanner. "I want an America that does what it wants and takes care of its own."

"Good, Jake. That's what I wanted to hear."

He left Washington after dinner and drove all night. The sun was just cresting the horizon when he pulled into the driveway and stopped to check his mailbox – advertisements mostly, and the *New York Times*. Unfolding the paper, he noticed the confirmation hearings had made the front page. The headline read, 'Long Live the King!'

He smiled to himself and eased the Mustang into the garage. Grabbing his garment bag from the trunk, he heard the phone ringing and hurried inside.

It was a reporter and the phone rang off the hook the rest of the day with talk show hosts wanting him on their shows, reporters wanting interviews, and politicians asking favors. He listened, took notes, answered questions, and politely begged off on TV appearances. "Too busy learning my new job," was his excuse.

It would take a couple days to pack, call around to find an apartment in New York, and close the condo. Then he'd return to New York for orientations and briefings before reporting to his new boss, Jacob Tanner, the U.S. Ambassador to the UN.

He'd also get a chance to see Merrill and Kyle again before they flew home. They were staying at the Plaza for a few days. Apparently, there were friends of the Clan in New York they had to see.

In the bowels of the rusting, fetid Russian trawler *Shkhara*, Pompous Zeda held the shiny new AK-47 in trembling hands.

An almost overwhelming mix of emotions – hate, power, sadness, revenge, desperation, exhilaration – swirled about in his mind.

The Georgian arms dealer handed Zeda a cell phone and said firmly, "Call in the wire transfer."

Zeda nodded to his brother who took the phone and began dialing.

As he watched with satisfaction, the dealer noted, "I will be back in three months. Where shall we meet?"

"The port of Morphou," the dictator-to-be answered.

"Must we always meet in a different place?" the arms dealer asked.

Zeda swung the rifle around until it was pointing at the insolent man's head. "If that is what I wish," he hissed.

The arms dealer coolly shook his head and raised his hands in mock surrender. He'd dealt with Schoen's tin-pot dictators too often to be taken aback.

"Morphou it is," he sighed.

Driving under the Hudson River, Mac glanced at the dashboard clock. 9:30 PM.

Emerging from the Lincoln Tunnel, he made his way to 42nd Street, headed east to Fifth Avenue, and turned south. Soon, the distant glowing halo of the Washington Square arch came into view.

Romanesque in design, it had been erected in 1889 to celebrate the 100th anniversary of George Washington's inauguration as President in New York City. Decorated with sculpted images of him, the arch stood sentinel over Greenwich Village's Washington Square Park. The land on which it stood had once been a potter's field and many of its residences still lay buried there.

Dave and Lynn Penn were surprised to hear his voice on the phone but were quick to offer their guestroom. Dave and Mac had worked at Dumas & Dickens together, and Lynn taught sociobiology at NYU. They were the stereotypical good-looking BMW-driving yuppie couple, but Mac did a good job of not holding that against them.

He found a parking spot along a dimly lit street of nineteenth century homes as it began to snow. Walking up the front steps of his friends' brownstone, garment bag slung over his shoulder, the porch light turned on and the door swung open.

"Where the heck have you been lately, man?" Dave greeted his old friend with a big smile and a hug.

"You wouldn't believe me if I told you," Mac answered with a grin.

"It's been a year since we heard from you," Lynn chided with a kiss on his cheek, and guided him inside.

"Yeah, sorry," he said sheepishly. "It's been, uh…a rough year."

"You okay?" she asked as they walked down the hallway to the kitchen and the welcoming aroma of fresh, percolating coffee.

"Fine. Starting a new career."

"We heard!" Lynn exclaimed.

"Sit down. Sit down," Dave said, gesturing at the kitchen table.

"Where are the girls?" Mac asked.

"Just put 'em to bed," Dave answered. "You'll get to see them in the morning."

"They're doing great," Lynn boasted with a mother's enthusiasm and poured the rich, steaming coffee into mugs. "Anna's in high school getting straight A's. Sarah's in middle school and growing up too fast."

"Can't believe they're that old already," Mac said, shaking his head. "How's your business doing?"

Dave had been the first man at the firm to take advantage of its new parental leave policy, and always left the office in time to make it home for dinner with his family. Paying for his family devotion with a stagnant career track, he finaly left and started his own consulting company.

"It was touch and go for a while, but I landed a national account a year ago and now we're flush. Busy as heck, but flush. And," he gave his wife a proud smile, "Lynn got tenure last fall."

"Whoa! That's great," Mac said, "and quick."

"Mmmm, I guess so," she said, trying to sound modest, "and I didn't have to kiss too many you-know-what's to get it."

"Sociobiology," Mac recalled. "You consulted with the United Nations Research Institute for Social Development a few years back.

"Uh-huh. And now you're about to become Deputy U.S. Ambassador to the UN," she smiled.

"Yep. I meet with Ambassador Tanner tomorrow to find out what I'll be working on. I'll get a hotel room after work and start looking for an apartment."

"Nonsense. You'll stay here until you get settled in somewhere," insisted Dave.

"Of course, he will," said Lynn.

Mac smiled. "Well...thank you. Hey, could I ask you some questions about the UN?"

"Of course," Lynn said enthusiastically.

Mac took a sip of his coffee. "To start with, what's your overall impression of the UN?"

"Oh, my goodness," she laughed. "I'll be up all night answering that one. Well, it has more politics, bureaucracy, and inefficiency than you can shake a stick at. It's frustrating as heck. You'll spend months working out a plan to do something, you'll take it through who-knows-how-many committees, it'll get twisted and changed by bureaucrats with their own agendas, and in the end it'll either be rejected by politicians in far-off nations you've barely heard of, or rendered ineffective by graft and ineptitude."

"Great," Mac chuckled.

"Why are you even considering this?" Dave asked.

Mac looked down at his mug. "Some people think I can make a difference."

The Professor placed her hand on his arm and said, "Well, then, make a difference for the whole world, okay?"

He smiled. "I'll try."

"Next question?"

"*Novum orbis regium.* A single, worldwide government. Is it possible?"

"Wow," Lynn exclaimed. "Well, uh…let's think it out. We have to start at the beginning. Human beings are social animals with no natural defenses –"

Mac and Dave exchanged grins.

"Hey, you asked, now listen," she smiled. "There's only one part of our anatomy that allows us to survive – our brain. In proportion to our body weight, it's the largest and most advanced of any living creature's. It allows us to prosper by helping us control our environment. Because we're social animals, we exhibit pack behavior – we congregate together, form complex social bonds, act as conformists, and so on. It manifests itself in the modern-world in group behaviors – living in neighborhoods, attending a church, going to sporting events, joining clubs, associating with people of like mind. To get along, we act myopically – don't ask too many questions, accept what we're taught, think in black and white. Everything else, anything different, is impulsively viewed as bad. So, when the outside world comes knocking on our door, we shun it out of hand. Outsiders become the personification of evil. Tensions rise, blood is shed, and suddenly an imagined evil is made real – Jews and Christians, Jews and Muslims, England and Ireland, the Union and Confederacy, the U.S. and Soviet Union, North and South Korea –"

"Cowboys and Indians," Dave suggested.

"Blacks and whites," said Mac.

"Exactly," Lynn nodded. "So, try getting 193 nations to agree on something, especially something as paradigm-shifting as your *novum orbis regium.*"

Mac considered this for a moment and said, "History reflects Man's struggle to shed his animal nature…to civilize ourselves, become higher beings –"

"Yes, but we still have a long way to go. We started as hunter-gatherers and the Mesopotamians gave us agricultural societies, Greeks created philosophy and democracy, Buddhists ascended to enlightenment, Romans created massive governing structures and architectural wonders, Europeans had a Renaissance and invented industrialization, the U.S. drafted a Bill of Rights and formed a secular government. Eventually, we outlawed child labor, slavery, indentured servitude, and colonialism. We enacted public education, suffrage, and Constitutionally guaranteed equal rights.

"The next step in our social evolution would be to eliminate the causes of poverty and crime. Too many children are raised in poor neighborhoods, attend underfunded schools, end up poorly educated, and become alienated adults. Poverty breeds anger and crime. Ignorance and cliquishness among the wealthier breeds contempt and division. There is no evil in the world, Mac, only inhumanity. No one is born with hate in their hearts. They become twisted by the circumstances of their lives or brainwashed by the ignorant among us. A world at peace with a single government, flourishing economy, and just society can exist *only* if the purity we're born with can be protected and allowed to flourish."

Mac got up and grabbed the coffee pot. "How do we do that?" he said, refilling their mugs.

Lynn took a sip and gathered her thoughts. "Well, first, the twisted people need to be reeducated. If they can't be, they need to be isolated – kept from doing harm without turning them into martyrs. That gets you to neutral. Next, you need to ensure everyone gets a well-rounded education – it overcomes all hardships, matures and expands the mind, advances ever more quickly, leads to new ideas and discoveries, pushes beyond the philosophical limitations of earlier generations, challenges tradition, dissipates absolutes, and allows each generation to better itself. Then we need to invent a new, fairer philosophy of capitalism – universalist and inclusionary instead of competitive and exclusionary. Next, we have to create an international governing structure and elect politicians who act globally rather than provincially. Then, we need to pass laws that allow people everywhere to have the same fundamental rights, citizenship, wage structures, workplace regulations, living standards, and so on. Then, we need to devise an equitable way to share the world's natural resources. And all this presupposes the creation of a world constitution."

"What an amazing document *that* would be," Mac said with awe. "What I wouldn't give to read such a thing."

"I could go on all night with my suppositions but suffice it to say that a *novum orbis regium* is possible. It's just that it would take generations to come to pass. Maybe a century or two down the road our descendants will be living in a Utopia, but not us."

The digital alarm clock in the Penn's guestroom read 2:23. The conversation had been quite stimulating, and so had the coffee. With little chance of falling asleep, Mac dressed, grabbed his coat, and headed for the door.

He walked over to Fifth Avenue and turned north. A misty fog gave the night a slightly surreal feel and everything that had transpired of late replayed in his mind. "Unbelievable," he whispered to himself, his breath visible in the chilled night air.

He passed closed shops and department stores, restaurants and cafés, the Empire State Building, and finally the brightly-lit buildings of Rockefeller Center. He walked up to the railing overlooking the ice rink and spied a solitary figure skating in broad circles below. As he turned to leave, a long rectangular marble monument caught his attention. On it were chiseled the words of John D. Rockefeller, Jr.

'I believe in the supreme worth of the individual and in his right to life, liberty, and the pursuit of happiness.

'I believe that every right implies a responsibility, every opportunity an obligation, every possession a duty.

'I believe that the law was made for man and not man for the law, that government is the servant of the people and not their master.

'I believe in the sacredness of a promise, that a man's word should be as good as his bond, that character - not wealth or power or position - is of supreme worth.

'I believe that the rendering of useful service is the common duty of mankind and that only in the purifying fire of sacrifice is the dross of selfishness consumed and the greatness of the human soul set free.

'I believe the greatest gift in the world is the unselfish giving of one's self and spirit to the betterment of that world.'

The words seemed to be meant for him that night.

He headed east on 44th Street, picking up a decaf coffee on his way through Grand Central Station. He came to a semi-circular stairway leading down to Raoul Wallenberg Walk, named in honor of the man who spirited tens of thousands of Jews out of Europe during WWII. Descending, he read the words cut into the stone wall beside the steps.

'They shall beat their swords into plowshares and their spears into pruning hooks. Nations shall not lift up sword against nations. Neither shall they learn war any more. – Isaiah.'

Reaching the bottom of the stairs, he noticed a memorial to Ralph Johnson Bunche, Under-Secretary-General for Special Political Affairs. Inscribed in a small stone alcove were the words, *'Peace, to have meaning for many who have known only suffering in both peace and war, must be translated into bread and rice, shelter, health, and education, as well as freedom and human dignity.'*

Could humankind ever learn to be so selfless?

Mac turned, looked across the street at the General Assembly Building, and sighed.

Later that morning, Mac stood outside the double glass doors to the U.S. Ambassador's office suite in the Secretariat Building. He was more than a bit nervous, this being his first day on the job, and Tanner was reputed to be a tough, no-nonsense type. Taking a deep, calming breath, he walked through the doors and found himself at one end of a large open room filled with cubicles. Looking around to get his bearings, he started down one of the aisles and came upon a plump, middle-aged woman hurrying in the opposite direction.

"Could you please direct me to Jacob Tanner's office?"

She gave a startled look of recognition which faded into pity. "Oh, it's you, sir."

"Uh, yeah…it's me. I can't be anyone else." He smiled. "Though sometimes I wish I could be."

She smiled back and without taking her eyes off him, pointed to a set of doors at the far end of the room.

"Thanks," he said and walked on.

Several staffers recognized him as he passed, but none said a word. More often than not, they looked the other way. One young man walking towards Mac actually turned and went the other way. He thought it all a bit odd but shrugged it off.

Walking up to Tanner's administrative assistant, he said, "Good morning, I'm –"

"I know who you are, dear," said Doris Finksetter, who had the pleasant habit of calling everybody 'dear.'

"I'm here to see –"

"Ambassador Tanner said to wait here, dear," she told him, pointing with her pen at the small sitting area between her desk and Tanner's office door. "Coffee, dear?" she asked and stood up.

"That would be nice, thanks," he smiled.

Once he had his cup of coffee in hand, he sat to wait. And wait. And wait. He flipped through a dozen magazines and finished three more cups of coffee. Finally, Doris' intercom buzzed, and a gruff voice said, "Send him in."

Doris gave Mac a sympathetic look and nodded towards the office door. "Go on in, dear."

Mac found the Ambassador hunched over his desk, writing furiously. Papers were strewn everywhere, even on the floor, and piles of reports and reams of computer printouts were stacked on the credenza.

Mac cautiously crossed the office and extended his hand. "Ambassador Tanner, I'm William Cameron MacCrarey."

Tanner continued writing. After a long, awkward silence, he muttered, "Sit."

Mac slowly lowered his hand, glanced at the two leather armchairs facing the antique oak desk, and sat down in the one not being used as a makeshift trash bin. Tanner held up a copy of the *Washington Post*. On the front page was Mac's picture.

"Let me tell you something, MacCrarey," he began in a low, ominous tone, "this don't buy you *shit* around here." He threw the paper at Mac. "Let me tell you something else. You were not *my* choice for Deputy Ambassador. You weren't even on my damned list! So, let me make this short and sweet. I'm assigning you to our office in Geneva. After you get there, don't ever call me, don't ever write me, don't even *think* about me unless I tell you to. Got it?"

Mac stared back, mouth agape.

Tanner returned to his writing. "Be in Geneva Monday. Now go. Get out of here!"

Mac had never been treated like this before. Without a word, he got up and left.

"You heard?" Tanner asked after the door closed, glancing at his speaker phone.

"Ja. Sehr gut," said Gerhardt Schoen. "Very good."

"I hope the Secretary-General will be pleased."

Schoen ignored the implied question. "Senator Jack Abrams was on the Senate Foreign Affairs Committee when you were confirmed, ja?"

"Yeah."

"How well do you know him?"

Tanner shrugged. "Pretty good, I guess. God-fearin' man. What else do you need to know, right?" he chuckled.

"Call him," Schoen ordered.

"Sure. What do you…oh, you mean…right now?"

"Yes, now, Jake," said another, all-too-familiar voice.

"Mr. Secretary-General!" Tanner gulped. "I didn't know… you…yeah, just let me –" He fumbled through his rolodex. "Here it is. One moment." He pressed the conference button and dialed. It took a few moments to get past the Senate operator and Ensign York, but finally Abrams was on the line.

"Jake! How the hell are you? Hey, listen, I can't tell you how sorry I am about the hearings –"

"Jack," Tanner interrupted, "I have someone on the line I'd like to introduce you to."

"Uh, sure, Jake," answered Abrams.

Tanner pressed the conference button again. "Mr. Secretary-General of the United Nations René Boujeau, Senator Jack Abrams of Virginia is on the line."

Abrams gave a faint gasp.

"Senator Abrams," greeted Boujeau, "so good to finally speak with you."

"Mr. Secretary-General," gushed Abrams. "What an honor to talk with you, sir."

"Mind if I call you Jack?"

"Of course not, sir."

"The Ambassador has nothing but good things to say about you."

"Oh, well, I just try to be a good American and do the best I can for the people who elected me."

"We all try, Senator, but few succeed."

"Kind of you to say, sir."

"Gerhardt tells me that perhaps you and I have a common concern. I was hoping perhaps we could help each other out."

Abrams had no idea what Boujeau was talking about, but said anyway, "I'd be honored, sir."

"This MacCrarey business –" he began and purposefully paused.

Abrams' heart sank. "I'm sorry, sir. I honestly thought I could keep him from being confirmed. I mean, King *Arthur*," he chuckled nervously, "Come on. Really? Who could have –?"

"What's done is done," Boujeau said, his tone darkening. "The Ambassador will do his part to contain the damage, but I need you to be my eyes and ears in Washington."

Abrams hesitated, but only for a moment. "Yes, Mr. Secretary-General."

"And should the day come when I need you to act, you will act."

"Uh, yes…of course, sir."

Mac nodded to Doris as he passed and wandered into the maze of cubicles.

"Mr. MacCrarey!" he heard someone call out.

All Mac wanted to do was get the hell out of there, so he ignored whoever it was and kept walking.

"Mr. MacCrarey!" the insistent voice repeated. "Mac!"

Reluctantly, he stopped and turned around. A fifty-something black man with a slightly receding hairline, graying mustache, and slight paunch hurried towards him. He was wearing a dark blue suit, colorful tie, and wing-tips.

"Do I know you?" Mac asked curtly.

"I'm, uh…a friend," the man said softly, looking around.

"I'm sorry, but I don't recall ever meeting you. So, if you don't mind –" Mac turned to leave.

The stranger grabbed Mac by the arm. "You know – a friend." He looked around again to see if anybody was close by. "A friend of the Clan."

Mac let out a sigh. "My apologies. I didn't know we had friends in the UN."

"Mafumbe Makatu," the gentleman said, extending his hand. "My friends call me T.J."

"How do you get T.J. from Mafumbe Makatu?" Mac said with a tired grin, shaking T.J.'s hand.

"'Cause my name used to be Thomas Jefferson Walker," T.J. replied with a smile and gently guided Mac to the outer doors of the suite. "In my younger, more radical days, I decided to change my name to emphasize my African roots…as if being Black in America wasn't enough," he laughed. "But now, in middle age, I prefer T.J."

"Well, T.J.," Mac said, "looks like I've been banished to –"

"Geneva," T.J. nodded. "Yeah, I know. But don't worry – you have your foot in the door."

"I'd say the door just hit me in the ass," Mac muttered.

T.J. chuckled. "Yeah, but so what? Go to Europe. Make the best of it. It'll all work out."

Mac gave a dejected shake of his head. "I have a Senator who's out to get me, my new boss doesn't want to see me, half of America probably thinks I'm nuts, the world'll judge my Clansfolk by my actions and I don't have a *clue* what the hell I'm supposed to do!"

"I'll help you," T.J. assured him as they reached the doors.

"How do you plan to do that?" Mac said wryly. "I'll be in Europe, you'll be in –"

"Geneva, Switzerland," said T.J. "I'm going with you. Merrill and the Keeper want someone on the inside to look after you. Geneva was looking for a financial wiz to liaise with the IMF. I have a Finance MBA, 30 years of experience, and just happen to speak German. A little paperwork, and voilà!"

"So now I've gotten you banished to Geneva, too."

"Not banished. Honored. Honored to help the last heir of Arthur."

Mac gave a self-effacing smile. "Well…thanks. I guess. I have to be there Monday. You?"

"Same," T.J. said with a friendly smile of his own.

The following Monday morning, they walked into the lobby of the United Nations building in Geneva. T.J. asked the young man seated behind the information desk where the station chief's office was.

Karl Koenig could have been a poster boy for German Aryanism. Recognizing Mac, he jumped to his feet, eyes beaming with delight. After politely giving T.J. the office number, he directed them to the elevators.

Mac thanked him and turned to leave.

Karl said excitedly, "Du bist ihm, ja?"

"Yes, I'm me," answered Mac. "And this is T.J. Makatu."

Karl nodded at T.J., smiled, and turned back to Mac. "May I have," he said in halting English, "your, uh, how you say…sig-na-tour?"

"Signature? You want my autograph?" Mac asked in surprise.

"Ja, bitte! Autograph!" He rummaged around his desk for a piece of paper and a pen. Handing them to Mac, he said, "I told my friends you were coming to our office, but they did not believe me. Now I will have proof."

Scribbling his name, Mac said, "Here's proof, such as it is."

Karl reverently took the piece of paper from Mac's hand.

"Your English is quite good, Karl. I've always been amazed and humbled at how well Europeans speak more than one language."

Karl shrugged and replied, "Why wouldn't we?"

Mac smiled and nodded. "Guten morgen, Karl," he said and turned to leave.

"Guten morgen, Herr MacCrarey."

He glanced back and said, "Call me Mac."

They made their way up to the receptionist's office for Geneva station chief, Viktor Kleinmann.

Walking in to the anteroom, Mac asked pleasantly, "Guten morgen –" he glanced at the name plate on her desk, "– Helga. May I see Herr Kleinmann, bitte?"

The receptionist could have been Karl's twin sister and she recognized Mac as well.

Her face flushed. "Herr Kleinmann told me to tell you he is busy, and he will see you later in the week."

Annoyed but not surprised, Mac asked politely, "How much later?"

Flushing again, she said apologetically, "Friday…after-noon…late."

Mac chuckled. "My schedule is, at the moment, quite clear so I am at his disposal. Could you direct me to my new office, bitte?"

She slumped in her chair and flushed yet again. "Ja," she sighed and stood. "Follow me, Herr MacCrarey."

"Call me Mac."

She smiled perfunctorily and led them back to the elevators.

They descended to the basement, walked to the end of the hall, and entered a dingy, windowless office barely large enough to be a broom closet. Dusty boxes and old manual typewriters were piled in the corners.

"Hmmm. Looks like I'll be working quite a bit from home," he quipped, "once I find one."

"Where's *my* office?" T.J. asked, not sure he wanted to know the answer.

Hilda's face brightened at once. "Oh! You have the office next to Herr Kleinmann's. I'll be your administrative assistant."

"Wanna trade?" Mac asked drolly.

"Hell, no," said T.J.

"Do I have an administrative assistant?"

"I'm afraid Herr Kleinmann has given orders to –" She hesitated.

"Not help me in any way." Mac guessed that Tanner had gotten to Kleinmann already.

"Ja," she said. "I am sorry."

"No apologies necessary," he said. "Herr Kleinmann is one to follow orders to the letter, yes?"

"And doesn't act without them," she nodded.

"Well," Mac sighed, looking around his new office, "I'll just get, uh…settled in."

"I know –" Helga started to say but then thought better of it.

"Yes?"

"I, well, I know of a home you may want to look at."

"That's very kind of you."

"It is my parent's home," she explained. "They just retired and are selling it."

"Perhaps you could arrange for me to drop by this evening?"

She smiled and nodded. "Ja! I will call them now."

The Schroedingers' townhouse sat along a tree-lined, cobblestone street near the old city center, just up the hill from several shops, cafes, and pubs. Dinner with Helga's family was immensely enjoyable and before the evening was through Mac had himself a new home.

Herr and Frau Schroedinger promised to be out by week's end. They'd been living at their new chalet on Lake Geneva a few miles out of town for the better part of a year, so there was little left to move.

After his meeting with Kleinmann Friday afternoon, Mac took a cab to the townhouse, handed a twenty mark note to the driver, and got out. With suitcase in hand and garment bag over his shoulder, he made his way up the walk to his new home. T.J. followed closely behind with grocery bags in each hand.

Mac noticed a large cardboard box sitting on the landing. "Wonder what that is," Mac said.

"No idea," T.J. replied. "Get the door and I'll bring it inside."

Mac found the key, unlocked the door, and stepped into the foyer.

"Geez o' Pete!" T.J. grunted, trying in vain to lift the box. "This thing weighs a ton!"

Mac stepped out onto the stoop and together they dragged it inside. Tearing off the packing tape and opening the flaps, He found a note resting atop stacks of books.

"It's from Kyle," Mac smiled. "'Honor and duty, wisdom and justice, kindness and love, passion and inspiration, friendship and loyalty, generosity and humanity…all are found in these pages.'"

After a dinner in his new kitchen and a few beers, Mac and T.J. slid the heavy box into the library. One by one, Mac took out the books and arranged them on the shelves by discipline.

There were books by Homer, Socrates, Plato, Aristotle, St. Augustine, Voltaire, Descartes, Kant, and Hume. Dante Alighieri, Sun Tzu, and Niccolò Machiavelli. Edward Gibbon, Benjamin Franklin, Thomas Paine, Thomas Jefferson, Alexis De Tocqueville, Abraham Lincoln, and Winston Churchill. Robert Ingersoll, Susan B. Anthony, Elizabeth Cady Stanton, Eleanor Roosevelt, and John Morris. Viktor Frankl, Bertrand Russell, Martin Luther King, Karen Armstrong, Elaine Pagels, Madeleine Albright, and His Holiness the Dalai Lama. Thomas More, Robert Louis Stevenson, Nathaniel Hawthorne, Alexandre Dumas, Walt Whitman, Henry David Thoreau, Charles Dickens, and Mark Twain. Victor Hugo, W. Somerset Maugham, Sinclair Lewis, Ernest Hemingway, Ray Bradbury, George Orwell, James Michener, David McCullough, Kurt Vonnegut, Charles Van Doren, Edward Rutherford, and Ken Follett. Nicolaus Copernicus, Galileo Galilei, Isaac Newton, Charles Darwin, Albert Einstein, Francis Collins, Carl Sagan, Stephen Hawking, and Stephen Jay Gould. There was also the Koran, the Dhammapada, the Torah, and the Bible, as well as textbooks on law, economics, philosophy, humanities, psychology, the arts, music, world history, physics, biology, sociology, and political science.

"I guess Kyle wants you to read," T.J. grinned, standing back and taking in the new library.

"It's gonna take *years* to get through all these," Mac said, hands on his hips.

"Best get started, then," T.J. told him, "and you're outta beer."

Mac grabbed a book at random. *The Count of Monte Cristo* by Alexandre Dumas. "Let's walk down to that café around the corner."

Petra the maître d'-owner-bartender-chef led them to a table beside the large plate glass window overlooking the sidewalk and busy street beyond. As they sat down, the waitress Katrina, Petra's daughter, dropped off menus and asked what they'd like to drink. They ordered a local draft beer and Katrina hurried off.

"Did you read any of those books back in school?" T.J. said as he scanned the menu.

"Maybe one or two. Had some humanities courses, Western Civ, philosophy, things like that. Never thought they'd be useful, but now they're the only ones I ever think back on."

"Maybe they're the only ones *worth* thinking back on," said T.J.

Mac smiled and nodded thoughtfully. "You're right."

"My daughters are in college now and the curricula are focusing less on the liberal arts than when we were in school. They seem to be preparing our kids for careers, but not for life, you know what I mean? They need to be exposed to music, theater, art, literature, poetry, history – things that give life color, texture, depth, meaning – you can learn how to program a computer or read an accounting ledger, but how will you be able to answer the great questions in life? When faced with moral dilemmas, how will you know what to do? When important decisions have to be made, how will you make the right ones? Kids need to get the broadest education they can." He reflected for a moment and chuckled. "Grown-ups, too."

"Guess I'll be getting one," Mac chuckled. "And I'll have plenty of time to do it. Kleinmann won't give me an assignment."

"Then read," T.J. said, tapping the cover of *The Count of Monte Cristo*. "Get through all those books and you'll be able to traverse any difficulty you face."

And that's how Mac began his new life as exiled Deputy U.S. Ambassador to the United Nations.

He often brought his books to Petra's café and sat alone by the window, reading and sipping espresso. Kyle and Merrill visited often to discuss the books he read, as well as to debate world affairs and their historical underpinnings. They'd hypothesize what the UN should do in this situation or that and discourse over the latest scientific discoveries.

Over the years, Mac and T.J. remained good friends, and he frequently flew back to Traverse to visit old ones. Camleton became a frequent destination for him and he got to know several of the families quite well. When visiting, he'd often re-read the binders, visit Arthur's tomb, and wander through the underground Library.

When it came to romance, though, Mac had no interest. His heart belonged to Genevieve and that was that.

Still, the intellectual side of his life was quite full and for now that was enough.

6

*"There can be no peace as long as there is grinding poverty,
social injustice, inequality, oppression, environmental
degradation, and as long as the weak and small continue
to be trodden by the mighty and powerful."*

         – His Holiness the Dalai Lama

*"Life's most persistent and urgent question is, 'How
responsible am I for the well-being of my fellows?'"*

         – Martin Luther King

*"Beware! Cling to no faith when faith brings blood! It
is mistaken law that leads you to sacrifice life…life
is God's most precious gift and no principle – however
glorious – can justify the taking of it!"*

         – Arthur Miller

Five years in Geneva. Mac had spent much of it reading and
the rest learning how the United Nations worked, and then
trying to make it work better. Eventually he earned Station

Chief Kleinmann's grudging respect and important projects started coming Mac's way. They were officially assigned to T.J., though, to avoid Ambassador Tanner's wrath.

Recently, Mac had been leasing transmission bandwidth on commercial satellites that geo-synchronously orbited above the 45th parallels. With enough leased satellite coverage, a secure electronic worldwide UN network could be created. Like an electronic quilt, it would link every office with every peacekeeping force in the field. Staff would be able to up-link to the global satellite network, nicknamed GLOSAT, any time, anywhere. GLOSAT would provide GPS positioning, video conferencing, high-speed data transmission, radio and cellular voice communications, live broadcasting of official UN meetings, and secure access to a database of military assets held by UN member nations for deployment in the field – all completely secured from other networks and independent of the Internet.

The first global test of GLOSAT had been the week before last and the results were encouraging. A few more modifications and the network would be ready for real-time field deployment.

On a warm Friday evening in early spring, Mac leisurely walked down the hill from his townhouse to Petra's. The café was small, not more than a dozen tables, with dark wood paneling and black-and-white floor tiles. Opposite the plate glass window that spanned the restaurant's façade was a bar, and on the mirrored-wall behind it were shelves of liquors. Classical music, tin-sheet ceiling tiles, and hanging brass lamps completed the warm and inviting ambiance.

Mac happily took his usual table by the window just as a beautiful young brunette came out of the kitchen wearing a form-fitting black dress and a white apron tied about her slim waist. She smiled and brought a menu over to his table. Leaning over, she whispered, "Try papa's special. It would make him happy."

He smiled and surreptitiously glanced at Petra standing behind the bar. Loudly enough for him to hear, Mac nonchalantly said, "You know, I think I'll try the special."

His friend's face lit up and he hurried into the kitchen.

Katrina smiled. "Thank-you. Anything to drink?"

"Nein, danke," he smiled back and she left for the kitchen to help her father.

Reaching into his valise, Mac pulled out his laptop, powered it up, and opened the Word file containing his notes and a first draft of the paper he was working on. It was a history of the United Nations, focusing on its relevance in the twenty-first century. In it, he made the case for several dramatic advancements – a much more central role for the UN in world affairs; the establishment of a global tax to provide UN funding independent of member nation dues; greater autonomy for the General Assembly from the Security Council; and the establishment of an independent Advisory Office to provide research and guidance on UN programs, projects, and peacekeeping missions.

Thanks to T.J.'s contacts, the paper was to be published in the *UN Chronicle* and with any luck it would be picked up by mainstream periodicals as well.

This all assumed, of course, that Kleinmann, Tanner, or Schoen wouldn't kill it first.

Mac clicked on the file and up came the Executive Summary.

History

The European powers had controlled much of the world in the centuries leading up to World War One. By 1900, however, industrialization, unionism, rising ethnic and nationalistic hatreds, the waning of colonialism, and the shifting of power from Europe to the Americas and Far East were quickly changing the political and economic landscape of the world. The concept of a world-order with the peoples of Europe steadfastly at the top was being challenged at every turn.

Then came World War One, then the Treaty of Versailles, and then the League of Nations. President Woodrow Wilson proclaimed that the League would make the world 'fit and safe to live in,' that every nation would, 'determine its own institutions, be assured of justice and fair dealing,' and be safe from 'force and selfish aggression.' But, alas, such hopes faded as the League's most powerful members placed their own national interests above those of others. Its impotence in staving off another world war made the League irrelevant, and by 1945 plans were being laid to replace it with the United Nations.

The conference to negotiate the UN Charter took place in San Francisco in April of 1945, the same month both Hitler and Roosevelt died. The hope for the United Nations, as reflected in the Charter's Preamble[1], was to create an institution that would

---

[1] UN Charter Preamble: 'We the peoples of the United Nations, determined to save succeeding generations from the scourge of war which twice in our lifetime has brought untold sorrow to humankind, and to reaffirm faith in fundamental human rights, in the dignity and worth of the human person, in the equal rights of men and women and of nations large and small, and to establish conditions under which justice and respect for the obligations arising from treaties and other sources of international law can be maintained, and to promote social progress and better standards of life in larger freedom, and for these ends to practice tolerance and live together in peace with one another as good neighbors, and to unite our strength to

ensure world peace. It would become the forum within which the world's problems would be resolved. It would be the police force, peacemaker and judiciary for the entire world. Its members would unite in, 'the suppression of acts of aggression or…breaches of peace,' to 'settle their international disputes by peaceful means,' to 'refrain…from the threat or use of force,' to 'develop friendly relations among nations based on respect for the principle of equal rights and self determination, and…strengthen universal peace… respect for human rights and…freedoms for all.' It would not, however, '…intervene in matters which…are within the domestic jurisdiction of any state,' nor would it, 'require the Members to submit such matters to settlement.'

And it would not lay the foundation for a world-wide democracy, nor create a one-world government.

Organizational Imbalance of Powers

The UN Charter established the Economic and Social Council, the Trusteeship Council, the General Assembly, the Secretariat, and an International Court of Justice in The Hague, Netherlands. The Economic and Social Council was empowered to, '…make or initiate studies and reports with respect to…economic, social, cultural, educational, health, and related matters.' The now defunct Trusteeship Council monitored the progress and

maintain international peace and security, and to ensure by the acceptance of principles and the institution of methods that armed force shall not be used, save in the common interest, and to employ international machinery and the promotion of the economic and social advancement of all peoples, have resolved to combine our efforts to accomplish these aims. Accordingly, our respective governments, through representatives assembled in the city of San Francisco, who have exhibited their full powers found to be in good and due form, have agreed to the present Charter of the United Nations and do hereby establish an international organization to be known as the United Nations.'

well being of numerous trustee territories around the world until they achieved complete self-governance. It was disbanded after the last trustee, Palau, became an independent country in 1994. The International Court of Justice was established as, '…the principal judicial organ of the United Nations…composed of a body of independent judges, elected regardless of their nationality from among persons of high moral character and recognized as competent in international law.' The Secretariat was created to be the executive branch of the United Nations, led by a, '…Secretary-General…appointed by the General Assembly upon the recommendation of the Security Council.' The Secretary-General's power and authority are absolute and broad, and as of this paper's publication date the Secretary-General of the United Nations is René Boujeau of Montreal, Quebec, Canada. The General Assembly was empowered to be the legislative branch of the United Nations. A representative from every member nation holds a seat in the Assembly, which receives recommendations on a variety of issues from its main committees – the Disarmament and International Security Committee, Economic and Financial Committee, Special Political and Decolonization Committee, Administrative and Budgetary Committee, Legal Committee, General Committee, Credentials Committee, and Social, Humanitarian, and Cultural Committee.

The last organizational branch of the United Nations is the Security Council. The Charter states that the UN, '…is based on the principle of sovereign equality of all its members.' Yet, some are arguably more equal than others. The UN made the same mistake as the League of Nations by giving special and unique powers to five nations – France, the U.S., the Soviet Union (now Russia), Britain, and China. These are the permanent members of the Security Council. The Charter states that '[The General] Assembly shall not make any recommendation with regard to [any matters] unless the Security Council so requests…[The General Assembly] members…agree to accept and carry out the decisions of the Security Council…[and] decisions of the Security Council…shall be made by…concurring votes of [its] permanent members' only.

Thus, the five permanent members have oligarchical power over all other UN member states. Virtually nothing – no resolution, military action, sanction, or request for membership – can pass until those five agree. But, if even one of the five exercises its veto power, the entire Security Council is stymied. Only unanimous decisions can take effect. One would be hard pressed to find five nations with more dissimilar policies and politics than France, the U.S., the Soviet Union (now Russia), Britain, and China. Thus, it is only when all five benefit from a decision that it gets passed. This is reflected in the fact that all UN peacekeeping and observer missions are within a thousand miles of the Middle East and its oil. This reflects the reality of religious conflicts and ethnic hatreds, of course, that have always existed at the crossroads of Europe, Africa, and Asia. But, it is clearly a reflection of the five permanent members' need for the region's oil.

Another example of self-serving Security Council actions involves civil wars and genocides within the borders of member states in regions where 'the five' have little strategic interest. Such events are conveniently ignored – a fact Joseph Stalin, Chiang Kai-Shek, Idi Amin, Saddam Hussein, and countless other dictators have understood all too well.

Why? Four reasons: First, the Security Council members don't want to put their country's soldiers into harm's way – body bags being unloaded back home is bad PR. Second, they wouldn't stand for interference in the internal affairs of their own country, so they adamantly refuse to interfere in the internal affairs of others. Third, their military industrialists make a good deal of money on the wars of others. And fourth, nearly half of all 'international enforcement' payments[2] from members have not been made, resulting in the UN's inability to undertake new missions. Even the United States, the wealthiest nation on Earth and a permanent Security Council member, is guilty of not fulfilling its payment obligations, even for missions it approved.

Conclusion

Putting them succinctly, here are my salient points: the Security Council rarely agrees on anything, the General Assembly is at the Security Council's mercy, the UN is hamstrung from intervening in the domestic affairs of sovereign nations, dictatorial nations do not fear UN reprisals and thus feel free to commit crimes against humanity, and when the UN does take action, its efforts are so under funded as to be nearly useless.

Thus, there is but one heartrending and unavoidable conclusion to be reached. Each time the UN allows a child to needlessly die, an innocent to suffer, a crime against humanity to go unpunished, or a nation to suppress the rights of its people, we take another step towards the UN's demise. And if that were to occur, we would fall backwards to a time of less civility and engender the cruelest, most vial incarnations of inhumanity among us to do as they wish.

Mac continued through the rest of his draft, making edits, until dinner arrived.

"Danke, Katrina," he said.

With her back to the bar, she gestured with her eyes to her father. "Papa is waiting to see if you like his creation."

---

[2] Article 42 of the Charter says: 'The Security Council…may take such action by air, sea, or land…as may be necessary to maintain or restore international peace and security,' but member nations must provide the funding, above and beyond their annual assessments, to pay for such, '…combined international enforcement action.'

He picked up his fork and took a bite. "Mmmm. Délicieux, Petra! C'est très magnifique."

"I am so happy you like it, my friend. Let me get you the perfect wine to go with it," and again he hurried into the back.

Katrina kissed Mac on the cheek before moving on to the next table. He took another bite and swapped his computer for *A Tale of Two Cities* by Charles Dickens. Though he'd read the book twice before, he relished the opportunity to do so again. It was a classic in so many ways, not the least of which was that it had as much relevance to the world today as it had a hundred and fifty years ago when Dickens first wrote it. Mac preferred books, fictional or not, with a strong historical underpinning – for it wasn't the past he was reading about, but the present and future.

'It was the best of times, it was the worst of times,' he read with a contented smile, 'it was the age of wisdom, it was the age of foolishness, it was the epoch of belief, it was the epoch of incredulity, it was the season of Light, it was the season of Darkness, it was the spring of hope, it was the winter of despair, we had everything before us, we had nothing before us, we were all going direct to Heaven, we were all going direct the other way – in short, the period was so far like the present period, that some of its noisiest authorities insisted on its being received, for good or for evil, in the superlative degree of comparison only.'

Another bite and something on the TV above the bar caught his attention. "Buddhist monks, the highly revered moral core of Tibet, led demonstrations against Chinese rule for the third straight day," the beguiling Jan Roberts reported from outside the Chinese Embassy in Washington, D.C. "The well-planned protests half-a-world-away were prompted by the upcoming anniversary of the 1959 Tibetan uprising against

Chinese rule, which led to the exile of Tibet's spiritual leader, the Dalai Lama.

"Yesterday, Radio Free Asia reported gunshots in the streets of Lhasa, Tibet's ancient capital. Last night, AP received cell phone photos of monks being severely beaten outside a monastery near Xiahe. This morning, according to official news reports, the government issued a curfew, closed Internet cafes, and shut down cell towers. By evening, thousands of Tibetans, many carrying the banned Tibetan national flag, joined monks marching on the provincial governor's palace in the city's center. The People's Armed Police, China's paramilitary force in Tibet, barricaded the surrounding streets and fired warning shots as the monks approached. Protesters hurled stones and bottles, and others broke through the barricades. Some began manhandling soldiers until the Minister of Peace, Kyong Mai, ordered his troops to fire.

Officially, only two deaths were reported, but observers say there were at least four dozen civilian casualties. This morning in New York, China blocked an effort by the UN Security Council to pass a resolution condemning the violence, and in London the Dalai Lama urged the Chinese government to begin a dialogue with monastic leaders as a first step towards restoring national independence. He also expressed disappointment with his fellow Tibetans for not showing greater restraint." She paused and signed off with, "I'm Jan Roberts, reporting from Washington, D.C."

Mac gave a grunt of frustration over the never-ending intransigence of some peoples and picked up his *A Tale of Two Cities* again. Before he could start reading, though, his iPhone rang.

He punched the speaker icon. "Mac."

"Is he there yet?" T.J. Makatu asked excitedly.

Mac smiled, "No, T.J. Not yet."

"Did he give you any clue?"

Mac chuckled at his friend's impatience. "Nope, none at all. Said something like, 'knowledge becomes wisdom only when steeled with experience.'"

"By 'experience' he's gotta mean an assignment, right?" T.J. said. "A *Clan* assignment."

Through the plate glass window, Mac noticed several men pass by.

"Holy –" he gasped.

"What?" T.J. asked eagerly. "What is it? Is he there?"

"Teej, you're never gonna believe this. I'll call you back."

Before T.J. could protest, Mac pressed End and stood up, his eyes fixed on the men walking up to the door.

Petra was wiping off the table next to Mac when the bell above the door jingled. He looked up and froze. "Is that who I think it is?"

Mac nodded slowly. "I think so. As improbable as it is." He turned to Petra and said, half-pleading, half-jesting, "What should we do?"

Petra, always a practical man, shrugged and replied with a smile, "Pull together a couple of tables and I'll get you menus and a nice bottle of Liebfraumilsch."

Kyle Dunham came through the front door with four rather imposing men dressed in long, flowing orange and yellow tunics draped loosely over baggy orange pants. Kyle gave Mac a wink and nodded to his silent escort. The four men parted, and there stood a small, nearly bald bespectacled elderly gentleman. With a wide endearing smile, he walked purposefully up to Mac.

"This is way past surreal," the heir of Arthur muttered to the Keeper who gave a quiet chuckle. The man stopped an arm's length away and Mac bowed slightly. "Your Holiness."

"Perhaps it is I who should be bowing to such a noble re-incarnation as you," the Dalai Lama said genuinely, and then did just that.

Mac smiled self-effacingly and said to the spiritual leader of the world's Buddhists, "Please, sit down." Looking at the tunicked men, he added, "All of you. Please." They bowed politely but remained standing, ever vigilant and loyal to their leader. "To what, may I ask, do I owe this honor?"

The Clan Elder answered. "His Holiness has a favor to ask of you."

Mac looked at the Dalai Lama with unabashed awe. "Yes, sir?"

"You have been listening to the reports from Tibet?" he questioned.

"Yes, sir," Mac repeated, nodding at the TV.

"My old friend Kyle has told me about you, and I believe your karma can be of immense value to my people's cause. You see, unbeknownst to all but a few, I intend to fly to Tibet… tonight…and I wish for you to accompany me." The endearing smile again graced his serene face.

Stunned, Mac stammered, "I…you…tonight? Me? With you?"

"Your presence as a celebrity, Arthur's last heir, *and* as an official representative of the United Nations will broaden public awareness of my trip and grant it validity."

"An official representative," Mac repeated, looking at Kyle. "Kleinmann doesn't know anything about this, does he? Neither does Tanner."

The Elder shrugged innocently and smiled. "What they don't know won't hurt them, eh?"

"Mmmm, it could hurt me," Mac quipped. "Disobeying superiors doesn't exactly help one's career, *eh?*"

Kyle leaned forward in his chair. "The blade of tyranny is about to be drawn across the throats of the Tibetan people. What are you going to do about it?"

Mac gave a slight jerk of his head. "You insult me by even asking," he replied, turning to the Dalai Lama. "I would be honored to accompany you, sir."

Kyle sat back, a proud smile etched across his face.

The last heir of Arthur recited from memory, "The word 'dalai' means 'profound knowledge' in Mongolian. The word 'lama' means 'teacher' in Tibetan. The title is a political and spiritual one, first conferred by one of the Khans in 1578 to the leader of Tibetan Buddhism. You, sir, are that leader's fourteenth reincarnation. In 1951, after 300 years of independent theocratic rule, Tibet was forcibly taken over by China. After a failed uprising in 1959, you left the country and never returned. So why return now?"

"If everything goes as planned," Kyle answered for His Holiness, "his return will be viewed by the international community as one of the United Nations' greatest diplomatic victories. Schoen and Boujeau will then have no choice but to publicly acknowledge your success, and —"

"And it'll split the Security Council apart," Mac finished. "China'll throw a fit and Russia will side with her against the three western nations."

"Of little consequence, after-the-fact," Kyle said smugly. "The Dalai Lama will have made his triumphant return and all eyes will turn to China. Economically tied to the West, she won't dare risk becoming a pariah. Her leaders will have no choice but to negotiate limited self-governance with His Holiness."

"You said, '*if* everything goes as planned,'" Mac commented. "What if it doesn't?"

Kyle's leaned forward again. "This is not a book you read in a café," he said with a nod at *A Tale of Two Cities*, "or a movie you watch from a theater seat. This is life, in all its gritty reality, lad."

"Understood." Standing, he said to the Dalai Lama, "When do we leave?"

The Dalai Lama's eyes twinkled as he took Mac's hand and eased him back into his chair. "Those who are truly wise… travel on full stomachs," he proclaimed, broke into a hearty laugh, and reached for a menu.

Gazing out at the darkness through the small cabin window of Michael's private jet, Mac guessed they were somewhere over the Ukraine. Well after midnight and unable to sleep, he tried his Dickens again but to no avail. Unbuckling his seatbelt, he got up to search for something to drink. When he returned, he noticed the Dalai Lama staring at him with a bemused expression.

"How long," he asked softly, "since you tried to end your life?"

Taken aback, Mac hesitated before answering, "A little over five years."

"May I ask why?" and his tone was so genuine and engaging, his interest so sincere, that Mac felt compelled to answer. When he'd finished, the Dalai Lama replied, "It is your life and you are free to do with it what you wish –" he paused to give Mac an evaluating look, "– but you will not try again."

Mac shook his head, both in answer to the implied question and in amazement at how insightful the man was. "Believe it or not, it made me realize how much I enjoyed life." He sat down. "In the last moments, instead of accepting death, I decided to live...*really* live."

"And yet," the Dalai Lama noted, "here we are flying into the tigress' gaping maw."

A fleeting look of apprehension crossed Mac's face. "It's the right thing to do."

"It is understandable to be afraid," His Holiness said without judgment.

Mac nodded slowly. "I guess knowing what's right simply takes learning. To always do what's right takes courage. I've spent a lifetime, especially the last five years, learning...now I have to work on my courage."

"That is a path you must travel alone, of course, yet you have already shown great courage. When you reached your crossroad, you dared to live. 'Few are those among the people who cross to the other shore...the realm of death so hard to traverse.' Your reliving of past experiences as you approached mortal death meant that you touched upon the releasing. That is to say, *enlightenment*. You reached the crossroad at which you were at once corporeal and ethereal – body and mind. The body is flesh and bone, yet immortal in the sense that it comes from the earth, returns to it, and allows life to begin anew. The mind is immortal in that its karma directs its rebirth in a new being."

"Are the soul and karma one and the same?" Mac asked.

Knowing Mac was referring to the Christian soul, His Holiness simply replied, "One's true essence transcends the mortal body."

"And what of heaven?"

The Dalai Lama smiled. "Buddhism teaches that there is a hierarchy of realms to which the reborn go – the realm of the gods, of titans, of humans, of animals, of the hungry ghosts, and of demons. To debate whether they truly exist is irrelevant. It is enough to say they are a metaphor for one's progression from being bound to earthly desires and pleasures to becoming unbound – released – from that which leads to dissatisfaction and pain. People existing within the realm of demons burn with the fire of passion, fated to suffer the pain of rebirth, aging, sorrow, despair, and dieing. People existing within the realm of the gods – nirvana – have achieved the unbinding through enlightenment, and suffer no more."

"So, nirvana is heaven?" Mac said.

"Yes…and no. It is the ignorant man who pursues what is temporal, the wise man who pursues the everlasting. Ignorance condemns one to earthly rebirth. Wisdom leads one to enlightenment and nirvana. Tranquility, joy, and peace are found along the path to enlightenment where rebirth ceases."

"To reach nirvana, then, is to cease to exist altogether… forever," Mac replied. "But to reach heaven, is for the soul to *live* forever?"

The Dalai Lama smiled and said as if addressing an apprentice, "In either, one finds peace. Until then, we must be wise enough to pursue 'whatever is true, whatever is noble, whatever is right, whatever is pure, whatever is lovely, whatever is admirable.'" He took Mac's hand. "You will help everyone live by those words. I see the reincarnation of Arthur in you."

The word spread quickly.

The Dalai Lama had many friends and tonight scores of them – political leaders, peace activists, Hollywood actors, fellow exiles – were making phone calls, posting, emailing, tweeting, texting, and making plans. By the time Michael

Abrams' jet touched down in the early morning darkness, Tibet was abuzz with rumor and innuendo, hope and angst. Hundreds had trekked to the out-of-the-way airstrip to see history in the making. And when the cabin door opened and the Dalai Lama appeared, he was greeted with cheers, shouts of encouragement, and tears of joy.

No sooner had his feet touched the tarmac than His Holiness knelt to kiss the ground of his homeland. As he stood, an old Jeep rolled to a stop beside him. With a wave to his people, he climbed in with his guards and Mac, and off they drove into the sunrise, cheers and shouts of joy fading away behind them.

The Jeep traveled up into the foothills of the Himalayas. Ecstatic welcomes greeted the Dalai Lama in every village they passed through. Finally, the road crested a ridge and the travelers found themselves looking down into a stunningly beautiful valley. Embraced by blue-gray mountains, the Tibetan capital of Lhasa stretched out before them, its roads and buildings sprawling in every direction, and the ancient Potala Palace on its bluff standing sentinel over the city, gleaming golden in the rising sun.

"Please stop," said the Dalai Lama.

The driver dutifully obeyed, pulling over to the side of the road. His Holiness got out and walked over to a small rise with a commanding view of the city. There he stood, staring out, tears trickling down his cheeks. Mac watched from his seat and in that moment truly appreciated the nobility of this frail little man.

When the Dalai Lama returned to the Jeep, he said as he climbed in, "A new day awaits my people, a day delayed far too long. Perhaps I should never have left," he sighed. "But, whatever this day brings, I shall never leave again."

With a nod to the driver, the Jeep lurched forward.

Word of His Holiness' arrival had preceded him and by the time they reached the edge of Lhasa throngs of the faithful awaited. From that point on, the driver could do little but inch forward at a snail's pace.

Indeed the word had spread, and not just to the faithful, for when the Jeep reached Barkhor Square two hours later, the People's Armed Police were waiting in force for them.

The soldiers of Kyong Mai, Beijing's appointed regional Minister of Peace and enforcer of security in Tibet, halted the Jeep. The Dalai Lama, his bodyguards, and Mac warily stepped out of the Jeep. On Kyong's command, the troops formed a straight line not more than ten paces away from the Dalai Lama…a line that looked to Mac like a firing squad.

Kyong stood glaring at the elderly man whom he'd never met and yet despised with every fiber of his being. With a sneer, he barked another command and every rifle was leveled at the Dalai Lama.

Mac's heart nearly leapt out of his chest. A wave of fear came crashing down on him obliterating all rational thought. A primal desire to run possessed him, yet at the same time he was completely paralyzed, unable even to blink.

The once exuberant and raucous crowd became motionless and silent.

"You will command your Monks and Tibetan *traitors* to disband at once," demanded Kyong.

"And if I do not?" the Dalai Lama said with a calm that Mac found both reassuring and so out of place as to seem absurd.

The Minister of Peace gave a disdainful snort. "And they say you are intelligent," he mocked. "I hold your fate in my hands, you *fool.* Do as I order…or die."

"You, Minister, have a choice in the matter," His Holiness replied so all could hear. "I, on the other hand, do not. We, you and I, are players on the stage of history, and this act is coming to an end. Whether we both walk off the stage alive, or only one of us, is up to you. But, be assured of this – what happens in the next few moments will be remembered forever. For me to obey your orders would be to embolden dictatorial governments like yours, and sanction the inhumane treatment of people everywhere." With measured deliberation, he shook his head. "No, Minister, I cannot obey you…so you must do what you must do."

A flash of rage crossed Kyong's face. He raised his right arm and the soldiers took aim. With his eyes fixed on the Dalai Lama, his heart filled with the glory of serving his country, the Minister did not notice the admiration his men had for His Holiness. They knew who he was. They knew he was famous the world over. They'd been raised by parents who believed, despite China's official atheism, in the 'three teachings' – Confucianism, Taoism, Buddhism – and they'd been ordered to point their guns at the personification of those teachings…a little man exuding serenity and a hopeful light.

"Fire!" Kyong commanded.

Screams echoed about the square. His Holiness' followers fell to the ground in fear. A veil of silence descended and each second felt like an eternity. Mac shook violently, his heart bursting in his chest as he awaited the inevitable explosion of gunfire.

"Fire!" the Minister screamed. Turning to look at his soldiers, he saw the hesitance in their eyes. "Fire!"

The line of men and women looked to their NCO, a career soldier they all respected, for guidance. He in turn glanced from the Dalai Lama to his Minister and back again. Knowing his soldiers were waiting for him to act, he adjusted his aim at the Dalai Lama, lifted the rifle barrel ever-so-slightly, and pulled the trigger. With a thundering crack and flash of red flame, the bullet rippled through the air, passing harmlessly over the Dalai Lama's head. His comrades, realizing what he'd done, followed suit with a volley of gunfire.

Anguished screams filled the Square. Every eye turned to the Dalai Lama. And there stood His Holiness, as majestic as the surrounding Himalayas.

Gasps of surprise and shouts of joy rose up.

At this, Kyong lost all semblance of self-control. He turned on his soldiers, screeching with anger, and snatched one of the soldier's rifles. Then he swung around and took aim at His Holiness. The NCO raised his rifle and pointed it at the Minister's head. As one, his comrades did the same.

Kyong, eyes widening in fear, froze. His hands began to shake, and the rifle clattered to the ground.

The Dalai Lama stepped forward and placed himself between the soldiers and the Minister. "Peace," he said.

His bodyguards led the Minister to the Jeep amid joyous shouts, and Mac felt his fear begin to subside.

The soldiers huddled together in animated debate. A consensus achieved, the NCO reverentially approached His Holiness. "My men and women have a…suggestion," he said.

"Please," the Dalai Lama encouraged, returning the bow.

"Could we surrender to you…and should Tibet gain her independence, would you allow us the same freedoms your Tibetans will have?"

"There would be no other path," replied His Holiness.

The NCO beamed, bowed again, and ran back to his soldiers.

The people in the Square formed an impromptu line, filing past the Dalai Lama with bows and good wishes. Mac, the muscles in his legs suddenly weak, sat on the ground beside His

Holiness. His body continued to tremble, and he felt ashamed by his cowardice.

Some of the Tibetans recognized him and shook his hand as they passed by.

With the sun setting behind the mountains, the last of the well-wishers departed for their homes. Mac was standing by the Jeep, staring at the ground, his arms folded.

His Holiness walked over and said genuinely, "You wouldn't be human if you weren't afraid."

"You weren't," he replied. "That was the bravest thing I've ever seen anyone do."

"I was simply coming to the end of a path I began traveling the day I left here. You are just beginning yours."

The NCO hurried over again. "Excuse me," he said with another bow. "We are hearing on the radio that many influential people around the world are pressuring Beijing to begin negotiations with you for an independent Tibet."

"That is wonderful news, my young friend."

"You'll be staying in Tibet then?" the soldier said hopefully.

"I intend to live the remainder of this life here," the Dalai Lama answered, looking around the Square and up into the mountains, "where I belong."

The NCO smiled happily and bowed again. But, before taking his leave, he stopped in front of Mac and said, "You are William Cameron MacCrary, that Arthur fellow?"

The Dalai Lama translated for him and Mac nodded.

"Some of my men and women recognized you. They were wondering what brought you here?"

"This brave man is here to give us the UN's blessing," the Dalai Lama answered.

The soldier bowed to Mac, crisply did an about face, and ran off.

"The UN's blessing," Mac repeated drolly. "Tanner's probably chewing nails and spitting rivets right now…and the Security Council's probably at war with itself."

"So, now we face a battle of words between diplomats. But, isn't that far better than a battle of weapons?"

Mac sighed, ashamed. "Of course."

Schoen pushed his chair back from the teakwood table and paced back and forth, never bothering to notice the extraordinary view the palace's broad white marble terrace afforded of Casablanca below and the Atlantic beyond. He hated being made to wait, particularly by inferiors.

"Come sit down, Gerhardt," René Boujeau commanded absently as he read the dossier in his hand and wiped his brow with a handkerchief. Despite the fact it was evening, and the Moroccan sun was touching the distant ocean, to men of northern climes the heat was sweltering.

Schoen dropped back into his chair. "Damn him," he muttered, "keeping us waiting like this. Who the hell does he think he is?"

Boujeau placed the dossier back into its manila folder and picked up his glass of iced tea. "He's Maurice Amin De-Morte, son of a French farmer and Moroccan peasant girl he took advantage of and tossed aside when she became pregnant. Shunned by her Muslim family, she gave birth to DeMorte in abject poverty. As a half-caste bastard, he lived the childhood of a street urchin. At sixteen, he joined the army and never saw his mother again. Funneling his rage into a Machiavellian rise through the ranks, he took any mission no matter how heinous and became a Colonel by the remarkably young age of 30… which is when you began providing him with funds and weaponry to systematically eliminate his rivals. Once the last was dead and buried, a rigged national election – which you helped orchestrate – turned our thuggish DeMorte into a President."

Schoen grumbled, "All the more reason to show me respect!"

"He's an animal, Gerhardt. Don't expect niceties from him." Boujeau tapped his finger on the manila folder. "He'll accept our terms?"

"Haven't all the others?" Schoen said smugly.

"Your talent for choosing the coldest, most vile puppets is unparalleled," grinned Boujeau. "How many does this make?"

"Twenty-two," Schoen answered. "North Africa, the Balkans, the Caucuses…and Cyprus will make 23."

Boujeau gazed past the balustrade at the far off Atlantic. "More than a trillion dollars in fighter jets, tanks, transports, arms, munitions…*millions* of soldiers under the command of our tin-pot dictators…and we in control of them," he marveled.

The doors leading from the palace ballroom to the terrace swung open and out walked Maurice Amin DeMorte followed by his phalanx of soldier-bodyguards. Despite his posh attire, he was still little better than a common ruffian.

Schoen and Boujeau stood as the President of Morocco approached.

"Gerhardt," greeted DeMorte in a guttural mix of French and Arabic. "When did you arrive?"

Schoen reluctantly shook the President's proffered hand. "Yesterday," he replied curtly, and nodded at Boujeau. "May I introduce the Secretary-General of the United Nations?"

Extending his hand again, DeMorte said cursorily, "I am honored," adding at once, "Why are you in my country?"

"To offer my assistance," Boujeau replied with a casual wave of his hand to an empty chair. "Won't you join us?"

As DeMorte sat, Boujeau took note of where the soldiers had stationed themselves and modulated his voice so as not to be overheard. "The United Nations would very much like to offer its financial assistance to your government, Mr. President."

Schoen extracted a document from the manila folder and placed it on the table with a fountain pen he took from his breast pocket.

"This agreement," continued Boujeau, "is for 100 million Euros in aid, deposited into an account of your choosing."

DeMorte's cold eyes flashed. "A hundred million Euros," he echoed.

"One-hundred million Euros *every year* our arrangement continues," Boujeau clarified, sinking his hooks into the man still further.

The President reached for the papers, but Boujeau's hand slammed down on them. "With this understanding," he said, his words now lacking all civility. "Our arrangement must be kept secret from everyone. *Everyone.*"

Schoen leaned forward in his seat. "If you do *not*, the consequences will be…quite dire." His words were spoken with such inhumanity that even a cold-blooded killer like DeMorte had reason to pause.

The President slowly pulled his hand back.

"Iron ore, lead, manganese, zinc, coal, phosphates," the Under Secretary-General ticked off, "these are your major exports, yes?"

"So?" DeMorte said impatiently.

"They are sold by legitimate export-import businesses on the world's international commodities markets, the revenues are wired to your Treasury, and the minerals are shipped to buyers overseas for processing." Picking up the pen and holding it out for DeMorte, he said, "Accept the millions in aid…but make sure every shipment leaving your country includes the amounts specified in these papers *beyond* the ordered tonnage and *off* the ships' manifests. I will arrange for the excesses to be off-loaded and sold on the Black Market."

"You keep the money?" said DeMorte.

Schoen nodded coolly. "And you receive 100 million Euros every year our agreement remains in effect. Eighty-percent of the money must be used to purchase military hardware – weaponry, armored vehicles, attack aircraft, etcetera – from the suppliers listed." The suppliers contracted with arms manufacturers in Security Council nations, but he didn't mention that. He also didn't mention that he and Boujeau held large shares of stocks in those companies.

"One day, should we have a need for your soldiers and military hardware," Boujeau said firmly, "they will be relinquished to Gerhardt's command and brought to bear on whatever target he says."

DeMorte huffed in disdain. "And how long will the agreement remain in effect?"

"As long as the shipments continue," the Secretary-General replied.

DeMorte took the pen from Schoen and leaned forward to sign the papers, but hesitated. He weighed his options and the consequences, thought again of the money, and scrawled his signature.

Schoen gave a grin that made even DeMorte's skin crawl.

"Thank-you, Mr. President," Boujeau said, his civility miraculously restored. "As a gesture of our good will, there is a ship in the harbor named the *Shkhara* loaded with small arms, shoulder launch missiles, Kevlar vests, and thousands of rounds of ammunition. It is our way of saying we wish for you – along with the other nations we have similar arrangements with – to stay in power. If you do, one day you will be part of the most powerful military force on Earth."

This seemed not to matter to the dictator-president who said, "Now I get the 100 million and I can do whatever I want with it?"

"You can do whatever you want with *twenty-percent* of it, yes," Schoen answered.

Something occurred to DeMorte and he said, "When he –" pointing at Schoen, "– takes control of my military, what will happen to me?"

"On that day, the world we've known will end," replied Boujeau. "To protect you from the fallout, you will be flown to South America and live in the style a man of your stature deserves. There is an estate in Western Brazil that Herr Schoen affectionately calls Viertes Reich. Stay there as long as you wish or use your considerable fortune to move on to a place of your choosing."

Schoen grinned again and slid a small piece of paper across the table. "This is the eleven-digit number to a bank account in St. Martinez where your 100 million Euros is waiting."

DeMorte snatched the paper out of Schoen's hand, stood, and stalked off.

Michael's jet landed in Geneva just before dawn. Mac said his good-byes, caught a cab back home, and got ready for work.

An hour later, he walked into his office. The headline of the newspaper sitting on his desk read, *"Dalai Lama and King of Camelot Free Tibet."*

"Oh, crap," he mumbled, and as if on cue the phone rang.

"MacCrarey," he said into the receiver.

"The Chinese Ambassador is livid!" Jacob Tanner shouted. "How *dare* you place the U.S. at odds with a major trading partner and Security Council member!"

"Jake, listen, His Holiness —"

"Who gives a *damn* about him? This is politics and economics, and you're fuckin' everything up."

"Isn't freeing the oppressed what the UN stands for?" Mac bit back.

"Shit, boy, are you really that fuckin' stupid? The UN is about letting the Security Council have its way and giving the little third-world peeps a forum to vent their spleens."

Mac shook his head and rolled his eyes. "You're such an —"

"Shut up and listen!" yelled the Ambassador. "I don't *ever* want you leaving Geneva again unless I tell you to, got it? In fact, don't even leave your fuckin' office! And keep your damned mouth shut!"

"Jake, that's bull —"

"Shut! Up! You're off every project you've been working on. T.J. what's-his-name is in charge now. Schoen's re-assigning you to something called the Genomapping Project."

"What's the Geno —?"

"How the hell should I know? Info on the project's coming from New York."

"Look, Jake, the Dalai Lama did something great. The UN should —"

The line went dead.

"Son of a —" Mac cursed and slammed the phone down. Pulling his laptop from the bag, he pressed the power button and went upstairs to visit Helga's coffee maker. By the time he returned cup in hand to his dingy little office, the PC was up, and his inbox had an email from one of Schoen's staffers.

"Great," he muttered sardonically and clicked on it. Attached to the email were several files on the Genomapping Project's history, scope, goals, staff, and the UN's involvement. Mac's job, apparently, was to handle public relations.

"An engineering B.S. from U of M, a Harvard MBA, and I'm gonna to be writing press releases," he grumbled.

Scanning the staff file, a familiar name caught his eye – Dr. Jonathon Joseph Kraeg. He hadn't seen the Professor – whose friends called him J.J. – since the Senate Foreign Relations Committee hearings five years ago. J.J. was a paleoanthropologist, Mac recalled, and according to the attached bio he was collecting and cataloging human DNA samples in Ethiopia, Kenya, and the Congo. A few phone calls later and he had the doctor on the line.

After exchanging pleasantries, Mac explained what was going on and asked, "Why DNA samples?"

"Ah, well," Dr. Kraeg began enthusiastically, "perhaps best to explain by using you as an example. Like Arthur, you're descended from an Anglo people who settled in the British Isles perhaps 20,000 years ago. They and you have Y-chromosomes that are part of the R1b haplogroup."

"What's a haplogroup?" Mac asked.

"A group of individuals that share a common genetic lineage," said the Professor. "Each member of the group carries the same genetic markers that have been passed down from generation to generation."

"Uh, okay…what are markers?"

"Markers are mutations in gene codes. Few mutations are fatal; most are harmless enough to remain in your DNA and get passed on. By sampling the genetic codes of indigenous peoples around the world, we can categorize the mutations into haplogroups. And, since the mutations occurred at different times and places, we can figure out how our prehistoric ancestors migrated around the world. The oldest continuous haplogroups have the fewest mutations, the newest haplogroups have the most.

"Perhaps the Genomapping Project's greatest revelation is that we're all nearly the same. Only *one percent* of our DNA accounts for *all* our evolutionary adaptations to different geographic environments – skin pigmentation, eye color, hair color and coarseness, hairiness, immunities, etcetera. In other words, the differences between races are little more than skin deep."

"Wow. That ought to kill racism once and for all," said Mac.

"One can only hope," agreed Dr. Kraeg. "The Genomapping Project also showed that everyone came from just one or two haplogroups that migrated out of Africa. They were the progenitors of the rest of us. The indigenous Amerindians of North and South America have the newest and most uniform haplogroup, meaning they came from a common set of ancestors in the very recent past. By genomapping mitochondrial DNA markers –"

"There are different kinds of DNA?" Mac interrupted.

"Two. The first is mitochondrial DNA, passed down from the ovum of your mother completely intact, unaffected by your father's DNA. By mapping mitochondrial DNA markers, we've traced the descendants of every haplogroup back to where I am now – Ethiopia. A single, common female ancestor of every human being alive today outside of Africa lived right here 150,000 years ago."

"Eve," Mac said, amazed.

"And so she's been dubbed by the paleoanthropological community," Dr. Kraeg said in all seriousness. "The second kind of DNA passed down intact and traceable through time is from the Y-chromosome inherited by sons from their fathers. Its DNA markers *also* bring us backward in time to this region."

"Adam?" Mac chuckled.

"Yes! Adam existed here in Ethiopia 60,000 years ago. One of Eve's female descendants mated with Adam and their descendants went on to populate the rest of the earth. Click on the map file in the email you received."

Mac did so and up came a map of the world with a broad arrow sweeping out of Africa through the Middle East into Asia. There, it split into several smaller arrows, one doubling back into Europe, another stretching down into the South Pacific, and a third arching up and across the Bering Straits into North America.

"A person inherits exact half-copies of each parent's DNA to create a whole new, unique person. Exact half-copies, that is, unless a mutation – a random, naturally occurring alteration in a chromosome – occurs. When a mutation occurs, it can be easily identified and tracked. As the inheritors migrate, they carry their mutations – or markers – with them to new lands. Each of us carries an evolutionary and geographic timeline in every one of our cells. The map shows the migration of humans across the globe and where each haplogroup ended up. M168 left Ethiopia 50,000 years ago, M89 left Arabia 40,000 years ago, M45 left Kazakhstan 35,000 years ago, M207 left Western Russia 25,000 years ago, and M343 – which defines you and Arthur as Anglo-Europeans – ended up in the British Isles 20,000 years ago."

"If everything's already mapped out," Mac asked, "then why are you still collecting DNA samples?"

"To better identify and isolate the haplogroups of the in-digenous people in Africa. Their extraordinary diversity and ability to thrive for millions of years may mean they have viral immunities and other genetic strengths that can be isolated and hopefully replicated. Remember, the less diverse a popu-lation is, the more susceptible it is to devastating diseases. The haplogroups outside of Africa have very little diversity. Look at what happened to the Native Americans – something like ninety percent of them were wiped out in a matter of decades by smallpox and other European diseases to which they had no natural immunities."

"Where does the UN fit into this?"

"It's well-respected in the third-world countries that field scientists like me work in. UN envoys can get the word out and demystify the project among native populations – get past the superstitions and mistrust, and all that. UN fieldworkers can help my project staff collect the blood samples."

They talked for an hour, and Dr. Kraeg said he'd be wrap-ping up his work at month's end. "I'll set up a meeting in Geneva for us with station chief Kleinmann," Mac told him, "to plan out our assistance."

"Excellent," replied J.J. "I'll be sure my travel plans include a layover there," and they said their good-byes.

Gerhardt Schoen paused the video playing on his laptop to pick up the ringing phone.

"Ja?"

"Mr. Under Secretary-General, Dr. Stone here," said the head of UNESCO, the UN Educational, Scientific and Cul-tural Organization.

"Ja?" Schoen said irritably.

"Sir," Dr. Stone nervously replied, "you asked me to keep you apprised of happenings in the Genomapping Project."

"Get to the *point*, Stone."

"Mr. MacCrarey has scheduled a meeting with the station chief and Dr. Kraeg on the 27th of this month in Geneva."

"Kraeg," Schoen muttered, trying to recall where he'd heard that name before.

"Yes, sir – from MacCrarey's confirmation hearing, sir."

Stone had Schoen's full attention now. "What is *he* doing with the project?"

"Lead field researcher, sir."

Was the Clan's hand at work in this? he wondered. "Keep me informed," he ordered and slammed the phone down.

He clicked on the Play icon to re-start the video Secretary-General Boujeau had sent him with a note saying, 'Might be useful to our plans.'

Schoen stood and began pacing back and forth behind his desk, trying to work out a possible connection between the Clan and the Genomapping Project.

The syrupy-smooth voice of Dr. Johnny Swaywell, prominent televangelist, delivering his latest Christian Vigil sermon wafted out of the laptop's speakers.

"Yet, through all this," Swaywell was preaching, "God still loves us. He wants to bring us home to Him, but He's waiting… waiting until we begin living by His laws. Not the laws of Man, not the laws of our secular Constitution – the laws of Moses, the prophets and, above all, His Son Jesus! Only then will He bring about the events foretold in *Revelations*. Then His love will bring us home in glory, and His wrath will smite down in agonizing death the evil ones among us…the ones who turned their backs on God."

"Come Jesus!" a parishioner shouted from somewhere in the massive sanctuary that Swaywell called the Crystal Cathedral.

"Believe me, my faithful followers, God *does* love us! He *hasn't* abandoned us. And there are signs all around us of His love. He gave us George W. Bush just before September 11 because He wanted America to bring Christianity to the Muslim nations by force. He sent AIDS to smite down homosexuals. He sent Hurricane Katrina to wash away the sins of New Orleans. He sent earthquakes and wildfires to California because of Hollywood's wickedness. He brought us the Great Recession to wash away our decadence. He gave us the Tea Party and Supreme Court decisions like Citizens United and Hobby Lobby to fight liberalism and abortion. And he gave us control of the White House and Congress to reverse decades of liberal, anti-Christian laws."

He paused and chuckled. "The liberal-media persecutes me for saying things like that. But, the more they do, the more convinced I am right!"

A handful of the faithful cried, "Amen!"

"Now...I'm afraid I must reveal to you something terribly evil," he said, his voice suddenly grave. "I learned of it only recently. It is called the Genomapping Project."

At once, Schoen stopped pacing and looked at the screen.

"It's being run by God-haters called evolutionary geneticists. Dirty atheists. And guess what they're trying to find out?"

"Tell us, Johnny!" a parishioner called out.

"Where human beings came from!"

Mocking laughter wafted about the sanctuary.

"We have news for them, don't we?"

"Yes!" the congregation cried.

"We already *know* where Man came from! It's written in the Bible! We don't need atheists telling us the same old lies about how we supposedly e-volved. God created us 6,000 years ago. Period. End of story."

More "Amens!" and a handful of "Hallelujahs!"

After a strategic pause and a slow, sad shake of his perfectly groomed head, he went on, "But that's just part of the bad news, my friends. The Genomapping Project isn't really a project at all. It's a well-funded campaign of lies. It's a plot to steal our *blood*. They're collecting *blood* from people all over the world!"

The mood of the parishioners changed in a heartbeat from righteous indignation to dumbfounded shock.

"I was as scandalized as you are now when I discovered their dark secret," he said with rehearsed sorrow. "I turned to the Lord for comfort and guidance. I prayed for three days and three nights, until *finally* He sent me a dream. But it gave me no peace. For in the dream, God showed me an army…an army of *clones*…*human* clones! Soulless monsters with dead eyes, herded together like cattle, armed by the godless dictators of far off nations, controlled by Satan himself and massing for the Final Battle with God's children…a battle to force Christians to renounce Jesus, or die!"

Gasps and murmurs abounded.

Someone screamed, "Help us, Jesus!"

A well-timed tear ran down the Reverend's cheek. "The hour is nearly at hand…the Rapture. Jesus is coming. Oh, come Jesus, *come!*"

In perfect unison, "Come Jesus!" echoed throughout the glass and steel-girdered cathedral.

"I know God will not abandon us. His justice will be unleashed, and He will smite down the unbelievers. Pray for God's justice, pray for His everlasting love, and pray for the strength to do what must be done…Amen."

A rousing "Amen!" and Schoen closed the laptop.

A wicked smile crossed his face. Charisma, religious conservatism, and a connection to the Genomapping Project. He reached for the phone.

"Dr. Stone," the voice on the other end of the line said.

"What does a lead field researcher do?"

"Ah! Mr. Under Secretary-General. Well, let's see, uh… Dr. Kraeg is travelling from village to village collecting blood samples –"

"Blood collecting?" Schoen said.

"Well, yes. Why –?"

"Get me the place and time of their meeting," Schoen said and hung up. A moment later, he was dialing again.

A click and the distracted voice of Rene Boujeau said, "Yes, Gerhardt?"

"Swaywell *will* be of great assistance to our secret project, Mein Herr. I assure you."

Dr. Johnny Swaywell, leader of the Church of Eternal Vigilance in Alexandria, Virginia, leaned over his oaken desk sorting through a folder of newspaper clippings and printouts from Internet news sites. Piles of articles were forming by topic – world events that would provide insight into the unfolding End Times; speeches by world leaders that might lead to the Evil One; technologies that could be used to persecute the faithful; moral abominations and liberal media attacks on his favorite conservative political leaders.

Once everything was sorted, he got up and crossed the plush burgundy carpet of his office to a floor-to-ceiling bookshelf that held just one book…one true book to answer every question and solve any problem. Swaywell's trusty King James Bible. No scholarly tomes, no classic works of literature, nothing that might contaminate the purity of the Reverend's thoughts could be found anywhere in his office. The rest of the bookshelf was filled with photographs of the good Reverend shaking hands with well-known politicians and business leaders.

Grabbing his Bible, he opened it to *Revelations* and returned to his desk. Sitting back down, he pulled several blank sheets of paper embossed with the Church's logo towards him. Time to read through each stack of articles and start writing his sermon for Sunday's telecast of the Christian Vigil.

In the outer office, a phone rang.

"Church of Eternal Vigilance. May I help you?" Betty, the Reverend's secretary, said in her a pleasant sing-song southern accent.

"I wish to talk with Reverend Swaywell," Gerhardt Schoen answered.

"May I ask who's callin'?" she said.

"UN Under Secretary-General Gerhardt Schoen," he replied. "Now get him."

"Oh! Oh, my," she gasped. Never had she received a call from the wicked United Nations before. "Just, uh…hold on…I, uh…wait one moment, please." She put him on hold and practically ran to the office door. "Reverend! There's a man saying he's a general secretary from the United Nations on the phone for you."

"A general –" Swaywell started. "Do you mean…a Secretary-General?"

"Yes, sir. A Gary somethin'…Gary Shun, I think."

"Leave me. And close the door." Swaywell sat there a long time staring at the blinking light on his phone, wondering what Satan's UN wanted with him.

Schoen waited on the line for what seemed to him an interminably long time, listening to the phone system run through a litany of church activities. Prayer meetings, potluck dinners, Bible classes, youth group outings –

"Mr. Secretary-General?" Swaywell said cautiously.

"Under Secretary-General. My name is Gerhardt Schoen."

"To what do I owe this…honor?"

"Reverend," Schoen replied humbly, "I heard you preaching about the Genomapping Project Sunday."

"Yes. Frightful, isn't it?"

"Indeed, and I happen to know one of the scientists collecting blood…for clones, as you say."

"Good Lord!" gasped Swaywell. He'd made the part up about clones, of course, but atheists were capable of anything. "Who?"

"A paleoanthropologist named –"

"A what?" Swaywell interrupted.

Schoen closed his eyes and took a deep breath. "A paleoanthropologist. Paleoanthropology is the hybridization of paleontology, the study of ancient life forms, and anthropology, the study of human cultural and social history."

"Uh…Oh, yes. Of course," said Swaywell.

Schoen tried a more simple-minded explanation. "He is a scientist proving evolution is real."

That hit the mark. "A Darwin-worshipper, eh?" the Reverend hissed.

"Ja, Reverend," Schoen replied in contrived disgust, "a Darwin-worshipper, named Dr. Jonathan Kraeg. He is meeting with a man you probably heard of…the heir of a king born in the shadows of the Roman Empire…the Empire that crucified our Lord Jesus Christ."

"Dear God. You're talking about William Cameron Mac-Crarey, aren't you? I remember his confirmation hearings, what…four years ago?"

"Five," Schoen said, balling his left hand into a furious fist and crushing the receiver with his right. "MacCrarey committed the sin of suicide, lied and coerced his way into the UN, created a satellite network that can spy on anyone anywhere on Earth, and now he's helped that heathen Dalai Lama take over a country!"

Swaywell was speechless, an unusual condition for him.

"You've read Tim LaHaye's *Left Behind* books?"

"Yes…yes, of course. Every good evangelical has."

"You preach that the United Nations is evil, ja?"

"I, well, yes, but –"

"Well, I can attest to that evil, Reverend. Someday the Antichrist *will* rise from within the UN…and I fear it will be MacCrarey."

"Oh, dear Lord," muttered the Reverend.

"And Dr. Kraeg and MacCrarey are meeting on the 27th."

"You…you must stop them!" cried Swaywell.

"How?" Schoen replied helplessly, smiling to himself.

"I…I don't know! I…you just have to!" stammered the Reverend.

"Nothing can stop them short of – oh, but I shouldn't speak of such terrible things."

"What? What will stop them?" said Swaywell.

Schoen hesitated, checking his reflection in the office window. "I couldn't…it would be a sin."

"What would be? Tell me!"

"I know when and where they're going to meet…and if an instrument of God's wrath just happened to be there at the right moment –"

"An instrument of God's wrath?" he echoed in near disbelief. "You mean an –" The word stuck in his throat as his pulse quickened. "Dear Lord," he whispered.

"Ja, Reverend," Schoen replied icily. "An assassin."

A wave of revulsion enveloped the good Reverend. "An assassin."

"A sin isn't a sin if its purpose is righteous...is it?" said Schoen.

"I...suppose —"

"I'm sure you have loyal, unquestioning believers who would do whatever God commanded them...don't you, Reverend?"

"I, well, yes...I suppose —"

"Is it not right to act for the sake of your ministry, your country, and your God?"

"Act," echoed the dazed Swaywell. When *should* a man of God put his words into action? he wondered. When *should* the righteous shed blood for their Lord? "MacCrarey...the Antichrist —" he mumbled. How long had he railed against Satan? Had he ever done anything to really stop him? And if he didn't stop the Antichrist, wouldn't he be guilty of *helping* Satan? Wouldn't he go to hell for that?

He drew in a deep breath, said a quick prayer — "Yes, Mr. Under Secretary-General, it is right to act. And I will."

"Call me Gerhardt," Schoen replied with a grin.

Senator Jack Abrams watched the tourists on Constitution Avenue from his office window in the Dirksen Senate Building. Finishing his coffee, he set the cup down on the credenza, grabbed his Armed Services Committee folder, and started for the door.

His private phone rang and he hurried back to his desk to pick up the receiver. "Abrams."

"Jack! How are you, my friend?" said a joyful Reverend Swaywell.

The Reverend was Jack's single largest campaign contributor because Jack was *for* home schooling, charter schools, grants for faith-based organizations, Israel, and big business; and *against* taxes, abortion, gays, separation of church and state, gun control, and big government.

"Johnny! How good to hear from you," he said with the faux enthusiasm and saccharin sincerity of salesmen and politicians. "How's life at the Crystal Cathedral?"

"Wonderful!" the Reverend replied. "Viewership and attendance are at all-time highs."

"Calling to have me on your show again?" Jack asked hopefully.

"Uh, sure…next month. But right now, Jack, I need a favor."

"Your wish is my command."

"Do you know Under Secretary-General Gerhardt Schoen?"

Surprised, Abrams said, "Well, I talked with him and Secretary-General Boujeau once. Why?"

"I talked with him today. He's asked me to find him…an instrument of God's wrath."

"A *what?*" Jack said.

Swaywell explained about the genomapping project and the paleo-something-or-other making clones, and how the End Times and the Antichrist were coming. "We have to stop him, Jack. Or else Satan –"

"Wait, hold on. Are you talking about an –" he lowered his voice, "– an assassin."

"Yes, Jack. I am, and I know how you're feeling. I reacted the same way, but God is calling me. And he's calling you!"

Abrams couldn't believe this. Swaywell wanted a homicidal fanatic to whack a nobody scientist just because Schoen asked him to. Then, he remembered his conversation with

Schoen and Boujeau five years ago. 'Should the day come when I need you to act, you will act,' Boujeau had said.

"And I agreed," he mumbled to himself.

"What was that, Jack?" asked Swaywell.

"Nothing. Look, Johnny —"

"*Revelations!* The Antichrist, Jack, *your* Deputy Ambassador to the UN!"

"What? *My* Deputy Ambassador?"

"MacCrarey's the Antichrist! It all fits. *Left Behind.* The United Nations. And he's meeting with that paleo guy in Geneva later this month!"

"MacCrarey's mixed up in all this," Jack said, piecing it altogether. "So it's not just the scientist that Schoen wants dead —"

"No. MacCrarey," Swaywell answered.

MacCrarey. How Jack hated the name. MacCrarey, who'd embarrassed him at the hearings. MacCrarey, who his grandfather had chosen for the Deputy Ambassadorship. MacCrarey, who'd split the Security Council. MacCrarey, who his biggest campaign contributor believed was the Antichrist. Wouldn't it be nice to be rid of MacCrarey once and for all?

"An instrument of God's wrath, you say?"

The Armed Services Committee meeting started in an hour, but Joint Chiefs of Staff General Curtis Powell wanted to meet beforehand at his Pentagon office.

"Jack, my boy," the four-star General drawled, extending his bear paw-of-a-hand. "Come on in!"

Abrams shook it and fell into his usual armchair beside the General's desk with a sigh. "How about opening up that Baptist bar of yours, Curtis?"

Powell gave a hearty laugh. "Rough day, huh?" He walked over to a bookshelf and grabbed the left side. Pulling, the bookshelf swung out from the wall to reveal a fully stocked wet bar. "What's your pleasure?"

"Scotch. Rocks," Abrams replied appreciatively.

"You're *really* havin' a rough day," the General laughed again, uncorking his best bottle.

"An odd one, Curtis."

"Care to tell me about it?" Powell asked as he filled two tumblers with ice and poured the rich amber elixir.

Abrams smiled weakly and took the proffered tumbler from Powell. He had no intention of sharing plans for murder with a four-star General. "You wouldn't believe me anyway," he said. Wishing to change the subject, he added, "So, what do we have to cover in committee today?"

The General pulled out a small humidor from a desk drawer. "Mostly Iran stuff," he replied, taking two cigars from the wooden box. Picking up a folder and tossing it over to Abrams, he said, "Here's the agenda and handouts. I'll walk you through it."

He snipped the ends off the cigars with a miniature guillotine that sat on his desk.

Half an hour later, the General refilled the Senator's tumbler for a third time and fell into the armchair next to him. Done with their official business, Powell chortled, "So, last Saturday mornin' I was sittin' in the Oval Office with the Joint Chiefs when all of a sudden this twenty-somethin' blonde runs in followed by a White House tour guide who was tryin' to catch her, ripps open her blouse to display her wares, and propositions the President right then and there."

"It's good to be king," Abrams laughed.

"And let me tell you, that little filly weren't no librarian," chortled Powell, lampooning the fact that the President's wife actually *was* a librarian. "O'course, Jameson's so damned straight-laced he wouldn't have known what to do with a filly like that anyway."

"Clinton woulda known what to do," Abrams joked.

"Hell, yeah. That ol' dog knew how t'hunt," and they laughed again.

"You should write a book someday, Curtis, what with all the crazy stuff you've seen."

Powell blew out a few smoke rings and pointed at a piece of paper on his desk. "No shit. Take a look at that letter over there. Some group out west is askin' for HDF activation," he said, rolling his eyes.

"What's HDF mean?"

"Oh, that's right. It was your granddaddy who was here then. Back in the Eighties old Ronnie Reagan told the DOD to ready the country for war with the 'evil empire.' So, we came up with a volunteer thing to train and arm American citizens in case of a Soviet invasion. Give away military surplus shit to paranoid types. Put a half-track in your garage and an M-16 in junior's crib, that sorta thing. The Secretary of Defense pitched a program he called the Home Defense Front, or HDF, to Reagan. And would you believe it? The old boy loved it." Powell chuckled and took a drag on his cigar. "Hook, line and sinker, son. Hook, line and sinker."

"So, what happened then?" asked Abrams, grinning and puffing away.

"Reagan put old George Bush the First in charge. Told him to set up HDFs all around the country. Anything DOD wanted, Georgie gave it to 'em – money, offices, staff, military hardware – you name it."

"Why haven't I heard of HDFs before?"

The General's good cheer faded a bit. "Well, actually you have, I'm sorry to say…you see, our own government created the militia movement."

"You're kidding?"

Powell shook his head and took another drag. "Wish I was, son. The DOD convinced somethin' like half the states to implement HDFs, but there was no central oversight, see? No monitorin' of who was joining up or why. Turned out that the volunteers were a bunch of paranoid nut jobs who believed the commies comin' for 'em, but so was everybody else – the federal government, Jews, Muslims, Blacks, immigrants, the ATF, the UN, you name it. At the time it didn't matter much – the folks signin' up were card-carrying Republicans. So, we shipped 'em weapons, did some counter insurgency training like homemade bombs, booby traps, sneak attacks, sniper hits, assassinations –"

Abrams sat bolt upright, dropping his cigar. "Shit," he cursed, jumping up.

"You okay, son?" the General chuckled.

"Yeah," muttered Jack, picking up his cigar and brushing ashes off his jacket and tie. "Assassinations, huh?" He walked over to the desk and picked up the letter.

Powell puffed on his cigar and continued his story. "Then, the Iron Curtain fell and the Russkies bit the dust, so Bush let the HDFs fade away. Only they didn't, see? They started buildin' up their *own* arsenals and trainin' *themselves* and buildin' compounds out in the boonies and believin' in every damned conspiracy theory that came down the pike. Then, September 11th happens, Wall Street collapses, the Great Recession hits, a Black man becomes President, Fox News says the country's goin' to hell in a handbag, and guess what? Them militia and neo-Nazi nut jobs think they were right along! Membership goes through the roof. Now there's more than a *thousand* of 'em."

Abrams read the letter.

> *To the Federal Office of the Home Defense Front*
> *Pentagon Building*
> *Washington, D.C. 21212*

> *Dear Sirs:*

> *We demand the activation of our Home Defense Front unit to prezerve our American sovrinty and protect our Christian way of life. The Reverend Johnny Swaywell says the end times are coming and we got to be ready. The world is about to be thrown into kaos by the United Nations and the Antichrist and Satan's armies. We need weapons and money right away, so we're asking for immediate activation of our HDF unit. Please reply ASAP.*

> *Yours in Christ and America,*
> *General Jonathan Robert Cobb*
> *White Freedom Nation*
> *P.O. Box 141*
> *Hulett, Wyoming 67667*

The Senator's mind raced and his heart pounded…for in his hands he held the means of William Cameron MacCrarey's destruction.

The sky was crystal clear and from the guard tower he could see the ancient, mile-high volcano shaft called Devil's Tower fifty miles north to the Montana state line. The land it sat on was the country's first national monument, which meant the land had been stolen by the Federal government.

"Sons o' bitches," muttered Jonathan Robert Cobb. The crisp winter air chilled him to the bone, and he stamped his feet on the weathered planks to keep warm.

Cobb was a pudgy, stubble-cheeked, make-believe militia General with dark blue eyes and a pale ruddy complexion. He wore second-hand Army-surplus fatigues and puffed a hand-rolled cigarette.

Glancing at his watch, he noticed it was time to head inside. He told the Sergeant next to him, "Your watch," and scanned the compound one last time as he walked to the ladder.

Barbed wire fencing enclosed a square with quarter-mile long sides oriented to compass directions. A dozen wooden, one-story buildings and four guard towers dusted with snow lay scattered about the compound that the White Freedom Nation militia members called home.

Sticking the cigarette in his mouth, he grabbed the rails of the ladder and started down one rung at a time. Cold and impatient, he decided to try what some of the younger soldiers did. Straddling the ladder, his army boots pressed against the outside of the rails, he loosened his grip and slid down. Approaching the bottom, he squeezed the rails with his hands and feet to slow down but discovered to his chagrin that a beer belly and gravity were too much for middle-aged muscles. Hitting the ground hard, the General's legs buckled and he landed on his ample posterior. Cursing, he got to his feet and dusted the snow off his fatigues as he started across the parade ground for Freedom Hall.

Inside the foyer, he took off his coat and boots while scanning the notices tacked to the bulletin board. One was the day's event schedule – family breakfast at seven, drills from eight to eleven, prayer lunch at noon, target practice from one to three, family dinner at five, vespers at nine –

"Damn. Vespers," Cobb groaned. He hadn't even started his sermon yet. Hell, he didn't even have a topic for it. "Oh, well," he muttered, deciding to watch his videotape of last Sunday's Christian Vigil sermon for ideas. With that pleasant thought, he headed down the hall to break bread with his fellow militia folk.

"Hey, boss!" Colonel Randall Joseph Collins called from the office as Cobb passed by. "Picked up the mail in town when I got the supplies this mornin'. Look what we got!"

The General backed up to the office door. Collins was standing behind a beat up green metal desk holding two letters and a small package. He was shorter and stockier than Cobb and also wore army fatigues.

"Who they from, Randy Joe?"

"You ain't gonna believe it," he said with awed reverence. "This here's from Senator Jack Abrams…and *this* one is from Reverend Johnny Swaywell *himself*."

"Holy mother of Jesus," Cobb exclaimed, hurrying over to grab the letters.

Ripping open the one from Abrams, he pulled out the embossed sheet of stationary and read it aloud. "'Dear General Cobb. The Reverend Johnny Swaywell and I have been close friends and confidants for many years, and it warms my Christian heart to know there are good, white, Americans such as yourselves still out there, willing to stand up for God and country. Effective immediately, your HDF unit has been activated. I must stress that your unit's activation is a singularly unique event. All knowledge of it must be kept secret at all costs. You are to report directly and only to me. My private telephone number is included below. Call me to receive your orders. With your help, our way of life will be preserved. God Bless you and God bless America.' And it's signed, 'Senator Jack Abrams.'"

"Praise the Lord," said Collins.

Cobb tore open the other envelop and began reading. "The Reverend's giving us a mission!"

"What kinda mission?" the Colonel asked excitedly.

Cobb read some more. "Seems we gotta take out a couple guys," the General explained, "in Geneva of all places."

"Where's that?" Collins asked.

Cobb rolled his eyes. "Europe. Didn't you study geometry in home schooling?"

"Killin' people," the Colonel said anxiously. "The Lord don't look kindly on that…'less there's a holy reason for it…is there a holy reason?"

"According to this there is. Seems to be tied to our HDF activation, too." He set the letter down and nodded at the small package in Collins' hand. "Open it up, Randy Joe."

The Colonel shook it gently and listened before tearing off the brown paper and packing tape. He opened the flaps and dumped the contents on the desk – a DVD and a handful of military insignia patches. One patch had two lightning bolts side by side that looked like the letters 'SS.'

"Shutzstaffel!" Cobb pointed, wide-eyed.

Another had a skull and cross bones. "Gestapo," said Collins.

The General picked up the DVD and read the label. "Dr. Johnny Swaywell, Christian Vigil, broadcast number 224, dated – Jesus, Mary, and Joseph! – dated *next* Sunday!"

"Praise the Lord," Collins said again. "Let's take a look!"

They hurried out the door and down the hall to the common room, a large square assembly area with hardwood floors and whitewashed walls. Rows of long tables and folding chairs were set up for a meal. Menfolk sat around talking and joking while womenfolk laid out a potluck dinner. Along one wall was a long cafeteria-style window that opened into a kitchen where coffee was brewing in industrial-sized urns and filling the assembly hall with a rich, warm aroma. At the other end of the room stood a raised stage with a flat-screen TV and DVD player on a rolling cart. Cobb hurried over, turned them on, and put in the disk.

An image of a huge glass and steel building appeared on the TV screen, organ music began to play, and everyone in the room stopped what they were doing to watch. Cobb said, "This here's Johnny's broadcast for next Sunday," and they crowded around.

The image changed to the Crystal Cathedral's interior and a deep, rich Ed McMahon-ish voice said, "And now…from the Church of Eternal Vigilance in Alexandria, Virginia…Dr. Johnny Swaywell is pleased to present another hour of the Christian Vigil. News and its meaning as revealed by America's most noted biblical scholar. Ladies and gentlemen…Dr. Johnnyyyyyy *Swaywell!*"

A tall, portly, well-groomed fifty-something man dressed in a perfectly tailored suit strolled across a vast stage, waving to his audience. A choir that could have given the Mormons a run for their money sang, *When the Saints Come Marching in*. Applause salted with cheers and an occasional 'Bless you, Johnny!' reached its crescendo just as the Reverend stepped up to the pulpit. He gave his signature smile, raised his arms, and slowly brought them down. The audience fell silent and sat down in unison.

"Welcome, my friends and fellow Christians," the Reverend began. "Oh, what a glorious day! Glorious, indeed." His voice was upbeat and rich. "For in the days to come, I promise you rewards in heaven…and why?"

He cupped his right hand to his ear and leaned towards the audience.

"HE'S COMING!"

"Yes! Praise the Lord. He's coming." Swaywell bowed his head to pray. "Oh, Lord, You have given us much and we thank you. Please forgive us if we fail to live our lives as Your only begotten Son taught us, for we are a weak people, Lord. *Weak.* But, we are here before You today to *try* and be better Christians, to preach to others Your word, and to tithe in Your name. Amen."

"AMEN!" the audience echoed

"My children, I'm pleased to announce that this past month the Church of Eternal Vigilance reached one hundred million congregants, world-wide. Fifty million tune in to our broadcast every week and half a billion receive our monthly *Christian Vigil* e-newsletter."

Cheers and applause.

"Half a billion Christians…and what does being a Christian mean?"

"WE ARE PERSECUTED!"

"Yes, and by whom?"

"JESUS-HATERS!"

"But, *you love* Jesus, don't you?"

"YES!"

"You believe in the literalness of the Bible. You know God sent his only Son to *save* you, a Son who wasn't afraid of persecution, a Son who *died* for you, a Son who *loves* you…like I love you."

A faint, "We love you, Johnny!" could he heard from the back of the cathedral.

"And I love you, child!" said the Reverend to laughs and applause. "I have been graced with the Lord's wisdom. The Lord uses me as His voice on Earth so that I may preach His word to you. That is a heavy burden, my children. Heavy indeed…but one I am bound by my love of God to bear. He says we'll be with Him in heaven soon because the End Times are coming…the times of the Dark One. The Evil One. The Son of Satan!"

Anxious, whispered conversations could be heard in the background.

"As it is written in *Revelations* and *Isaiah*, God's prophecy is coming to pass even as I speak. How do I know? Because the Lord sent me a dream, a vision, a *nightmare*, some would say, of what is about to happen. The Dark One is here. Now! On Earth!" declared the Reverend ominously. "He is among us this very minute…the *Antichrist!*"

A collective gasp went up, both on the DVD and in the common room.

The good Reverend held up a handful of newspaper clippings and printouts of Internet articles. "He will destroy America and create a single, global government. Listen to what's happening," and he read aloud excerpts from articles on world events, quoted political leaders, referred to media opinion pieces, all the while drawing parallels with Biblical times and prophecies by citing Bible verses. "We must be forever vigilant, and vigilance is why the Lord put me here on Earth in these, the last of days." He leaned against the podium as if a great weight had just been placed upon his shoulders. "God has revealed the Dark One's name to me, and before my sermon ends today, I shall reveal it to you."

Murmurs of anticipation sounded in the background and an anguished congregant cried, "Who is he?"

Swaywell gave a grim smile. "First, let me tell you who he is *not*. He was raised here, but he is *not* an American. He has fooled the liberal media, he's fooled our elected officials who put him in the United Nations, but he has *not* fooled me. He claims to be the descendant of an English king, but he's *not* the *King* of Kings.

"I've watched video tapes of him. I've read the press accounts of him. And Lucifer's hand is at work here, people. He wants the Dark One to be the leader of the seventh great kingdom, the first six having long since faded into history – Egypt, Persia, Greece, the great Roman Empire, the Third Reich, and the Soviet Union. His seventh will straddle many lands and rest upon the ruins of the first six. This *novum orbis regium*, the new world order, will rise from the vile United Nations – enemy of God and America! The Dark One, the Antichrist, is already rising through the ranks of the UN. Remember my dream about scientists collecting human blood? The Antichrist is in league with those scientists to create an army of clones and lead them into battle at Armageddon."

"Help us, Jesus!" someone cried.

"There will come a time when all seems hopeless. Yet rejoice, for even in the darkest hours the Lord will not forsake those who have taken Jesus Christ into their hearts. You are the Lord's chosen people, and I am His messenger. Whatsoever He speaks to me, so shall I speak to you. Together, we will warn our fellow Christians of the Antichrist's coming…and together we shall be victorious."

A smattering of applause rippled through the sanctuary.

"In our victory, we shall see Jesus riding His chariot of fire out of the heavens brandishing His sword of vengeance, reaping the followers of the Evil One with each mighty stroke, and sending them to hell for all eternity!"

"Praise the Lord!" cried someone.

"Praise Jesus!" shouted another.

"Are you ready to hear the Antichrist's name?"

"YES!" shouted the audience.

"Are you sure? Do you promise to spread the word? Tell your neighbor? Call your congressman? Write your local newspaper? Will you do that for me? For God?"

"*YES!*" they shouted again.

"Very well, then…the Leader, the spawn of the Evil One, the Antichrist who will bring the Apocalypse down upon us is…William Cameron MacCrarey, Deputy U.S. Ambassador to the United nations!"

The screen switched to the shocked faces of the congregants. A prim elderly woman was crying. Shouts of anger and calls for mercy abounded. An 800-number appeared at the bottom of the screen and the picture changed to a phone bank of clean-cut, youthful operators eagerly writing down pledges. Swaywell's voice could be heard reading *Revelations* chapter 7, verse 9 to chapter 22, verse 6, finishing with, "'And behold, the time is near. Let the evil doer still do evil, and the filthy still be filthy, and the righteous still do right, and the holy still be holy. Behold, I am coming soon, bringing my recompense, to repay everyone for what he has done.' One thousand two hundred and sixty days…that is how long William Cameron MacCrarey shall rule until his army of the damned clashes with the army of the East at ancient Armageddon in a battle such as the world has never seen. Cities shall lie in ruins, nations shall fall into economic chaos, crime and terrorism shall become common place, millions shall die of famine and pestilence, secular humanism shall reign, America shall fall to the Liberals —"

"No!" someone cried.

"Help us Jesus!" cried another.

"We'll fight to the death, Johnny!" shouted still another.

"– but in the end," Swaywell concluded, "we shall sit at the right hand of God."

The picture faded to black.

Anxious conversations broke out amongst the brothers and sisters of the White Freedom Nation. "Quiet down, everyone," Cobb shouted. "Quiet!" and the din subsided. "Senator Abrams has activated our HDF unit." He held up the letter. "We are now at war. The Reverend Swaywell –" and he held up the other letter, "has given us our first mission." He paused to look at the faces of his friends and family. "We are to kill William Cameron MacCrarey!" and cheers shook the hall.

"Who gets the killshot?" asked Collins when they were alone in the office. "You gonna do it, Jon Bob?"

Cobb thought for a moment and shook his head. "We need someone young and hungry."

"Well," the Colonel began with some hesitation, "my boy Willie's the best shooter we got. Tough, too. And smart. Taught him real good. Loves Jesus and hates everybody who don't."

The General considered it before asking his friend, "You sure you'd be okay with Willie going? It'll be dangerous."

"God'll watch over him," the Colonel replied without a doubt in the world.

The General sighed. Willie truly was the best man for the mission. "Alright then. Let's call him in here."

7

"Mommy!" she squealed in delight as she ran into Genevieve's outstretched arms.

"Hi, Sweetie," Genevieve smiled. "Did you have a nice day at school?"

"Yeah! I had cake and I got presents and we sang songs and it was really fun."

"Oh, that's great, honey," her mother said with a hug. "Here, hold my hand while we walk to the car, and tell me *everything* that happened today."

So, little Cameron Kristine MacCrarey told her mom all about her fifth birthday at Milliken Elementary School in the little town of Old Mission. Genevieve buckled her daughter into the car seat with an occasional, "Wow!" and "Uh-huh" as the story of her daughter's day unfolded. They were half way home when Cameron paused long enough for Genevieve to squeeze in more than two words in a row.

"I have a surprise for you at home," she said.

"What, Mommy?" Cameron said, her big blue eyes sparkling in anticipation.

Genevieve looked at her in the rear-view mirror. Her long curly blonde hair cascaded over her shoulders and framed her beautiful alabaster face. "It's a surprise," she teased.

"Is it my daddy?" Cameron asked excitedly.

Genevieve was caught completely by surprise. She'd never told Cameron who her father was. She'd never even told her father he was a father! From time to time, she saw his picture in the paper or heard his name on the news, but never tried to contact him. He lived in Geneva – at least she thought so – and still owned a condominium on the peninsula not far from her and Cameron.

"Um…no, Sweetie."

"Oh," she said softly, the smile on her face fading as she turned to look out the window.

Genevieve felt like the world's worst mom. "What made you think it might be your father?"

Cameron shrugged. "Sarah's dad took her to the Disney Store for *her* birthday."

Genevieve sighed with relief and said with a smile, "We can go to the Disney Store this weekend, okay?"

The smile returned to her daughter's face. "Okay! Promise?"

"I promise."

"Yay!" Pause. "But, I'd still like to meet my Daddy…someday."

She was the worst mom again. "Someday," she echoed.

Someday…how a simple word could carry so much meaning. How it had the power to change a life…or two. She thought back to when Cameron was born, recalled looking out the window of her room at the gently falling snow and whispering to her newborn baby girl, "I'll take you to meet him someday, Cameron…someday."

"Someday," she repeated absently, looking in the rear-view mirror at her lovely daughter and knowing that 'someday' had finally come.

But, would Mac want to see them? She'd left *him*, after all. And he hadn't wanted to see her when he was in the hospital.

But, what if he *did* want to see them? She imagined catching his eye across a crowded room. His face would light up and he'd walk over smiling the way he did when he thought of how much he loved her. She'd throw her arms around him, and –

"Mommy," Cameron said, looking at her mother in the mirror, "why are you crying?"

The four of them were talking and eating when Mac's phone rang. Pressing Answer, he said, "Guten abend?"

From four time zones away, he heard Professor Lynn Penn's voice. "Do you have satellite TV?" she asked excitedly.

"Why, I'm fine, Lynn, thank-you so much for asking. And you?"

She giggled. "Sorry, but you just have to see what's on."

"Yes," Mac smiled, looking over at the TV set mounted above Petra's bar. "Satellite. What station?"

She told him and made him promise to call her back afterwards.

"After what?" he said.

"You'll see," she answered and hung up.

"That was Lynn Penn," he told Marion, T.J., and Dr. Kraeg. "Wife of an old friend of mine from New York. Petra," he called to his new friend who was sitting behind the bar doing paperwork. "Mind if I switch the station?"

"Nein. Go ahead," he said with a wave and returned to his papers.

"What's Lynn doing research on now?" T.J. asked as Mac got up to grab the remote.

"The last time I saw her she was researching the, 'psycho-social ramifications of religious fundamentalism, cross-normalized with the demographic, biographic, and psychographic statistics of her control group,'" Mac recited, "or something like that," he chuckled.

T.J. nodded thoughtfully and then asked, "So, what's Lynn doing research on now?"

Everyone laughed.

"She and her staff have been documenting the social, political, moral, and ethical positions America's fundamentalists are taking on Presidential, Congressional, economic, media, and social issues," Mac answered as he flipped through the channels. He found the one Lynn said to put on, and then turned up the volume. "Her study'll show the extent to which fundamentalists influence politics, the economy, and social norms."

A commercial was ending for a retirement home called Covenant Acres with the 't' shaped like a cross. Then the screen switched to a minister in a tailored suit standing behind a pulpit.

"– the Lord sent me a dream, a vision, a *nightmare*, some would say," the Reverend was preaching.

Mac furrowed his brow. "Swaywell."

"Who is he?" Dr. Kraeg asked.

"Big time televangelist," explained T.J. "Critical of the UN."

"– the Antichrist is among us this very minute –" Swaywell continued.

"Why did Lynn want us to watch this garbage?" griped T.J.

"No idea," muttered Mac.

"– the Leader, the spawn of the Evil One, the *Antichrist* who will bring the Apocalypse down upon us is… William Cameron MacCrarey, Deputy U.S. Ambassador to the United nations!"

Mac's jaw dropped.

"Oh my God!" gasped Marion. "He's been talking about *you!*"

"Unbelievable," muttered Dr. Kraeg, shaking his head in dumbfounded amazement at the ignorance of some people.

T.J. smirked, "Geez, first King Arthur, now the Antichrist. Who's next, Brad Pitt?"

"Funny," Mac said dryly, "very funny."

When the 'Amens' came and the organ music began, Mac switched the channel back.

"The Clan should hear about this," T.J. said to Mac.

"Knowing Kyle and Merrill," he smiled humorlessly, "they already have."

Dr. Kraeg brought his luggage downstairs from the guest room and set it by the front door.

"Do we have time for lunch?" asked Mac.

"A quick one. My flight leaves at two."

"Petra's, then?" Mac suggested.

"Fine, gives me a chance to say good-bye to him and his charming daughter, Katrina," he winked.

They talked about the Genomapping Project as they strolled down the quiet cobblestone lane to the bustling cross street at the bottom of the hill, and turned right. They were greeted by a warm breeze carrying the scent of edelweiss entwined with the aroma of Petra's latest culinary delight.

"Man, I'm hungry," said Mac with a grin. A pudgy twenty-something man leaning against a lamp post across the street caught Mac's attention.

Spying his targets, the young man stepped into the street.

To Mac, the man looked like a fish out of water – short-cropped dirty blonde hair, pink cheeks, and a high forehead beaded with sweat. He was wearing ill-fitting fatigue pants, army boots, Men-in-Black sunglasses, and a sand-colored hoody. As the stranger approached, Mac could make out the words on the sweatshirt – 'God, Guts, and Guns Made America Free' – printed in English over a symbol of some kind, something akin to a black and red pinwheel.

As the man stepped onto the curb, he awkwardly swung his right hand around his torso as if to pull up his sagging trousers, but when his hand reappeared it held a pistol.

By now, Mac and Dr. Kraeg were in front of Petra's plate glass window.

No sooner had he seen the gun than a sickly, familiar sense of panic radiated out from Mac's chest, through his torso and into his limbs. He stopped dead in his tracks, unable to move or take his eyes off the pistol.

The Professor, who'd paid the man little attention, kept walking until he called, "Dr. Kraeg?"

Instinctively, Dr. Kraeg turned and said, "Do I know you?" Then he saw the pistol.

He grabbed Mac's arm and started for the café door, but his friend was fixed to the spot. The Professor stopped, the man raised the pistol in a malevolently graceful move, and without a moment's hesitation fired point blank three times into Dr. Kraeg's chest.

The Professor gasped in shock and pain, his body falling back into the window, and collapsing to the sidewalk like a rag doll.

Mac's heart leapt at the booming crack of the gunshots and felt as though he might pass out. Then, in what seemed like slow-motion, the pistol swung his way. An icy chill ran down his back. A primal desire to run screamed at him from deep within his foggy mind, but he'd lost all physical control.

With a grim smile, the American raised his gun to Mac's head. "William Cameron MacCrarey," he said as if passing judgement.

Another booming crack exploded in Mac's ears! Heart pounding, he waited for the searing pain of lead tearing through his flesh and bone…but it didn't come. Instead, his would-be-assassin began to sway, a look of shock and con-fusion crossing his face, and then he fell face-first onto the pavement.

Someone grabbed Mac's arm and began dragging him into the café. Turning his head with supreme effort, he saw Petra's determined face, and in his free hand a smoking hunting rifle.

"Your man succeeded," Schoen told the Reverend over the phone. "The Darwin-worshipper is dead."

"Oh, dear God," Swaywell whispered, closing his eyes, anxious revulsion and delight contending with each other in his mind.

"Unfortunately," Schoen went on, "your assassin was killed during the attack."

Swaywell muttered a quick prayer and said with sermonic sympathy, "He was a brave warrior of God. Is there a more noble way to leave this life than dying in the service of the Lord?" He waited for an affirmation from Schoen, but it never came. "And what news of MacCrarey?" the Reverend finally asked.

"The bastard's cheated death again," he answered bitterly.

"Satan protects him," said Swaywell.

Schoen closed his eyes and clenched his jaw. "Perhaps," he forced out through clenched teeth, "you're right."

"Nooooo!" wailed Randall Joseph Collins.

Cobb patted him on the shoulder as he stared at the dusty planked floor of the barracks. "I'm sorry, Randy Joe," he muttered. There was nothing else to say.

In his hand he held a handwritten letter from Johnny Swaywell saying their, "brother in the war against evil," had succeeded in his mission but, regretfully, "William Cameron MacCrarey, in league with Satan, struck down your wonderful son. Yet, take comfort in knowing that he died the death of a martyr, for he unquestioningly did God's will. And rest assured that you will one day see him again, sitting at the right hand of God."

"When will they bring him back?" Collins sobbed, his face buried in his hands as he sat in the metal office chair beside his friend.

Cobb grimaced. "I'm afraid we…can't bring his body back, Randy Joe. If we try and claim his body, the government'll know we were involved."

"*Nooooo!*" he wailed again. "*Nooooo! Nooooo!*"

Unnerved, the General drew back and slapped Collins hard across the face, knocking him to the floor. "Sorry," Cobb disingenuously muttered.

The Colonel, stunned into momentary silence, lay on the floor rubbing his cheek.

"I swear to God," he professed with tremulous voice, "before I see my son in heaven, I'm gonna kill that bastard Mac-Crarey."

Rene Boujeau sat behind his desk in the Secretariat Building paging through the latest UNFICYP report as Schoen paced back and forth across the office.

Annoyed by the constant footfalls, Boujeau dropped the papers on the desk and said, "What's vexing you now, Gerhardt?"

"Not vexed…eager," he said, hurrying to the office door and closing it. "We are ready, mein Herr…finally, after decades of toil, we are ready –" He lowered his voice. "– for Viertes Reich!"

Boujeau didn't particularly care for Schoen's pet name for their brilliantly executed plan. To compare it with Hitler's brutish Third Reich was like comparing Shakespeare with Stephen King. Both were great writers but in completely different leagues. Still, he permitted his associate this one indulgence… well, the ridiculous Clan business, too.

The Secretary-General stood up. "The last of our acquisitions have been made? And Cyprus? Zeda is ready?"

"Ja," Schoen replied with dark pride.

The Secretary-General slid the papers to one side and pressed a button under the lip of his desk. The glass atop the desk began to glow. A brilliant blue image of the UN logo and a virtual keyboard materialized. Boujeau stepped aside for Schoen, and a few keystrokes later a satellite image of the world spread across the desk.

"The new composite map?" asked an impressed Boujeau.

Schoen nodded. "From GLOSAT. Refreshed every 60-seconds." He pressed Egypt and the screen began zooming in. He held his finger there until only northern Africa, the Middle East, Europe, eastern Russia, and the Caucuses filled the desk. A few more taps and keystrokes, and a list of assets appeared beneath the name of each country. "These are the United Nations official asset depots and their locations." He typed a command and a login box appeared. Another set of commands and a list of military armaments – fighter jets, tanks, armored troop transports, mobile cannons, automatic weapons, troop counts, and so on – began scrolling down beside each depot's name. "These are our *personal* assets," he said hungrily. "I embedded them in an encrypted GLOSAT shadow database. Only you, I, and General Mendenberg have access to it." He pointed at Libya. "Using our assets, General Mafti has captured the final remnants of the King's Royal Guard in Tripoli and dissolved parliament. We will be hearing about it on the news today. He has complete control of the country now."

"And we have complete control of him," Boujeau smiled cooly.

"We have all of North Africa except Egypt," said Schoen. "Twenty-three countries across Africa, the Middle East, the Balkans and the Caucuses. Once we have Cyprus, our preparations will be complete." Just thinking about it excited him, emotionally *and* physically. "Only America possesses a greater military force than we do now."

"So now we must neutralize her," Boujeau said matter-of-factly.

"Ja, mein Herr," Schoen acknowledged, "but there is still
–" He faltered.

"What, Gerhardt?" the Secretary-General said impatiently.

"There is still…MacCrarey."

Boujeau closed his eyes and replied irritably, "MacCrarey
is isolated, removed from all projects, and assigned to nothing
but the Genomapping Project. Yes?"

"Ja, but he is *not* an ordinary man."

"He managed GLOSAT, so what?" scoffed Boujeau. "If it
hadn't been for his Holiness, Lhasa would have been a miser-
able failure and MacCrarey would have been disgraced."

"Do not underestimate him!" demanded Schoen.

Boujeau did not tolerate insolence, even from his Under
Secretary-General. Half a foot taller and considerably broader
than the wiry German, Boujeau stepped to within inches of
his face.

Schoen did not move, nor did his defiance falter.

"No more of this nonsense," Boujeau said with the intona-
tion of a man unwilling to be disrespected again.

"Without the UN, MacCrarey will have no power base left
and no pulpit to preach his Clan's pathetic pipe dreams from.
Therefore, he must have a high-profile failure. Turn the tide of
opinion against him. Then, you can fire him at will, without
repercussions."

Boujeau looked down at Schoen for a good long moment
and stepped back. "You have something in mind?"

Schoen gestured to the pile of papers. "Make him Mission
Commander of UNFICYP."

A smile crossed Boujeau's face. "Just before Zeda strikes?"

Schoen nodded again. "He awaits my orders, mein Herr."

"And Tanner?"

"Also awaiting my orders."

Drs. Jay Michener and Robert Ingersaul were at the funeral. So were Merrill and Kyle.

Dr. Kraeg's wife and two grown daughters wept beside his grave as the family's Episcopal priest concluded the committal service. "Forasmuch as it hath pleased Almighty God of His great mercy to take unto Himself the soul of our dear brother here departed, we therefore commit his body to the ground. Earth to earth, ashes to ashes, dust to dust, in sure and certain hope of the Resurrection to eternal life through our Lord Jesus Christ. Amen."

The obligatory "Amens" wafted away with the cool breeze and mourners began their tearful good-byes. Ashamed to have faced his worst fear a second time and failed, and feeling more than a little responsible for J.J.'s death, Mac walked head down to the waiting Astin Martin, Clarice following close behind. Without a word, he climbed into the back seat, soon to be joined by the two Elders.

"Petra told me what happened," Kyle said without looking at him. "Lhasa…again?"

Mac turned to the window and said nothing.

"For five years you've studied. You know right from wrong, prudence from foolishness, heroism from cowardice. But, you must take that knowledge and –"

"Steel it with experience," Mac said peevishly. "Yeah, I know."

"And steeled experience, infused with courage and compassion, becomes nobility," said Kyle. "The lives of heirs have never been easy, lad. It is your burden to bear as Arthur's last heir." He let a silence fall between them to give Mac a moment's reflection. "Will you continue to accept that burden? Will you honor your promise to the Clan?"

Again, silence.

Mac's iPhone rang.

Kyle held up a hand. "Answer my question."

Mac gave a brusque nod.

"Good," said Merrill, "because you're about to get your next steeling experience."

Mac gave the Elder a questioning look before clicking Answer. "MacCrarey."

"Boujeau wants you in The Hague," barked Ambassador Jake Tanner. "Today! New assignment."

Mac stared at Merrill. "A new assignment?"

"What are you, a fuckin' parrot? *Yeah,* a new assignment. Be grateful you're doing *anything*," groused Tanner.

"Can this wait? Dr. Kraeg's funeral was today and –"

"Get your ass on the train now!" roared Tanner and the connection went dead.

Mac threw the phone down. "Shit," he muttered. "Clarice, is there a train station nearby?"

Mac stepped off the elevator and into the second-floor lobby of the International Court of Justice in The Hague. The outer office of the Chief Judge's chamber was open, so he walked in. To his left was a conference room, and around the table huddled René Boujeau and three other men in animated discussion.

Two were lean and swarthy, dressed in black fatigues, the third was as opposite as could be – northern European to a tee with blond, almost white, short-cropped hair.

Gerhardt Schoen.

One of the strangers gestured at the door and they all fell silent. The Under Secretary-General turned and stared at Mac with emotionless blue-gray eyes. Boujeau got up and closed the door behind him as he walked out of the room.

Without a handshake or salutation of any kind, Mac asked, "What's this I hear about a new assignment?"

"A singularly *special* assignment," Boujeau said with a hackle-raising smile. "Your favor with the fickle press, your make-believe ancestry, and your obvious disdain for my command has placed you in a class of *one* for this assignment."

"Something tells me that's not a good thing," Mac smirked.

"Effective today, you're the Commander of UNFICYP."

"The Cyprus peace-keeping force?" Mac exclaimed. "Me? You need a *General* down there, not a…a —"

"A what?" snapped Boujeau. "A pencil-pusher? A bureaucrat? A nobody? A *fraud?*"

"A civilian," Mac retorted. "UNFICYP is a stalemate and a money pit, and I've never led a military operation in my life! You've got the wrong man."

"I have the right man for what I expect to be done."

"And what exactly is that, Boujeau?" Mac brazenly replied.

The Secretary-General took a menacing step forward. "You will call me 'sir.' I am the Secretary-General of the United Nations and you will show me the deference I am owed." He gave a boastful huff. "There are those in this world who *kneel* in my presence."

"No one should be made to kneel before another," Mac said coolly as he, too, took a step forward.

"One day, even you will kneel before me."

"Never," Mac scoffed. "Nor would I allow anyone else." For a moment, he thought Boujeau might take a swing at him.

Instead, the Secretary-General threw the Robin's egg-blue folder he'd been holding at Mac's head. The heir of Arthur batted it away, sending papers fluttering across the carpet.

"Select your team," Boujeau ordered and turned for the conference room. "Schoen will brief you before you leave."

An hour later, the conference room door opened and everyone but Gerhardt Schoen silently filed out.

"Kommen sie hier," said Schoen with a curious intensity.

"The Secretary-General said you'd brief me on UNFICYP?" Mac asked indifferently as he walked in.

Schoen said not a word as he stood, eyes probing every inch of Mac's face and frame.

"The briefing, Schoen?" Mac asked impatiently.

The Under Secretary-General gave a derisive snort. "I wished merely to look upon you with my own eyes." The two men had never actually been in the same room before. "While you're still alive," he added with an ice-cold grin. "Now, be gone…once and for all."

On Sunday morning Mac boarded a train in Geneva bound for Florence. From there, he took another to the Roma Termini and from there another to the port city of Taranto in the heel of Italy's boot. On the morrow, he would sail for Cyprus and assume command of UNFYCIP.

With no peacekeeping experience, no training, no detailed orders, no *anything* to prepare him for the mission, Mac understood all too well he was being set up to fail. He also understood he had no choice. Orders were orders, and Kyle and Merrill expected him to follow them.

Just before midnight, Mac joined the disembarking travelers as they made their way off the train and onto the trackside platform. Crossing through the narrow station to the sidewalk beyond, the claustrophobic world of his day opened onto a harbor-scape ringed by jagged volcanic mountains. Fishing boats moored for the night bobbed up and down, wooden shanties dotted the rock-strewn beach, and the black Mediterranean seemed to go on forever. In stark contrast were brightly lit shops, cafes, and hostelries lining the street to his left and right.

"I was getting worried about you," said a familiar voice.

On a bench beside the ticket office sat T.J. Makatu.

Mac gave his friend a tired smile and walked over to give him a quick hug. "Hope you haven't been waiting too long, buddy."

"Mmmm," T.J. said with a half-grin. "No matter. I've been busy reading up on UNFYCIP…and 'O Captain! my Captain!' you are screwed."

Gerhardt Schoen stood on the deserted Cyprian beach next to the tall, gaunt man he'd first met five years before in a darkly lit café. Together they watched as the *Shkhara,* silhouetted against the moonlit sky and whipped about by the Mediterranean, steamed into the secluded cove and dropped anchor. Soon, a deck crane swung a cargo skiff over the rail and lowered it into the choppy water. Lashed to its deck were two Jeeps and dozens of crates.

The Under Secretary-General nodded at the ship and said, "Your last shipment. Now you have everything you need." He handed Zeda a cell phone. "I call. You attack —" he pointed at the flapping map Zeda held in his hands, "— here." Along the demilitarized zone, a small village was marked with an 'X.'

Zeda stared at the map, his face hard and expressionless. The man's dark hair thrashed wildly in the wind, starkly contrasting with his lifeless black eyes. With a hasty nod, he rolled the map back up.

"Take what you want from the land. Do what you wish with the people. And build up your army with the money I give you." Schoen looked out upon the black sea. "A great war is coming. The armies of many nations including yours will be brought together, and the world shall be recast into its proper order."

"You will take my army?" Zeda said in his Greek-accented English

Schoen answered, "I will take *my* army, you will be rich, and Cyprus will become part of the new world order my ancestors fought and died for. But for now, during your conquest of the island, I ask for only one thing…the death of William Cameron MacCrarey."

0730 hours – Day 1.

In transit to the Island of Cyprus.

Mac, T.J., and the four members of the UNFICYP administrative team sat together in the galley of a British naval patrol ship bound for Nicosia. As she pitched and rolled, T.J. opened his army-issued thermos and poured a round of coffee. Everyone had been given assignments and this was their first face to face meeting as a team.

Mac nodded to Perry Spencer, a fair-haired Royal Air Force Colonel and fighter jet pilot who'd been recommended by the British Ambassador. Perry looked as if he'd just stepped out of a recruiting poster. "Give us a run down on the UN administration and command of peacekeeping forces," Mac said, his voice loud enough to be heard above the creaking of the ship and the deep rumble of her engines.

"Yes, sir. And may I begin by saying congratulations," said Perry with a pleasingly classic British accent.

"Call me Mac and what the hell are you talking about?"

"When we make landfall in Nicosia, you'll officially have the equivalent rank and authority of a Brigadier General."

T.J. laughed, "Him? A General?"

"If that's true," Mac said dryly, "then my first command is to have him," hoisting a thumb at T.J., "thrown in the brig."

T.J. and Perry laughed, but the others sat stone-faced, not risking a faux pas.

"Lighten up, gentlemen," T.J. told them. "This command's gonna be a bitch, so let's try and make it bearable. Continue, Perry."

"Under the UN Charter, member states are to carry out the directives of the Security Council, refrain from the use of force, and settle disputes by peaceful means. Military hardware is for self-defense only. All nations in which UN personnel are deployed must give their consent prior to a peacekeeping mission commencing, and peacekeepers are to treat all sides fairly and equally."

"We can't take the offensive and the best we can hope for is a perpetual stalemate. Fair summary?" said Mac.

"Yes, sir."

"Taylor," T.J. asked, "what can you tell us about the island?"

Taylor Johnson was a Liberian-born member of his country's UN delegation. His Cambridge education, talent for languages, scholarly knowledge of Islamic affairs, and experiences with civil strife at home uniquely qualified him for this mission. Like Perry, Taylor came from a fiercely independent nation and held no blind loyalty to the U.S., the UN, or any other nation. That was one of the key criteria Mac and T.J. had used to select the team.

"Cyprus is the third largest island in the Mediterranean," Taylor began. "Only Sicily and Sardinia are larger." He too spoke with an accent – native Liberian mixed with upper-crust English. "It is 240 kilometers from east to west, 100 kilometers from north to south. A DMZ – demilitarized zone – divides the island roughly in half. In the Greek south is the Troodos Mountain range, the port cities of Larnaca, Limassol, and Paphos, and the highest point on the island at 6400 feet – believe it or not – Mount Olympus. In the Turkish north is the Mesaoria Plain, the Pedias and Kariyoti rivers, and the port cities of Famagusta and Morphou. The capitol Nicosia is cut in half by the DMZ like Berlin used to be. The island's economy is agricultural – citrus fruits, olives, almonds – and husbandry – goats, sheep, pigs, et cetera.

"The land is rocky. There are frequent earthquakes. It's hot and humid in the summer, rainy in winter. There'll be moderate temperatures when we land, increasing precipitation over the next few weeks."

"Gee, a real garden spot," T.J. said sardonically.

"With all due respect," said Perry, "why is it important to know the geography and natural resources of the island?"

"Do you know who James Michener was?" Mac replied.

"Of course. Author. Wrote *Hawaii, Centennial, and The Source.*"

"Among others, yes," Mac said. "In his autobiography, Michener wrote that to truly understand a people, you have to understand their land. Consider the rain forest in Brazil where food literally falls from the trees and lands at your feet. Now, think of an African desert with no tree or bush in sight for hundreds of miles. Wouldn't the cultures of the people living in such places differ greatly? To truly understand the Cypriots, we must understand the symbiosis that exists between them and their land. The physical and *meta*physical connection they have with their world. Only then can we move on to their society, traditions and history to fully construct appropriate solutions to their problems."

Perry gave Mac a respectful nod. "Understood."

"How about a history lesson?" T.J. asked Taylor.

"Well, the Island's been a stepping-stone for conquering empires throughout history. First Greece, then Phoenicia, then Rome, then the Byzantines, then the Ottomans, and finally the British."

Perry spoke up. "By 1900, Great Britain ruled most of the Middle East. Since 1948, fifteen of the UN's thirty-three peacekeeping missions have been in former British colonies, as are eight of the current fourteen."

"Why do you suppose that is?" asked Mac.

"There was something fundamentally flawed in Britain's approach to setting borders and transitioning colonies to independence. Too Eurocentric and economically driven. But centuries-old animosities among ethnic and religious groups played a major part as well. And no one but the groups themselves will ever resolve those animosities."

Bolstering Perry's point, Taylor went on, "Cyprus became independent in 1960. Its constitution created a republic designed to balance the interests of its 730,000 inhabitants, 78 percent of whom are Greek, 18 percent Turkish, four percent British. But, by 1963, the Turkish minority withdrew from the government in protest of Greek attempts to take political control."

"The Greeks are Orthodox, the Turks are Sunni," said Perry, "and they're all bloody stubborn."

"Stubborn and violent," Taylor agreed. "Fighting broke out in '63 and in '64 UNFICYP, the United Nations Peacekeeping Force in Cyprus, came into being. Now there's a 100,000-man National Guard made up of Turks and Greeks, 1,000 of whom are on active duty at any given time patrolling the DMZ with UN units."

"Thank you," said Mac, turning to his last team members. "Gentlemen, tell us what we'll be facing in the coming months."

Mustafa 'Moose' Sifas spoke up first, his accent a blending of Turkish and British. "As the token-Turk on this mission, let me say you have an impossible task ahead of you, Mac."

From a well-to-do Izmir family, he'd attended Oxford and afterward went to work at the UN in New York. For twenty-two years, he'd served as civilian advisor to various Middle Eastern and international organizations as well as two peacekeeping missions. The nickname Moose came not only from his name, but from his dark and imposing visage. But, he was actually quite gregarious and genteel.

"According to Boujeau's files, you are not only administering the peacekeeping mission," said Moose, "but you will be the mediator at next month's unification talks."

"Oh, great," Mac muttered.

"It will be the twelfth time since 1968 such talks have been held, all of them ending in failure…especially for the mediator. T.J. has explained to me your, uh, situation, and I must tell you that Cyprus is the perfect place to discredit you. Your failure will change nothing yet keep you from ever being assigned to a UN project or mission again."

"Considering we have yet to dock, it's a little early to count us out, don't you think?" T.J. chided.

"No," Moose answered without hesitation. "Mac was down for the count when he boarded this ship."

Mac's stomach was doing somersaults.

"Mmmm," grumbled T.J., turning to the last team member. "Aro, can you give us a chronology of events since Cyprus gained her independence?"

Aro Petous was a second-generation Greek-American, born and raised in south Detroit. He was swarthy and rugged-looking, street-smart and uncouth, yet spoke fluent Greek, had a Masters Degree in International Relations from U of M, and was currently working on his Ph.D. Moose had met Aro on a liaison mission to ISIS-occupied Syria two years before and recommended him for UNFICYP.

"Sure," he replied. "But, first let me echo Moose's opinion. Mac's fucked."

Mac let out a breath as though he'd been gut-punched.

"Second, the Turks have been fucked ever since the island got its independence. They were banned from holding government jobs, they were treated like second-class citizens, they were terrorized by right-wing Greeks for two generations, so they wrote their own Constitution in 1985 and established an independent government."

Moose countered, "Do not view the Turks as victims, my friend. The Turkish army invaded Northern Cyprus in 1974, and in 1975 refused to allow Greek refugees who'd fled south to return to their homes. We, too, are guilty of prejudice and discrimination."

"Look at what led up to that, though," Aro pointed out. "In 1968 and again in 1974, a coup d'etat backed by the military government of Greece overthrew the Cypriot government. *That's* why the Turkish army invaded."

"And the UN refused to stop either the coup d'etat *or* the Turkish military intervention," said Perry.

"Yup, though in 1985, the Turks accepted a proposal from the Secretary-General to establish a unified Federal Republic of Cyprus. But, the Greeks refused. In 1991, the Security Council wanted to form a bi-communal, bi-zonal republic which also ended up in the shitter. Same story ever since. One side gets militant and terrorist attacks thwart unification efforts, or nationalistic politicians get elected and refuse to talk peace."

"The UN's achieved *nothing* in half-a-century and we're supposed to fix it in a month?" said Mac.

"What do you mean 'we,' Kemosabe?" muttered Aro.

The others laughed, but Moose said, "He may be joking, but Aro is making a good point. When *you* don't succeed at the unification talks, Mac, or if something goes wrong on the island while you're commander, only *you* will be blamed."

"After that," said Aro, "you'll be nothing but a fucking pencil pusher in some forgotten back water of the UN."

"If this is as hopeless as you all say, why the hell did you sign up?"

No one answered. They looked at the table, the floor, the wall, anywhere but at him.

"Yeah, that's what I thought," he smirked. "You're just as idealistic as me."

1300 hours – Day 1

The turnover of command was accomplished with little fanfare, though it too seemed to hold portents of failure. There was a brief, perfunctory ceremony on the parade grounds before a mass of dispirited-looking soldiers, and a quick salute from the former Mission Commander who promptly made a beeline for his staff car and beat a hasty retreat.

In his new office, Mac found no words of guidance from the departing Commander, no records of what had transpired during his tenure, and no instructions as to what needed to be done to prepare for the unification talks. Dispirited, Mac and T.J. walked over to the command center, then to the mess hall and finally to the officer's residence in search of senior military staff who could give them the lay of the land. To their dismay, they discovered that every commissioned officer had been ordered off the island just prior to Mac's arrival.

In the coming days, Mac found that the UN troops under his command gave him the deference a Brigadier General was due and followed his orders. But, they were *only* following his orders. He knew that if he wanted their respect, he was going to have to earn it.

1000 hours – Day 22

Despite their inauspicious start, Mac and his team accomplished a good deal during their first three weeks on the island. Now, with the unification talks a week away, Taylor was in New York making final arrangements, T.J. and Perry were in charge of day-to-day operations at HQ, and Moose, Aro and Mac were leaving on a tour of the DMZ patrol camps. It was mostly a symbolic task meant to bolster morale and garner positive P.R., but the troops also expected it of a new Commander.

Sitting in the lead Jeep, Mac's driver led the convoy out of the UN compound on a cool, sunny fall morning for the first leg of their four-day tour. Passing through the western gate, they slowly made their way through a crowd of onlookers. To Mac, the Turks and Greeks were indistinguishable from one another. How replete history is, he reflected, of peoples so much more alike than different who nevertheless end up on different sides of an issue and fight to the death over it.

There was one person, though, who did stand out. He was tall and gaunt with dark intense eyes that stared unblinkingly at Mac. Aro and Moose saw him as well, anxiously exchanging worried looks and hushed words.

The convoy moved on, the stranger faded into the crowd, and the ill-ease of the moment passed.

1245 hours – Day 22

Aro raised his voice above the sound of grinding gears and whining engines to say, "We have over 100 patrols along the demilitarized zone at any given time. Each patrol has four soldiers and covers a three-mile stretch of land. At the deserted city of Varosha, we have the largest UN encampment outside Nicosia, almost 1,000 soldiers. We'll spend the night there."

"Why is it deserted?" Mac yelled over his shoulder from the front seat.

"Varosha lies right in the middle of the DMZ. In the mid-'60s, both sides claimed the city for themselves and neither was willing to compromise. The UN had no choice but to evacuate it."

Mac nodded. "Who was that man by the way?" he asked.

Knowing at once who he was referring to, Moose and Aro again exchanged worried looks.

"Pompous Zeda," Aro answered. "Greek separatist and suspected terrorist. Intel suggests he may be up to something, but no idea what."

There'd been something in Zeda's eyes that still haunted Mac. "Please pass on whatever additional Intel you get."

"Will do," Aro replied.

They came around a bend in the road and a long, broad valley came into view. "Pull over," Aro told the Sergeant who obeyed with a jerk of the steering wheel and a shuddering stop.

Mac gave his traveling companions a questioning look.

"You're gonna get some perspective," Aro told him, hopping out. "Come on!"

Mac followed him up a small hill and no sooner had they reached the peak than Aro pointed at a spot far off in the valley. "Look."

Gazing in the direction of Aro's outstretched finger, Mac spied a military encampment with soldiers milling about in the Turk-controlled northern foothills. To the west lay open fields of grass dotted with outcroppings of rock and groves of olive trees. To the east lay the deserted city of Varosha.

"And look there."

To the south sat another camp along the bank of a dried-up river bed.

"Greek separatists?" Mac asked.

"Yup. Keeping a close eye on their Turkish enemies over there. This has been Cyprus for three-quarters-of-a-century. I wish I could say the unification talks'll change it, but they won't. *Nothing* will." He turned and stomped back down the hill.

Mac took one last look at the two camps and distant Varosha. Feelings of frustration, helplessness, and an odd sense of foreboding swirled in his mind as he made his way back to the Jeep.

2345 hours – Day 26

Once their coast-to-coast tour of installations along the DMZ was over, the team promptly returned to HQ in Nicosia. Mac was packing for the unification talks in New York City when a knock sounded at his door.

"Come in," he said as he continued packing.

Colonel Perry Spencer walked in. "Mac, we picked up a transmission from one of our patrols. T.J.'s already in the CC. Moose and Aro are on their way."

"Coming," Mac replied, dropping a Garcia tie into his garment bag and reaching for his jacket.

By the time he and Perry arrived at the Communications Center, the others were huddled around the radio set. "What's up?" he asked, walking towards them.

"We're not exactly sure," T.J. answered. "Sergeant, play back the last transmission."

"Yes, sir," Staff sergeant Sean Kelly replied. The tall young man had short black hair, large light brown eyes, a muscular frame, and a broad firm jaw. If the Greek gods had ever taken mortal form, they must have looked like Sean.

A sound of commotion came through the speakers. A frantic female voice cried, "This is Patrol W2 out of Varosha Base calling HQ. A Turkish village near the DMZ is under attack. Repeat, under attack!"

Suddenly, the sound of an explosion blasted out of the radio's speakers.

"Request assistance immediately!" she pleaded. Running footsteps could be heard, then a man yelling in the background – "Oh, my God!" she screamed – the crack of semi-automatic gunfire, electronic feedback screeching through the speakers, and the signal went dead.

Everyone turned to Mac.

"Any other transmissions?" he said weakly.

"No, sir," Sean answered with a professional calm.

"Should we contact the nearest patrol, Sean?" Mac asked. "Have them check it out and radio back?"

The Sergeant gave his CO a *Why are you asking me?* look. Real commanders never called non-coms by their first names *or* asked for their opinions. "Is that an order, sir?"

"Uh," Mac hesitated, looking around at his team. "What do you think?"

Moose said urgently, "It's a terrorist attack."

"Whose?" Mac said. "Why?"

Moose gave Aro an exasperated look before turning back to Mac. "Who knows? Who cares? The question is, what are you gonna do about it?"

Sean Kelly interrupted. "Got another patrol, sir." The men huddled around the radio again. "Took a few tries, sir. At least three teams are off the air. I have W7."

The Sergeant noticed the Mission Commander's hand was shaking slightly as he took hold of the radio transmitter. "W7, this is Mission Commander MacCrarey. What's going on out there?"

"Sir, this is Lieutenant Denali. We're on a ridge north of the village. There's gunfire in the streets everywhere!"

"Any sign of W2?" Mac asked.

"None, sir."

Mac gave his team an imploring look.

That was all the encouragement Perry needed. "It'll take a day to get sufficient hardware and troops out there to mount a defense, Mac."

"It'll be *over* by then," Moose argued.

Aro began to say something when a deep voice crackled out of the speakers.

"This is General Pompous Zeda. I hereby declare war on the Turks and the United Nations. All UN soldiers must leave my island within 48 hour…or they will die. Do you understand me, Commander MacCrarey?"

Mac stared blankly at the radio.

"The UN does not negotiate with terrorists," Perry reminded Mac.

"Hell, every nation *says* they don't," said Aro, "but politics and public opinion polls make 'em do it anyway."

"You can't give in to these bastards," Perry argued. "Once you do, they'll walk all over you."

"There are lives at stake here, Mac," T.J. said.

"I demand the return of my soldiers immediately," Mac ordered, his words sounding impotent even to him.

Zeda gave a contemptuous laugh. "Where are my manners? You are new to my island, King of the Anglos. Let me send you a welcoming present." The transmission ended.

"'King of the Anglos,'" T.J. muttered. "Apparently our friend reads western newspapers."

"What do we do?" Mac asked, a quaver in his voice.

T.J. wanted to tell his friend to grab his balls and act like a General but bit his lip.

"Ready the troops," Perry answered as if it were obvious. "Get intel! Ask NATO for overheads and any military support they can offer."

Mac ran a trembling hand through his hair but said nothing.

T.J. grumbled, "*I'll* contact NATO."

"I'll ready the troops," Perry nodded. "Aro, Moose, we need to know *everything* about this son-of-a-bitch Zeda. Sergeant, stay in contact with the patrols and keep us posted."

"Yes, sir!" Sean said.

Perry looked from Aro to Moose to T.J. "We reconvene in thirty."

0015 hours – Day 27

"NATO will down load satellite photos of the village by 0200," T.J. told the others, "but they have to get approval from NATO Command before they can commit troops. I also notified Tanner's office of our situation."

Mac grimaced. The last thing he wanted was for his bosses to know his command was turning into a shamble.

"It's protocol, Mac."

Perry said, "We'll have 200 troops ready to deploy at sunrise and another 300 by 1030 hours. Fourteen armored transport vehicles and a dozen light armor tanks are standing by."

"Call up the Cypriot National Guard troops," T.J. suggested to Mac.

"Excellent suggestion, sir," Sean piped in.

Mac nodded blankly. "What do we know about Zeda?" he asked feebly.

"Born in Morphou in 1969," Aro replied, "five years old when the Turks invaded, lost his parents and sister during the fighting, grew up in a refugee camp, fell in with the resistance movement as a teenager, rose through the ranks, took control after killing off his rivals."

"None of our Intel indicated anything like *this* was in the works," Moose added. "There's no way he could have stockpiled enough weapons on his *own* to pull this off."

"Why now?" Mac asked.

"Damned good military strategy, really," Perry answered, trying not to sound condescending. "There's a brand-new UN Commander on the island who's not a soldier, the weather's poor, no moon tonight, element of surprise."

"Perhaps more than *military* strategy," Aro suggested.

"The unification talks?" Moose said.

"Yup. Zeda's a marginalized, hate-filled Greek nationalist who would rather *kill* or *be* killed than make peace with the Turks."

"And he thinks this attack will keep the talks from getting underway," nodded Moose.

"Fucking A."

"So…what do we do?" Mac anxiously asked.

"What choice do we have?" Moose said in frustration. "We go after the bastard!"

"Call up the National Guard," T.J. repeated.

Mac's ability to focus was waning. He just stood there, unable to make a decision.

Perry shook his head and told the others, "I'll assemble the troops. Sergeant, you're with me."

0645 hours – Day 27

Fog lazily drifted about the parade ground as the soldiers waited in their transports for orders.

Mac asked T.J. as they stood next to the lead Jeep, "Any further communications from Zeda?"

Before T.J. could reply, Sergeant Kelly ran out of the CC and, pointing to the foothills, yelled, "Incoming!"

Mac and T.J. ran to the nearest guard tower and climbed up. The rest of the team followed close behind. Binoculars up, Perry and Sean anxiously scanned the gray hills.

"Damned fog," Aro griped, "can't see more than a hundred fucking yards."

The Sergeant handed Mac the binoculars, gesturing toward a patch of black fog along the far side of the clear-cut security zone that stretched from the fence to the nearby hills.

"What's that?" Mac muttered, looking through the binoculars.

"Vehicles, sir."

Mac felt sick. "How many?"

"If it's an attack, they'd be coming in column formation to hide their numbers."

"Yes…of course," Mac said. "Air support?"

Sean shook his head. "Weather's too bad."

"Oh. Right." Sean was no longer saying 'sir' when he addressed him, Mac noticed. He turned to his team. "Suggestions?"

Perry jumped in, "Bring up the artillery and sharp shooters. Deploy the troops in defensive positions."

"Yes, sir!" Sean said and unclipped the portable radio from his belt.

Mac watched the patch of black fog gradually take the shape of an army transport bouncing its way across the security zone.

"Truck bomb?" T.J. asked Perry.

"Zeda's present," Perry agreed. Wheeling around, he told Sean, "Order the artillery to fire as soon as they're ready!"

"Yes, sir!"

Soldiers set up mortar tubes on a small rise near the fence. Sean relayed the command and a moment later they began firing. The first shells exploded behind the target. Two more thumped out, one landing to the right of the transport, the other just to the left.

"Bracketed!" Perry shouted.

Another thump and this time the shell struck just in front of the truck, its explosion forcing the transport slightly to the left.

The soldiers lining the fence opened up with their M16's, peppering the truck's armor, shattering its windshield and headlights, and puncturing its front right tire, pulling it even further to the left.

Watching through his binoculars Perry called out, "There's no driver!"

Mac gave Sean a questioning look.

"Definitely a truck bomb," the Sergeant explained. Leaning over the railing of the guard tower, he yelled at the artillery unit, "Blow the damned thing to hell!"

Another thump but the transport was too close now. A moment later it smashed through the fence line. Soldiers scattered in every direction. Hitting the rise the artillery crew had used, the truck launched into the air, came down with a bounce, and veered sharply to the right. Tipping over on two wheels, it careened into the back wall of the mess hall and came to a shuddering stop.

Soldiers dove for cover or dropped to the ground and covered their heads. The next few seconds seemed to last an eternity as everything fell still and silent. A few daring soldiers peered out from their hiding places. A pair of enlisted men lying on the ground nearest the mess hall cautiously got up and approached the transport.

"Come on," said Perry and he started down the ladder.

A young private looked inside the truck, jerked his head back in revulsion, and fell to his knees retching. Perry and the others ran up and peered inside. Mac trailed behind.

"Oh, shit," breathed Aro.

"Fuck!" Moose cried.

"Damn bastard," spat Perry as Mac finally reached the transport and looked inside.

Stacked like cordwood from the front seat to the back gate were the disemboweled bodies of the missing UN patrols.

"This can't be happening," he choked out, a crushing pressure building up in his chest.

"Radio contact with Zeda," Sean said, radio to his ear.

Mac stood staring at the carnage, mouth agape.

The Sergeant shook Mac. "Zeda wants to talk to you!"

Mac closed his eyes. "This can't be happening," he whispered.

Sean debated slapping his Commander back to reality. Perry must have read his mind because he quietly said, "Son, I'd hate to see you court-martialed for something we'd all like to do right about now."

T.J. grabbed Mac's arm and dragged him towards the CC. "Get your act together, man," he said, just loud enough for Mac to hear. "You're the heir of Arthur, for chrissakes."

He pushed Mac through the Comm Center door and pressed the radio transmitter into his trembling hand. "*Talk, damn it!*"

The Mission Commander forced out one word. "What?"

"In your lifetime, King of the Anglos," Zeda began ominously, "have you had everything taken away from you? Did you grow up in squalor? Have you had to beg and steal to feed yourself? Have you had every shred of self-respect stripped away?"

Mac said nothing.

"I can smell your fear, MacCrarey," Zeda said with vengeful satisfaction. "Go home and take your pathetic peacekeepers with you. Or I swear to god I will slaughter every last one of them…and then, I will kill *you.*"

8

"The biggest people with the biggest ideas can be shot down by the smallest people with the smallest minds. Think big anyway. Give the world the best you have, and you may get kicked in the teeth. Give the world your best anyway."

– Kent Keith

"If a man be gracious and courteous to strangers, it shows he is a citizen of the world."

– Sir Francis Bacon

"The more complex the world becomes, the more… [it] must always rely upon the man with broad human knowledge. Governing requires knowledge of men, a balanced judgment, a gift for conciliation and, above all, a constant weighing of good versus bad. Only men with broad educations can perform such tasks."

– James A Michener

1100 hours – Day 27

The BBC announced that the governments in Ankara and Athens publicly blamed the other for the violence in hastily called press conferences.

1230 hours – Day 27

The head of Turkey's State Department issued a press release saying his people would not participate in next week's unification talks, unless the Greek militants surrendered to the UN.

1340 hours – Day 27

The President of Greece went on TV to say that his people would not attend the unification talks until the UN restored peace on the island.

1630 hours – Day 27

NATO faxed over a signed refusal to intervene.

Schoen and Boujeau were quite pleased with how events were unfolding. The battle was just beginning, NATO would keep its nose out of it, their Mission Commander was emotionally incapacitated, the media was denouncing UNFICYP as weak and ineffective, and the unification talks were likely to be called off.

2015 hours – Day 27

Perry knocked on Mac's door. Hearing a faint "Yes?" he walked in and gave a perfunctory salute. "I called up the National Guard troops, Mac."

No answer.

"With their help, I reestablished UN patrols along the DMZ. The Turk guards'll camp to the north of the line, the Greeks to the south every mile or so."

Mac, who hadn't left his quarters all day, gave a half-hearted nod.

A slamming door sounded somewhere down the hall, running footsteps, and Moose appeared in the doorway. Winded, he said between breaths, "You'd better…come over…to…the CC."

The rumpled and mussed Mission Commander followed Moose and Perry like a beaten dog across the compound and into the Comm Center. Sergeant Kelly was sitting at the radio console flanked by Aro and T.J.

To Mac's surprise, Taylor Johnson was standing between them.

"Flew in from New York as soon as I heard," Taylor told his boss.

"Guard Unit 3 come in," Sean Kelly was saying into the radio transmitter. "This is Base. Repeat. Guard Unit 3 come in."

"Report, Sergeant," Perry ordered.

"Now the National Guard patrols are going missing, sir. Unit seven and eight, five and four, now three!"

T.J. furrowed his brow. "Aren't those all *Greek* Guard Units?"

Sean nodded knowingly. "Yes, sir," he replied gravely.

"You thinking what I'm thinking?" Aro said to Moose.

"They're defecting," he answered.

"Damn it," muttered Perry.

"Should we send out more soldiers?" Moose proposed.

"And leave the base even more vulnerable? No fucking way," said Aro.

"What choice do we have?" countered Moose.

Glassy eyed and hands trembling, Mac whispered, "Order all UN soldiers back here."

The others turned and stared at him in dumbfounded silence.

"What did you say?" Perry asked, hoping his ears had deceived him.

"Order all the patrols back here to Nicosia," Mac said again.

"Stop our patrols? Shut down all our bases?" Aro yelled. "Are you fucking nuts?"

"Mac," Perry said calmly, "we'd be abandoning the entire DMZ. Zeda could come and go as he pleased."

"I'm not letting anyone else die on my watch. Bring everyone in." Mac started for the door.

"Damn it!" Aro screamed at him. "You're handing over the whole fucking island to him!"

"These are soldiers, Mac," T.J. implored. "They know the risks. *Don't* call them in."

"The order stands," Mac mumbled without looking back, and out the door he went.

Perry turned to Sean and nodded. The Sergeant started radioing the bases and patrols.

T.J. shook his head and muttered to himself, "Kyle and Merrill aren't going to be happy about this."

"Sit," Schoen said curtly, pointing to the chairs in front of his desk.

Jake Tanner and Jack Abrams obeyed.

"I want your input on something very important."

"Yes, sir?" said Tanner.

"Between the two of you," Schoen explained, "you know most of the senators and representatives, and even a few governors."

"True," Senator Abrams said smugly.

"Then, tell me this – who is fairly well-known and ambitious, has an overly simplistic view of the world, fancies himself a good Christian soldier, and is humble enough to heed the counsel of –" and here Schoen chose his words carefully, "– both the wise and of God?"

Jack gave a snort and looked at Tanner.

The Ambassador grunted, "Hell, yeah."

"Who?" Schoen asked impatiently.

"Senator Mitchell Thomas," Jack answered.

Schoen smiled to himself. "Thomas…from the confirmation hearings?"

Jack nodded. "Hails from southeastern Ohio down near the West Virginia state line. Bible college-educated, ordained evangelical minister, old-fashioned Midwestern values. Mayor of his home town and then a state rep. Made a name for himself mandating prayer and prohibiting sex education in the schools. Banned pornographic magazines and videos from party stores. Voted to close abortion clinics. Started a ballot drive to outlaw homosexuality. Made up a list of banned books and introduced a bill to keep them out of public libraries."

"The librarians filed a first amendment suit against him in Federal Court," Tanner chuckled, "so he introduced a bill to fire every last one of 'em!"

"I heard he even barged into a synagogue during Rosh Hosanna," Jack smiled, "started screaming that they were all going to hell for not believing in Jesus."

Tanner nodded. "Heard that one, too."

Jack continued, "He was in the state house for maybe six years before he ran for the U.S. House. Won by the largest margin in a generation and fell in with the 'Contract with America' crowd. Gotta windfall of corporate contributions and two years later won his first bid for Senate. Now he's big with the Tea Party."

"Intelligent?" Schoen asked.

Abrams and Tanner both laughed. "Hell," the latter snorted, "he makes W look like a Rhodes Scholar."

"Great with legislation on personal morality," said Jack, "but pretty much everything else is foreign territory. He's a follower when it comes to bills on business, the military, the sciences, matters of state, etcetera."

"Oratory skills?" Schoen asked.

"Fiery preacher-type. Give him a teleprompter and he's your man."

Schoen stood and paced back and forth behind his desk. "Get out," he ordered without so much as a glance at his guests.

"Uh…excuse me?" Jack said incredulously.

Tanner tugged at his sleeve and shook his head.

"Get out!" yelled Schoen, picking up a stapler and threatening to throw it.

Tanner was already half-way to the door when Jack jumped up and ran after him.

Tanner closed the office door behind him and Schoen picked up the phone. A moment later, a click and Boujeau said, "Who did they pick?"

"Senator Mitchell Thomas," Schoen replied smugly.

"Very well," and another click.

Schoen began dialing again. Two rings and the Reverend Johnny Swaywell answered his private line. "Yes?"

"Reverend, this is Gerhardt Schoen."

Swaywell was momentarily taken aback. The two of them hadn't spoken since the whole 'instrument of God's wrath' business. "Yes…Gerhardt. What…what do you want?"

"I'm returning a favor," the Under Secretary-General replied.

"Favor?" the Reverend said warily.

"The world is on the brink of great change, Johnny. The End Times are coming and the United Nations will be the cause, I fear…unless we create a powerful counter-force to stop it."

"What could possibly be powerful enough to stop the United Nations?" Swaywell asked incredulously. "Besides prayer, of course."

"Next year, your country will have a general election. I want your people to run for public office. Tell your evangelicals to file for every local, state, and national seat in play. Also, network with other preachers and begin a national campaign to register voters of faith."

"The United States would be the counter-force?"

"Ja. Only the U.S. is militarily and economically powerful enough."

"What you propose takes money, Gerhardt. More money than we evangelicals have. And in America, campaign finance laws ban church interference in elections."

Schoen turned to his PC and typed in the Reverend's email address and a bank account number. "Look at your in-box."

The Reverend didn't have a computer of his own. His secretary typed everything for him, handled his e-communications, and kept his social media accounts current. "Betty!" he called.

She appeared in the doorway.

"Look for an email and print it out. Hurry!"

A minute later she handed him a sheet of paper. He shooed her away, scanned the page, and said into the phone, "What's this?"

"A key to the riches of Solomon," Schoen answered. "A number to a St. Martinez bank account…with more money than you can possibly imagine. Take what you need, contribute to whomever you deem worthy, and get your faithful elected."

Swaywell's mouth fell open. "Praise Jesus," he breathed. "But, campaign finance laws –"

"Johnny, you are a smart man. I'm sure there are ways to get the money to God's candidates. And *Citizens United for Freedom vs. the Federal Election Commission* allows you to form a political action committee. Use it to pay for TV and social media ads to support God's candidates."

"Yes. Yes, Gerhardt!" Swaywell said excitedly.

"Do not tell anyone about our conversation or where the money came from. Understood?"

"Yes, of course. I'll give this my undivided attention." With delusions of grandeur dancing in his head, he wondered aloud, "Do you think…perhaps with enough money…we could find a *Presidential* candidate worthy of God's blessing? Someone with the moral strength to rule America by God's commandments, and to stand up to the United Nations?"

Schoen smiled. How easy this was. "Do you, by any chance," he said innocently, "know Senator Mitchell Thomas?"

1330 hours – Day 28

Most of the UN soldiers were back in Nicosia when word came in that Bash El was under attack.

"A Turkish constable says Zeda's soldiers are executing people in the streets –" Sean Kelly told the team while trying to keep his emotions under control, "– burning down buildings, raping women –" He couldn't go on.

Moose and Aro began arguing over what to do. Perry and T.J. went over military assets and timeframes. And the heir of Arthur remained in his quarters.

By evening, Turkey and Greece had graduated from political rhetoric to military threats, and the media was speculating on the possibility of war.

2325 hours – Day 28

Mac was officially relieved of command and ordered to appear before the Security Council at the earliest possible time. He heard the news through the locked door to his quarters.

0430 hours – Day 29

Sleep had come in fitful respites. Lying in his cot, Mac heard something outside, something terribly out of place, and perhaps even out of time. He must be mistaken, he decided, sitting up to listen. The sound was getting louder, and soon there was no question of what it was – the deep, pounding, rhythm of hoofbeats! Hundreds of them!

Jumping out of bed, Mac ran to his window and looked out.

Where were the barracks and parade ground? The fence and guard towers? All he could see was a misty field, stands of green trees, and a tall steep hill silhouetted against a blood red dawn.

Sliding the window open, Mac climbed out and let himself down. No sooner had his feet touched the ground than the window and his quarters disappeared. Now he was standing alone in a vast, dew-dampened field. The air was cool, and the pungent aroma of wild flowers and moist, rich earth filled his nostrils. He could see his breath as he looked around, trying to decide which direction the sound of hoofbeats was coming from. He started towards the hill but had barely taken a step when the edges of the field dissolved into red morning sky. Turning all the way around, he realized he was standing on top of the hill now. Below him, banks of misty clouds hung over the valley, and a sea of tents and smoldering campfires hugged the hill's base. From behind, he heard the sound of hoofbeats again and swung around. Cavalrymen on horseback, hundreds of them, were charging straight for him in columns, two side by side!

Rich thick air drew deep into his lungs. His pulse quickened, and his muscles tensed. The ground shook and the power of the horses permeated to his core. Every sight and sound, motion and smell, filled him with life-affirming urgency. The intensity of his senses, the sharpness of his mind, the exhilaration of the moment set him free, and yet made him one with everything around him.

And all fear was gone. Never again would it control him. From this moment on, his will would command his life. With the noble horsemen storming past him to either side, he raised his arms into the air and let out a life-affirming primal yell! They plunged down the hillside into the swirling mist and he started after them. At once he was standing amidst rows of tents and filthy disheveled-looking men were stumbling out to see from which direction the sound of hoofbeats came.

They were clearly soldiers, but their dress and weaponry were of no modern army's. Their clothing consisted of crude wool and animal hides clad with broad leather belts, and their swords, lances, and bows were handmade. When they saw the horses thundering down the hill, they yelled for the others to wake, snatched up their arms, and ran.

The cavalrymen, dark as night, their swords glistening with the red of the dawn, fell upon the camp. A war cry went up from the riders as the sound of clanging metal and the screams of pain joined the pounding of the hoof beats. Straight and true they drove their horses to the far edge of the camp and turned, one column to the right, the other left, flanking the fleeing soldiers in both directions.

Mac again started after them but instead found himself standing on the rim of a deep hollow, the tall hill looming above him. The soldiers were huddled together below, exhausted and afraid, weapons at the ready. Sitting deathly still atop their steeds, bloodied swords in hand, the horsemen lined the rim of the hollow. Mac wondered what would happen next. Would the vanquished strike back? Would the horsemen charge and slash? He watched and waited, but nothing happened – the mist hung in the damp air, the horsemen sat unmoving on their mounts, the silent soldiers stood their ground below. What was going on? Who were the leaders and why didn't they act? To do nothing was unthinkable. Someone had to act!

And in the next moment, Mac was sitting astride a horse, its reins in one hand and a blood-drenched sword in the other. He was clad in dented, tarnished armor held together by fraying leather straps. The deep, rhythmic breathing of his steed and the feel of the sword's handle in his palm soothed and at the same time exhilarated him. The other horsemen were turning to look at him now, and he realized he held their fate in his hand. The power to decide what the day would bring – murder or mercy, death or dishonor – was his to wield.

A heavy burden it was, but as easily as drawing a breath he knew what had to be done.

The words formed in his mind, adrenaline coursed through his veins, and he called out, "Oesc of Kent, come forward and hear me!"

Barely had the echo of the words faded than a massive brute of a man with long straggly white-blonde hair charged from the huddle of soldiers. Garbed in a hodgepodge of animal skins matted with filth and blood, the Saxon warlord raised his sword high over his head and let out a blood-curdling scream. Closer and closer he drew, his face crimson, his gray-blue eyes wild with bloodlust and hate.

Mac turned his horse slightly to the left, the sword in his right-hand dangling at his side. The warlord's blade slashed through the air and just before it struck, Mac gripped his sword's hilt with all his might and swung it up in one, swift flowing arc. It met Oesc's with a thunderous clang, the force of its blow twisting the warlord's torso away from Mac. Bringing the sword down, he struck the Saxon hard on the back with the blade's flat side, knocking him to the ground. With a flick of his reins, Mac sidled over and placed the tip of his sword on Oesc's chest. "Surrender and mercy shall be granted unto you and your soldiers."

The hollow began to fade. The hill melted into the mist. And Mac was lying in an army cot, the pale light of dawn shining through his open window. Had it been a dream? A memory? He looked at the clock – 0610. The last few days replayed in his mind, but the helplessness and fear did not. He stood, walked to the window, and into the dawn's light stepped Arthur!

Grabbing his jacket, he ran out the door, sprinted across the muddy compound, and burst into the CC. "Taylor," he commanded, his voice strong and confident, "you and I are going to New York. T.J., call Michael, tell him to send the jet, and we'll need wheels when we touch down. Perry, work up an offensive strategy and re-deploy the troops. You're in charge 'til I return. Moose, Aro – work the diplomatic channels. Try to calm things down. I need a day. Sean, take a Recon Unit out. Find out where Zeda is and shadow him." Then, he smiled confidently and said, "Don't count us out yet, gentlemen. Now get to it."

"Yes, *sir!*" Sean answered, snapping to attention.

"Fuckin' A! Now we're talkin'!" Aro cried as he Moose ran out of the room.

T.J. reached for the phone, grinning ear to ear.

Perry gave a crisp, respectful salute to the Mission Commander who'd finally arrived, and headed for the door.

1615 hours – Day 29

Michael Abrams' limousine passed through the security gate along Raoul Wallenberg Avenue and into the United Nations complex.

"The General Assembly breaks for the day in thirty minutes," Taylor Johnson explained to Mac. "The Secretary-General will be holding a televised press conference in the Assembly Hall right afterwards about the UN's typhoon relief in French Polynesia."

"I need to address the Assembly right before Boujeau goes in front of the cameras," Mac said. "That way the reporters will already be there, hear what I have to say, and file it with their stories. With any luck, the public will get behind us, the politicians will follow suit, and the Security Council will have to go along."

"Got it. And, uh…by the way," Taylor hesitated, not wanting to be the bearer of bad news to a man who only hours before seemed on the edge of a nervous breakdown, "UPI just reported that Ankara's declared war on the Greek Cypriots. Athens is expected to reciprocate later today."

To Taylor's surprise and relief, Mac grinned. "It was just a matter of time, and besides –" The limo came to a stop and he reached for the door handle. "– that strengthens our hand."

The Ambassador from South Africa, who was addressing the Assembly from the podium on stage, was the first to notice Mac walking down the aisle. He halted his speech and said, "Welcome Deputy Ambassador MacCrarey. You've had a rough go of it on Cyprus, yes?"

The chamber filled with murmurs of surprise and curiosity as all eyes turned to watch Mac bound up the steps to the stage. He warmly greeted the South African Ambassador who bowed slightly and graciously stepped aside. Stepping up to the podium like a man who was anything but beaten, he said boldly, "Bloody attacks on the people of Cyprus are underway. Pompous Zeda intends to rule the island with an iron fist. What are you going to do about it?"

A stunned silence descended upon the hall.

"The UN does not act until both sides of a conflict reach a stalemate. Then we do nothing but maintain it." He paused. "That must end! We must evolve into *creators* of peace, anytime and anywhere people are in jeopardy. We must lead the world by example. We must defend others against naked aggression and injustice." Another pause. "Will you, the emissaries of your nations, stand tall with the peoples of the world? Will you place what's right ahead of what's expedient or beneficial? Will you do what has to be done to end the rule of oligarchs and dictators?

"I admit, I have not been the Mission Commander Cyprus needs. Two mornings ago, I looked into the back of a truck and saw the butchered remains of peacekeepers…yet I did nothing. An entire village was massacred – every man, woman, and child…yet I cowered in my barracks. By not acting, I gave a mad man free reign.

"But from this day forward, I promise to act *every* time a person is in need, whether that need be a helping hand or a sword!" he declared, his tone defiant and stirring. "I will be the bearer of peace. I will save the imperiled. I will stop those who would do harm." He paused. "I will fight for the people of Cyprus, and I implore you to stand with me! Send armed UN peace*makers* to Cyprus now!"

The Ambassadors replied with a smattering of applause.

"The UN Charter empowers the Security Council to send soldiers to a nation like Cyprus. But why doesn't the Charter allow the General Assembly to send soldiers? Why can't we –" he purposely used "we" to side with the Ambassadors, and not with Tanner and the U.S., "– act unilaterally to end conflicts, or better yet, to prevent conflicts?" Yet another pause. "I'll tell you why! Because the five, permanent Security Council members don't want a General Assembly with free will, a General Assembly with the military might to intervene in the sovereign affairs of any nation, anywhere, anytime! That *frightens* them. It frightens the leaders of many countries. Well, guess what? It should! That's the point! That's why the General Assembly ought to have that power. As a republic of nations –" this was the first time he publicly inferred that the UN was an actual government "– we should have the power to pursue and enforce whatever is in the interest of the common good. Therefore, I say we send a message to the world that the 'might' of the Security Council does not make 'right' anymore. I say we pass a resolution to send armed forces to Cyprus. I say we recast our peacekeepers as peace*makers* from this day forth. I say today is our Independence Day!"

The Ambassadors responded with vigorous applause and excited chatter in a hundred different languages.

The Ambassador from India shouted, "So moved!"

"Second!" the Ambassador from Italy called out, and the chamber erupted with cheers.

The Ambassador from South Africa grabbed Mac's hand as he stepped back from the podium and shook it. The President of the Assembly rapped his gavel and asked if there was anyone who wished to debate the resolution. The Ambassadors of all five permanent Security Council members raised their hands. The President gleefully ignored them and called the vote.

There was excited laughter and more cheers as the President's assistant entered an improvised resolution into the computer. It appeared on the overhead screen, and interpreters housed in glassed-in offices to either side of the chamber floor relayed the resolution's words to their Ambassadors. They in turn cast their yeas or nays via touchscreens at their desks. The computer tallied the votes and the final count appeared on the overhead screen just below the resolution.

It passed by an overwhelming majority.

The President whispered to his assistant, "Keep it on the screen until the reporters and Secretary-General arrive for the press conference." She smiled back and did just that.

Mac gave the ambassadors a humble nod of gratitude and walked back up the aisle, shaking proffered hands as he went.

1701 hours – Day 29

Gerhardt Schoen and René Boujeau had watched the General Assembly meeting on their offices PCs, and by the time they walked in, the Chamber was abuzz. The Secretary-General's face was red with anger as he leaned towards Schoen and hissed, "Get rid of MacCrarey anyway you want."

From the podium, the press secretary was saying, "…and that'll be on the fifteenth. Remember, annual renewals of your press credentials must be submitted by the twenty-second." He turned to the Secretary-General and smiled. "Alright, let's get started with the briefing. All yours, sir."

Stepping up to the podium, Boujeau unfurled his notes and perfunctorily began running through his scripted comments. Reporters, many of whom had come in towards the end of the General Assembly meeting, started shouting questions. He ignored all of them, until Jan Roberts said, "Mr. Boujeau! Is this the General Assembly's Independence Day?"

Brusquely snatching up his papers, he muttered something under his breath and started for the stage door, but then thought better of it. Stomping back, he petulantly replied, "The naiveté and disrespect exhibited by the *former* UNFICYP Commander is appalling! His appeal directly to the General Assembly for military intervention on Cyprus is reckless beyond compare. The Security Council is well aware of the island's troubling state of affairs. The loss of life is regrettable. But, it is the Security Council's responsibility to decide whether and when to send in troops, *not* the General Assembly's! We cannot have woefully uninformed Ambassadors or delusional Mission Commanders doing whatever they damned well please. The sage and prudent guidance provided by the Security Council to member nations is a *critical* check and balance on our operations. It is enshrined in our Charter and I will not allow it to be amended. I can only guess that *former* Mission Commander MacCrarey's many personal failures and weak-kneed mental state is what led him to abandon his troops during a crisis and come here to plead for help. His woeful inaction has been criminal, and I hereby order him to appear before the Security Council on charges of insubordination, dereliction of duty, and involuntary manslaughter!"

0815 hours – Day 30

As soon as he and Taylor passed through the front gate of the camp, Mac ordered the Jeep to stop. A leader had finally arrived, and he wanted everyone to know it. Getting out, he marched cocksure across the compound and into the CC to meet his team. Only Sergeant Sean Kelly was missing.

"Perry, any other attacks?"

"Yes, sir. Fishing village. All dead."

"Damn it." The muscles in Mac's jaw tensed and his eyes flashed with anger. "Is Sean's Recon Unit still tracking Zeda?"

"Yes, sir," Perry answered.

Mac turned to T.J. "Let's do a GLOSAT GPS lock-on."

"You got it," T.J. said, reaching for his laptop.

Aro said, "What the hell's a GLOSAT GPS lock-on?"

"You upload the precise latitude and longitude of an object into GLOSAT," Mac told him, "or you bring up a live image, cross-hatch it, and GLOSAT's geosynchronous satellites will track it from here to kingdom come."

T.J. said, "Got a GLOSAT satellite image of the island."

"Corporal," Mac said to the man sitting behind the radio console, "contact Sergeant Kelly." The Corporal nodded and a moment later Sean Kelly's voice sounded through the speakers.

"Kelly here, Corporal. This damned well better be important."

"Sergeant, this is Mac."

"Yes, sir. Sorry, sir. We heard what happened in New York, sir…outstanding."

"Thanks, Sergeant. I doubt the *threat* of more troops will send Zeda scurrying back into his hole, so until help arrives we're on our own. And who knows how many people Zeda will have killed by then."

"Yes, sir," Sean replied stoically.

"So, let's catch the bastard ourselves and end this thing."

"Yes, sir!" said Sean. "Do you have a plan?"

"Hell, yeah I do," Mac said cockily. "Where's Zeda now?"

"Camped out in a hollow right below my position, sir."

"Can you pick him out?"

Sean lifted his binoculars. "Yes, sir. Talking with his unit commanders."

"Good. Fire up your laptop. We're sending a live satellite image of your sector. There'll be a cross-hatch on the screen that you can control with your keyboard. Use the zoom and pan controls to place the cross-hatch on Zeda. Perry will be able to see what you're doing and put a GLOSAT lock on the SOB. Understood?"

"You got it, sir."

"Once we have a lock-on, we'll know where he is at all times and you can bring your Recon Unit back to camp."

"We'll be back by noon, sir," Sean assured him.

"Good work, Sergeant. Mac out."

Perry spoke up. "Without at least another four battalions, our peacekeepers won't stand a chance against Zeda's army."

"We're peace*makers* now, Perry, and all we'll need is a single strike team…with a little luck," Mac grinned.

1225 hours – Day 30

They watched Zeda all morning via video streaming from GLOSAT. Using topographical road maps of the island, they calculated where he was heading and finalized their plan.

"I still say your nuts if you think this is gonna work," Aro repeated for the umpteenth time as he helped Mac load the Jeep.

Mac smiled. "Well, if it doesn't, you can tell me 'I told you so'…at my funeral. Has Zeda reached the Olympus Mountain Range yet?"

Perry glanced at the laptop sitting on the front seat. "In the foothills now, should be at the ridge by dusk."

"Lady luck is still with us," Mac grinned. "Let's go."

A few minutes later, he, Sean, T.J. and Perry drove out of the compound leading a single troop transport.

1840 hours – Day 30

The sky was gray, the weather cold, and a misty fog drifted between the olive trees in a neglected orchard stretching up to the crest of a ridge. There, the strike force was digging in and Sergeant Sean Kelly was hustling about dolling out orders.

"Where is he now?" ex-Mission Commander MacCrarey asked.

"His convoy's coming up the mountain as we speak," Perry answered, "They should be on the other side of the ridge in ten, maybe fifteen minutes."

Mac nodded. "Sergeant!" he called out. "Bring everyone over here, please."

A minute later, the men and women who'd volunteered for Mac's mission were standing at attention in front of him. "We have one chance at this, people," he began. "You've been on grave duty for days, so I don't have to tell you what's at stake. Now is the time for few words and great action." He walked along the line of soldiers looking into their eyes as he passed. "Avenge the fallen, defend the living, and stand tall. The world is watching." He stepped back, snapped to attention, and gave them a perfectly executed salute. "Deploy!" he ordered.

They saluted back as one, broke ranks, and hurried to their assigned positions. Sean turned to leave, but Mac grabbed his arm. "Sergeant, this plan is mine and mine alone. Even though it's just this side of a suicide mission, I'm going through with it no matter what. But –" he added earnestly, "– without someone watching my back, the chances of success are slim to none."

"You going to stop Zeda from killing anybody else?"

Mac gave a solemn nod.

"Then I've got your back, sir."

"You can refuse, Sean. This isn't an order."

The Sergeant debated with himself for a moment before saying, "You remember a news story about a pro-ball player who left the NFL to become an Army Ranger?"

Mac thought for a moment. "I think so."

"He said it was his duty as an American. Said he couldn't let others less fortunate than him die for his country." A distant look crossed Sean's face. "What a lucky man he was…sports hero, media star, beautiful wife, money, fame. Got sent to Afghanistan…he was an agnostic."

Mac furrowed his brow. "And?"

"One day he was out on patrol with his unit and got shot dead. The Army said it was an Al Qeada ambush. But, a few years later I met someone from his unit. We were stationed in Sinai, got drunk one night, and he told me the NFL guy was fragged – killed by friendly fire. Three shots from an M-16 in the forehead." Sean turned to the grove of olive trees and stared past the ridge beyond. "Soldiers face death in battle, so how do Armies get them to fight? Religion. God. Rewards in heaven. Yes, there's king and country and all that, but religion is what soldiers cling to in foxholes when the shit's hitting the fan. Boot camps and military academies are like churches. There, God and country are one and the same. Blind obedience to orders and unquestioning belief in God are one and the same. An atheist or agnostic is a threat of the worst kind – a counterpoint, a *traitor*. When his brothers-in-arms shot him dead, they thought they were being patriots and good Christians!"

Sean took a picture out of his pocket. "My wife," he said, handing it to the ex-Mission Commander.

"She's beautiful," Mac said, handing it back.

"Yeah. Even more so now that she's pregnant."

"Congratulations."

He gave Mac a fleeting smile. "I'm an agnostic…does that bother you?"

"No," Mac answered without missing a beat. "What difference does it make? All that matters is the nobility people show each other in life."

"I've kept my agnosticism to myself during my military career, but I shouldn't have to. The Constitution says I have the right to believe or *not* to believe. It says I can speak my mind without fear of persecution. It says no one can tell me what to think or do, as long as I don't hurt anybody. But sometimes… sometimes it feels like I don't have *any* of those freedoms. And it's getting worse!" He shook his head in frustration. "I love my country, Mac. And I'm proud to be a soldier. I want to be there for those who need us, and to fight for the freedoms we cherish – not only for my wife and baby, but for everyone…all over the world. That's why I'm here…why I volunteered for a tour of duty with the UN." He slung his rifle over his shoulder. "And if you feel the same way, and you really don't care that I'm an agnostic, then I've got your back, sir." He held out his hand. "You got mine?"

Mac smiled and shook Sean's hand. "Hell, yeah!"

The faint sounds of straining engines rolled over the crest of the ridge.

Hunched over the laptop, T.J. called out, "It's now or never!"

"How much further?" Mac called back.

"About a hundred yards!"

"May I please have your .45, Sean?" Mac said, holding out his hand.

Undoing the flap of his holster, Sean asked, "Is that an order, sir?"

"No more orders between us, Sean, and its Mac from now on. Okay? You and I are friends and patriots, doing what's right for everyone…all over the world."

"Patriots of the world?"

"Of the world," Mac smiled.

Sean held out his Colt .45 Peacemaker. The ex-Mission Commander's fist closed around the handle and he grabbed a small drab-green backpack from the back seat of the Jeep.

"Ready?" Mac said.

"Hell, yeah!" answered Sean.

And they took off running. The freezing mist stung Mac's face as he sprinted through the trees and past the UN soldiers already in position. He and Sean stopped at the tree line, the sounds of Zeda's convoy growing louder. A few steps beyond the trees, the ground dissolved into grey sky.

"Just below that drop off," Mac explained, "is a narrow road cut into the mountain. Coming up the road single file is Zeda's convoy." He crouched down and cautiously edged towards the drop off. He spied the convoy a few dozen yards away and waved for Sean to join him. "Our GLOSAT lock puts Zeda in the lead Jeep," Mac said, taking out the Peacekeeper and laying it on the grass. "No shooting anyone unless absolutely necessary. Agreed? There's been enough killing on this island."

"Agreed," Sean answered, reaching around for the M-16 slung over his shoulder.

Mac reached into the drab-green back pack and pulled out a light gray block of what looked like modeling clay. Burrowing into the wet earth, he placed the block in a shallow hole and pushed in a small thin cylinder with a red cap. He rummaged around the pack until he found a pen-like plunger, clicked it once, and the red cap began flashing. Mac winked at Sean, picked up the .45, and inched closer to the drop off.

Just then, a soldier in a ragged blood-splattered uniform sitting in the second Jeep spotted the ex-UN Commander, and began shouting something in Greek. Mac gave the man a smug grin and a mocking salute.

"Fire!" he called over his shoulder to Sean.

The Sergeant put his M-16 on full automatic and began blazing away over the heads of Zeda's men and into the gray void beyond. The convoy came to a grinding halt as the soldiers scrambled for cover. With that, Mac leapt over the edge, falling through the air until his body hit the lead truck's canvass rooftop. The force of his fall carried him through as though it were wrapping paper. Slamming into the Jeep's back seat, he let out a grunt and muttered, "Shit, that hurt," as he slowly sat up.

The driver looked over his shoulder. Surprise at finding Mac sitting there registered on his face, and he reached for his holster. Before he could draw his gun, Mac had his .45 pressed against the man's head.

"Drop it, buddy," he said calmly. The driver complied with a curse, Mac glanced over at the passenger, and found himself once again staring into the black unblinking eyes of Pompous

Zeda. "Afternoon!" Mac quipped, and with an amiable smile added, "I'd duck if I were you."

Zeda muttered something in Greek that Mac guessed wasn't meant for polite company and reached for his pistol. The ex-Mission Commander shrugged and began to lie down. "Suit yourself," he grinned and placed his thumb on the plunger.

Zeda understood at once what was about to happen, repeated his explicative, and reached for the door handle. Mac pressed the plunger and detonated the C4. The earthen wall beside the Jeep rushed forward with a thunderous explosion, showering the Jeep with chunks of reddish dirt, torn roots, and fist-sized stones. The force of the blast hove the truck to the far edge of the road. The air cleared of debris and Mac sat up to find the driver buried up to his neck, and Zeda hanging onto the open passenger-side door, legs dangling in midair over the abyss.

The heir of Arthur leaned forward, grabbed the door, and swung Zeda towards him. Pulling the dazed madman into the Jeep, Mac showed him the .45, grabbed his left arm, and maneuvered him over the seat and out the other side of the Jeep. Crossing the rubble-strewn road, he dragged Zeda up through the trench the C4 tore out of the mountainside.

A soldier in one of the convoy trucks started firing. Bullets splattered into the trench wall, one passing so close to Mac's head that he felt the ripple of the pressure wave. Sean opened fire again and sent the Greeks scurrying back into their hiding places.

"Thanks!" Mac yelled up to him. "Fall back!"

The Sergeant gave a nod, fired a few more rounds for good measure, and backed up to the tree line. Mac and Zeda emerged from the trench and made a beeline for the orchard. Rallying yells could he heard below, and soon Greek soldiers were clambering up the trench. Mac was pulling Zeda through the olive trees with Sean covering the rear, when cracks of gunfire sounded and bullets began slamming into tree trunks.

Then, the air shuddered with shock waves as the UN soldiers opened fire from every direction! Two Greeks dropped like rag dolls, the others scampered back into the trench, and a cheer went up from the peacemakers.

"Outstanding!" Mac called out. "Let's fall back and head home!"

Another cheer went up and everyone cautiously backed down the hill.

T.J. and Perry hurried forward to take Zeda into custody. "Let's get on the radio," Mac told them with a weary smile, "and tell the world Cyprus is safe. And from this day forward, the United Nations will stand up to any foe, anywhere, anytime."

At base, the official order from Secretary-General Boujeau to appear before the Security Council was waiting for former UN-FICYP Mission Commander William Cameron MacCrarey.

"And this after we captured the most wanted man in the world," T.J. griped. "We stop Zeda, his henchmen scurry back to where ever they came from, the island's at peace, and *you're* the bad guy?"

"No worries," Mac grinned. "I'll go to New York...in a roundabout sort of way."

T.J. gave his friend a knowing smile. "The Hague first, *then* New York?"

"But of course, *and* another visit with the General Assembly."

The two friends laughed and walked out of the CC for the last time.

After a few well-placed phone calls from Michael's jet, the news began spreading like wildfire. By the time the plane landed at The Hague, the news from the BBC and UPI had generated so much buzz that a sea of reporters was waiting on the tarmac.

Three men stepped out of the cabin. Mac stood to one side of Pompous Zeda, T.J. to the other. Cameras flashed and reporters yelled questions as military guards hurried forward to escort their infamous prisoner to the World Court for arraignment. That accomplished, Mac walked over to the reporters and held a not-so-impromptu press conference. When it was over, the stories filed by the reporters declared the massacres at an end, the world a safer place, and the UN soldiers heroes.

Later that day, Athens and Ankara announced that the unification talks would proceed.

"The Charter of the United Nations must be rewritten!" Mac declared before the General Assembly. It was hard for him to imagine that only three days had passed since he was standing behind this podium.

The pent-up frustration from years of being under the Security Council's thumb burst forth in raucous cheers and enthusiastic applause. He wasn't surprised. Since the General Assembly's birth in 1946, countless Ambassadors had longed for true democracy among the nations of the UN...to be Ambassadors without a net and serve the world's peoples with unfettered compassion. "I take it you agree," Mac said with a smile. Laughs and cheers shook the hall. "Well I'm glad...because I took the liberty of drafting the amendments on my flight from The Hague." There were more laughs and applause as the screen behind him lit up, displaying rows of Charter chapter and article numbers. He explained, "Article 12 of Chapter IV and Article 25 of Chapter V must be revoked completely. The rest of Chapter V and the other chapters listed here must be dramatically revised to make the Security Council an advisory body only. From that point on, all matters brought before the UN will be dealt with by the General Assembly democratically. One nation. One vote. Period."

Excited applause rippled through the hall.

"Articles 10 through 15 should be amended to allow the General Assembly, not the Security Council alone, to intervene in Article 52, Paragraph 2 regional conflicts, *if* a simple majority of nations in geographic proximity to the conflict agree on a course of action. After a concurring vote by the General Assembly, the agreed upon action would take effect immediately. *No* concurring vote by the Security Council would be required.

"By way of example, the nations nearest to Cyprus are Greece, Turkey, Syria, Lebanon, and Israel. Getting them to agree on something under *normal* conditions is no small task," he conceded dryly to more laughs, "but the prospect of an all-out war between Greece and Turkey is so horrific, that an agreement by a simple majority of their neighbors would be easily reached. Still, for my amendments to work, one more step has to be taken. A neutral party has to step between the brawlers and hold them back. Usually, that ends up being a country or countries who want something from one side or the other. Or who wants to use them as pawns in a cold war which has nothing to *do* with the brawlers. Or the countries intervene *after* a full-scale war breaks out, don't commit enough resources, and the war goes on forever! And guess what?" he said heatedly, "The intervening countries more often than not are the ones on our Security Council!"

To this, more than a few jeers and boos were offered up by the Ambassadors.

"So, who can be trusted to intervene immediately, remain completely neutral, and bring to bear enough force to create peace? The UN, of course."

More applause.

He gestured to the screen behind him. "You can see how these amendments would allow us to build up the power and have the authority to be the neutral peacemaker. The next step is to call a Charter Amendment Conference, debate my proposed amendments, hone them, and formally draft a resolution to ratify." Hands on hips, He grabbed the mic from the podium and began pacing. "But, here's the rub. To ratify these amendments, your home governments first have to approve them. That could take months, maybe years. In the meantime, the Security Council nations will be *pressuring* your politicians *not* to ratify them. They'll also be pressuring, or trying to bribe, *you* not to ratify them when they come back here. So, let's be realistic – there's a snowball's chance in hell that my amendments will ever pass. But –" he stopped pacing and turned to the Ambassadors, "– ask yourself this. Is it the right thing to *try?* Is it the right thing to say to the world we need a true international democracy with the heart and nobility and strength to end war, keep the peace, and stand up for the oppressed and downtrodden? If it is, then vote to call for a Charter Amendment Conference! Send a message to the Security Council that the right of self-governance is the right of everyone and every nation. Tell them we want to live by our *own* words and deeds, not theirs. Tell them that the rule of the *many* by the *few* is over!"

Amidst the consenting cheers, the Assembly President called a vote on the resolution his assistant had already typed up and displayed on the screen. The tally was displayed, the vote passed, and a Charter Amendment Conference was in the offing. During the applause that followed, the President consulted the Assembly calendar and announced with a rap of his gavel, "The conference will commence September the fifteen." And with that, the session was adjourned.

The *USA Today* labeled Mac, "the Savior of Cyprus." The *Record Eagle* in Traverse called him the, "the King of Peace." The *London Times* proclaimed that, "the world has taken the greatest step towards a one-world government since the zenith of the British Empire." The *New York Times* headline read, "The Birth of a New Camelot."

Positive PR was life for a politician and going up against overwhelming opposition was career-ending for a diplomat or a Commander-in-Chief. Boujeau was all three so he knew he had little choice but to rescind his charges of insubordination, dereliction of duty, and involuntary manslaughter against Mac. He was far from happy about it.

"Gerhardt," he seethed as he leaned menacingly over his office desk in the Secretariat Building, "Mr. MacCrarey has managed to turn himself into an international *superstar*. You apparently underestimated him."

Schoen's faced reddened. "Arthur is inside him," he bristled, "and I have *never* underestimated *him*."

T.J. set the *New York Times* down and got up from the kitchen table. "Unbelievable," he smiled, walking over to the counter. "Coffee?"

"Sure," Mac said with a grin.

Lynn Penn, Professor Emeritus at NYU, hurried into the kitchen dressed in a stylish pant suit, holding her coat in one hand and a briefcase in the other. "T.J., please be a dear and pour me a cup. I'm running late for my first lecture."

"Sure thing," he replied, reaching for a travel mug.

"I'm glad you two were able to stay over, but I'm getting too old for late-night drinking binges." She tossed a couple aspirin in her mouth as T.J. handed her the mug.

"But as our gracious host, you were obliged to stay up late and celebrate with us," Mac said facetiously, holding up the *New York Times*.

Lynn's husband Dave – who was sitting at the table in his robe – chuckled and cringed, dropping his head into his hands. "Ugh," he moaned. "Give me some aspirin, dear. Please?"

"At least I can hold my liquor better than my husband," she giggled, tossing him the bottle and turning for the door. "Oh!" She stopped and spun around. "Mac, can you stay over again tonight? There's a lovely new girl in our department at the University and I can ask her to come to dinner."

Mac reached for his coffee mug, trying to think of an excuse. "I, uh…we're leaving for Geneva this afternoon. Right, Teej?"

"We are?" his distracted friend replied. Mac gave him a pleading look. "Oh, yeah! Right," he nodded. "This afternoon."

Lynn rolled her eyes. "You'd be *so* happy if you just settled down and started a family."

"So you've told me," Mac muttered.

Dave laughed and cringed again.

"Just you wait. You'll meet a lovely girl, fall in love, have babies, and you'll wonder how you ever lived without them."

Mac's face went blank as his mind drifted off to a place and time years ago.

Lynn smiled broadly and said, "Who were *you* just thinking of?"

"No one," Mac lied.

"Lynn, leave him alone," Dave moaned.

"Fine," she said petulantly, "if you won't tell me, then I'll tell *you* about the new girl. Now, she's a little plump, but that just means there's more of her to love –"

"Lynn," Mac cut her off, "why do you think I haven't dated in all these years?"

"Well, I…I figured you were just particular."

"Yes, very particular. So particular, in fact, that in the whole wide world there's only one woman I want to be with. *One.* And she doesn't want to be with me. So –" He took a moment to quell his emotions. "– so that's the way it is."

"You really love her…you love her so much you don't want to live without her."

Mac took a sip of his coffee, staring at the table.

Lynn gave him a hug. "So, go and find her," she said.

Mac shook his head. "I can't."

"You mean you won't."

Mac took another sip.

"What's her name?"

He hesitated for a moment. "Genevieve," he whispered.

"Guten morgen, United Nations Ambassador's office?" said Helga Schroedinger. "Yes, Herr MacCrarey does work out of this office. Let me put you…Nein? Would you like to leave a message?" Pause. "I could take your number and have Herr –? Very well, then. Auf wiedersehn."

"Who was that?" Mac asked, coming through his office door as she hung up. He handed her a file.

"She wouldn't say. Just wanted to know if you worked here. She was American. Long-distance."

"Probably another reporter," Mac said dismissively, heading back into his office.

"So, everything went well with the General Assembly?" Helga called after him.

Mac turned around. "We couldn't have asked for better," he smiled, glancing at her phone. "The President of the Assembly asked T.J. and I to organize the Charter Amendment Conference. We've got our work cut out for us, so we best get started. Please schedule a planning meeting for Friday."

"Ja," she replied with her customary smile. "Right away."

Late the following Monday, Mac was wrapping up some paperwork and dealing with emails when his secretary knocked on his office door. Without waiting for a reply, she walked in.

"Yes?" he said distractedly, typing away at the computer on his credenza, his back to the door.

"You have a visitor," Helga announced.

"Who?"

"You will find out, ja?"

Still typing, Mac muttered, "A surprise, huh? Why does that worry me?"

She giggled and closed the door behind her.

He kept typing and a moment later the door opened again.

"Have a seat," Mac said with courteous detachment. "Be done in a sec. Did my secretary offer you some coffee?"

His visitor did not answer. Mac clicked Save and asked, "Would you like some coffee?"

"I prefer tea...remember?" his guest said.

Mac froze. His heart began to race – it had been five years since he heard that voice…*her* voice. "I…I don't think I heard you correctly. Could you –?"

"A cup of tea would be nice," she replied pleasantly.

It really is her voice. She's here…right here!

He felt light-headed. How many times had he imagined what this moment would be like?

A menagerie of emotions swirled around in his mind as he struggled with what to say next. That he thought about her every day? That he missed her terribly? Or maybe he should apologize for…for, well, he wasn't sure what, but it seemed like a good idea to apologize anyway.

He slowly turned around and there, standing in the doorway was a woman more beautiful than even his dreams had recalled. "Genevieve," he breathed.

She smiled and said almost as a question, "I wasn't sure you'd want to see me."

Mac dumbly gestured for her to sit down and then pointed to his credenza. There sat a picture of Genevieve in a silver frame. She was standing on the deck of his condominium, the summer sun setting behind her over Traverse Bay. "Chamomile with lemon," he said as if in a trance.

"You remembered," she smiled again.

Mac nodded and without another word he got up and walked out of the office.

"Chamomile with lemon?" he grumbled as he stood in the kitchenette dunking a tea bag into a porcelain cup emblazoned with the UN logo. "After five years that's all you could think of? Chamomile with lemon?" He shook his head. "You stupid bonehead."

He slowly walked back to his office arguing with himself.

Why is she here? Maybe she wants me back. No, stupid… Does she? *No.* Maybe she has something to tell me. Maybe she needs my help. Yeah, that's it – she needs my help. Gotta be it. I mean…she doesn't want me back…Does she? *No.*

Reaching the doorway, he took a deep breath and walked in.

"Thank-you," she said amiably, taking the tea cup.

Mac collapsed into the chair beside her. "Can I get you anything else?" he asked, starting to stand up again.

"No, I'm fine," she replied in her just-calm-down voice.

"How did you find me? I mean, I'm *glad* you found me, but… it's been a long time and all, and so I was…just wondering –"

"Simple, really," Genevieve answered with a smile. "I just listened to the news. And…I had some vacation time, so… here I am."

"Here you are," Mac said, staring as if still unsure she was real. "It's been a long time."

"A long time. A lifetime…in a way," she agreed, looking into her tea cup.

Mac simply nodded.

"Curious why I'm here?" she asked with a weak smile.

"No…well, yeah, but –" he stammered, feeling oddly self-conscious.

Stop talking with your hands. My hair alright? Geeze, this office is a pigsty –

"There's someone I want you to meet," she blurted out.

Mac's heart sank. His gaze fell to the carpeted floor. "Someone…special?" he said feebly.

"*Very* special," she replied.

He felt a knife drive into his chest. "Very special," he echoed. Her husband, maybe? A fiancé? He forced himself to look at her, sat up straight, and said as chivalrously as his aching heart would allow, "I look forward to it."

"Tonight, then?" she said, standing to leave. "There's a cute little French bistro on Lac Strasse. It reminded me a bit of that place you proposed to me in. Remember?"

"I remember," he said wistfully.

"Eight? I'll meet you there?"

"Eight," and he got up to walk her to the door. "He must be very special, Genevieve. And very lucky. He has you." He felt like his insides were being kicked out.

Realizing he misunderstood, Genevieve considered telling him then and there.

But, no – not this way. "Until eight, then," and she walked out.

He followed her into the lobby. "It's been wonderful seeing you again."

"And you," she said with a fleeting smile.

The elevator dinged, the door slid open, and a moment later she was gone.

Alone again in his office, he mindlessly picked up a folder from his desk and stood there motionless. The folder began to shake as feelings of sadness, regret, loss, and frustration began to get the better of him. "Damn it," he whispered, wiping his eyes with the back of his sleeve. "Damn it."

He worked until 7:30, doing his best to keep his mind off their dinner date.

It didn't work very well.

Leaving the office, he decided to walk to the café, believing the cold air and exercise would steel him for what was sure to be one of the worst nights of his life.

It didn't work very well.

Turning onto Lac Strasse, he spied the bistro and suddenly his legs felt like lead. He was about to meet Genevieve's lover, the man who was living the life Mac let slip through his fingers. "Damn it."

After dragging himself to the café entrance, he took a deep breath to calm himself.

It didn't work very well.

"Why am I doing this?" he mumbled, pulling open the door and stepping inside.

The middle-aged, tuxedo-clad maître d' asked as if it pained him to say, "May I help you?"

"I'm meeting a man and a woman here for dinner."

"There is no couple waiting to be interrupted by *you*, monsieur," the man replied.

Given that he was about to be put through hell, the last thing Mac wanted was to be insulted by a prick in a tuxedo. "Look, Pal," he growled, "Just tell me —" and then he faintly heard his name above the din of table conversations, clinking silverware, and clanking plates. Looking past the maître d', he saw Genevieve waving as she half stood from behind a table by the window.

The maitre d' gave a disdainful wave of his hand and tossed a menu at Mac. Self-consciously, he crossed the dining room, chose the chair opposite her, and sat down, leaving an empty chair between them.

"Thank-you for coming, Mac," she said, the words cordial but apprehensive.

"I've been looking forward to it," Mac lied, trying to smile.

"I doubt that's true," she grinned.

He sighed. "I'm trying. This isn't easy, Genevieve —"

"I know," she said. "It's not easy for me either. I…I thought about telling you before, but…I wasn't sure it was the right time…and then you wouldn't see me at the hospital, and —"

The knife in his chest twisted. "You knew him already when I was in the hospital?"

This was getting worse by the minute.

"Let me finish, please," she told him. "I never heard from you after you were released. Then, a little while later, I read that you'd become the Deputy U.S. Ambassador to the United Nations. You'd moved on…you'd put us behind you –"

"I put you behind me?" he said incredulously. "You put *me* behind *you*." No sooner had he said the words than he realized how childish he sounded. He sighed.

"You left me a long time before that, Mac," Genevieve said firmly.

She was right, and he knew it. He gave a weak nod.

"I stayed with you as long as I could," she said. "We had what everyone dreams of, and you let it slip away!"

Those might as well have been his own words.

He pushed his chair back and stood up. Respectfully, he said, "I'm sorry, Genevieve. For then…and for now."

A tear rolled down her cheek. Picking up a napkin, he leaned over the table and dabbed it away. Out of respect for the woman he still loved and always would, he sat back down. He'd make this one, final, honorable gesture and lose her forever.

"You're right, Gen," he said. "We had what everyone dreams of and I let it slip away. But not because I stopped loving you. It was because I was so disillusioned with my life. There was something I had to find…had to do, but I couldn't… reach it. I was lost…weak…I gave up." He took her hand. "But, for what it's worth, I found it, Gen. And I'm doing it!"

She made herself smile, for his sake. "I'm happy for you, Mac," she said, taking the napkin from his hand and dabbing her eyes.

"I almost killed myself, Genevieve. Did they tell you that at the hospital? If someone hadn't found me, who knows what –"

"*I* found you, Mac," she told him.

Mac's mouth fell open.

"I found you," she repeated, squeezing his hand.

"You…you may have saved my life –"

"Yes," she said softly. "And look what you've accomplished with it? Deputy Ambassador, hero of Cyprus, directing a Charter Amendment Conference – those are *amazing* accomplishments, Mac. And then there's the last heir of Arthur business!"

He chuckled. "Yeah. Pretty crazy, huh?"

"Wonderful, I'd say." She let go of his hand and took a deep breath. "Would you like to meet the most special person in my life?"

The knife twisted again. "Yes…of course."

She turned to look at the maître d' who was glaring at Mac like a father meeting his daughter's boyfriend for the first time. She gave him a nod and he started across the restaurant. As he passed by each table, Mac noticed a little tuft of blonde hair appear and disappear. When the maître d' rounded the last table, there holding his hand was a beautiful little girl. When she saw Genevieve, she pulled away from the maître d' and ran into her mother's arms.

"Mommy!" she cried. After a long hug, she pulled away and looked up into Genevieve's eyes. "Have you been crying again?"

The Frenchman glowered at Mac as he stood behind the little girl like a watchdog.

"Oh, I'm fine, Sweetie," Genevieve said and smiled up at the maître d'. "Thank you, Antoine."

With one last malicious look at Mac, the Frenchman took his leave.

Mac glanced around the dining room half-expecting another man to join them. "Where's her father?"

"He's here," Genevieve said. "Look closely."

Mac glanced around the restaurant again.

"At *her*," she admonished with a smile.

"Oh, uh….okay –" he replied, furrowing his brow

"Look at Mac, Sweetie," Genevieve said to her daughter.

The little girl shyly looked over at him. He smiled and leaned forward. Her hair was long and wavy like her mother's, but blonde not auburn. He thought of the first time he'd seen Genevieve at the carnival midway in Traverse and how the breeze coming off the bay had blown her long, red hair about her shoulders. The little girl had bright blue eyes, big and soft, but not quite the same shade as Genevieve's. Her glowing face was as beautiful as her mother's, though slightly different in a familiar way.

"What's your name?" Mac asked, smiling at her.

"Cameron," she said with a giggle and buried her face in the crook of Genevieve's neck.

The dawning realization came with a rush of adrenaline. When he was young, his hair was blonde. Her eyes were the same shade of blue as his. And her name –

Genevieve smiled and said to her daughter, "Cameron, remember when I said we were coming here to meet your daddy?"

She looked up with a glowing smile and nodded eagerly.

"Well, Sweetie…this is your father."

To Mac, the moment seemed completely surreal, yet the little girl stealing shy glances at him across the table was very real indeed. He reached across the table and touched Cameron's cheek. She giggled again and nestled in closer to Genevieve.

She was love alive in the flesh, and a tear came to his eye.

Cameron saw the tear roll down his cheek and slid off her mother's lap. She stood beside her and said, "I'm sorry."

"Why?" Mac asked, wiping away the tear.

"Because I made you cry," she answered sadly.

Mac knelt down beside her. "You didn't make me cry, Cameron. It's just that I…I've always wanted a little girl, *just like you.*"

Her beautiful face lit up and she threw her arms around him.

Genevieve picked up the cloth napkin and dabbed her eyes again.

They sat at the table for hours, talking and laughing, and catching up on the last five years of their lives. Even after Cameron had fallen asleep in Mac's lap, Genevieve went on telling stories that only the proudest of mothers could tell. When the last of the evening's guests left the bistro, she and Mac had to accept that this wonderful evening had drawn to a close.

"Stay," Mac blurted out as Genevieve stood up from the table.

"They're about to throw us out," she smiled.

"I meant…stay here in Geneva."

Genevieve was completely taken aback. "But…Cameron and I are flying home tomorrow."

"Don't go…please!" he said.

"Well…I…I have another week of vacation time –"

"I'll find a place for you to stay. I'll take off from work," he promised. "What do you say?"

Genevieve looked at him, and then at her sleeping daughter lying in his lap. A smile crossed her beautiful face and she nodded.

"Great!" he said, a bit too loudly he realized as Cameron stirred in his lap. "Whoops," he whispered.

Carefully he stood up, resting her head on his shoulder, and reached out for Genevieve's hand. She leaned forward and they softly kissed, holding their daughter between them.

"Thank God she looks like her mother," Mac chuckled.

Four thousand miles away, his old friend Duron laughed. "No doubt."

"She has long, silky, blonde hair. Big, bright blue eyes. A cute little dimple on her right cheek —"

A beep sounded in his ear. "Hey, hold on for a sec." He looked at his phone to see who was calling. "It's Kyle. Can you stay on the line for a minute?"

"Just call me back tomorrow, buddy. Okay?" Duron told him.

"Will do," Mac promised.

"I'm happy for you, *Dad*," said his friend. "Talk to you later."

"Later," Mac echoed and tapped the screen to connect the Keeper. "Merrill tell you the good news?"

"Indeed, he did," Kyle cheerily replied. "The Clansfolk are overjoyed to welcome another heir into the fold. They're already wondering when they'll get to meet her!"

"Soon, I hope," Mac replied. "For now, I'm looking forward to spending my first week with her…and getting to know Genevieve again."

"Don't let her go this time, laddy."

"Not sure that's on the table, Kyle. She came to Geneva so I could meet Cameron, not to get back together."

"Think with your heart, Mac, and everything will turn out just fine."

"Mmmm," Mac hedged.

Kyle chuckled. "You've always been a Doubting Thomas. Perhaps it's time you believed in happy endings, eh?"

"Maybe," he smiled.

"Well, lad, my next comment is *not* up for debate. Keep Cameron close to you," cautioned the Keeper. "Her heredity, like yours, demands great vigilance."

Mac had learned that all too well the past year. "I will, Kyle," he promised. "You can count on it."

Mac couldn't recall a happier week in his life. He and Cameron had had a wonderful time getting to know each other, and when the weekend came, T.J. and Marion offered to watch her for the evening.

Helping Genevieve with her coat, Mac gently pulled her long auburn hair out from beneath the collar. "I always loved your hair," he said wistfully.

"Thank-you," she replied with a kiss.

Cameron crinkled up her nose and giggled.

Giving his daughter a hug, he promised they'd be home in time to tuck her into bed. She and Genevieve had been staying in the Makatu's guest room.

Sitting in a secluded corner of the bistro Mac and Cameron had met in a week and a lifetime ago, they talked about Merrill and Kyle, the Clan and their hopes, his and Cameron's ancestry, the UN and the conference, J.J.'s death and his close calls in Lhasa and Cyprus. Perhaps someday they'd talk about why there were only two heirs of Arthur left, but not now.

"How do you deal with it all?" Genevieve wondered aloud. "Its immensity…its danger?"

He gave a slight, dismissive shrug. "I have no choice, really. I'm doing what my birthright expects of me. But," he smiled, "it's what I *want* to do as well…for the Clan's sake… perhaps for everyone's sake."

"I just can't imagine the burden you must feel."

He smiled and shook his head. "Not a burden at all. It's an honor, and it gives me purpose. I'm the most fortunate man in the world." His smile dimmed. "Except in matters of the heart. I missed all of Cameron's life, and I missed five years I could have spent with you. And now you're leaving." He leaned forward, took her hand, and kissed it. "If this is our last night together…if I never see you and Cameron again, I just wanted to say…I love you."

In that moment, with those three simple words, he gave to her the most precious gift he had to give. With them came the possibility of happiness, or the finality of living the rest of his life without her – the only woman who made him feel emotionally whole. "Stay," he said with a hopeful smile.

Genevieve pulled her hand away. "You broke my heart," she said softly but bitterly.

"I *know*. I know. I'm *so* sorry, Genevieve. I was lost. I gave up. But, I fixed that part of my life. You're the other part I need. I *want*. More than anything. And our life together could be wonderful!"

"I have Cameron," she said, absently rearranging the silverware on the tablecloth. "I don't want *her* heart to be broken."

Mac felt his chest tighten. "After what I did to you, you have every right to doubt me. And you and Cameron have every reason to leave tomorrow. But, stay anyway. Please."

She said nothing.

Two questions had repeated themselves in Mac's mind all week, and time was running out to ask them. There didn't seem much to lose by asking them now, so he said, "Gen, why were you at my condo the night I tried to kill myself? And why did you try to see me in the hospital?"

She hesitated. "You had a right to know."

"What? That you were pregnant? Nothing else?"

She tried not to look at him.

"This might be our last night together, Gen. Please tell me."

She crossed her arms as if cold and said, "I thought, maybe…we could try again. I thought maybe Cameron would fill the emptiness inside you that I couldn't."

"It wasn't my heart that was empty, Gen. It was my soul. You were *everything* I dreamed of, and at the same time everything I never knew I wanted. You saved my life and you created Cameron. I could give you everything I have, and be your slave for a *thousand* lifetimes, and still never repay you for all you've given me." He got up from his chair and knelt down beside her. "I loved you. I *still* love you. I'll *always* love you."

Genevieve broke down and cried. Mac wrapped his arms around her.

Someone grabbed him from behind and pulled him away. Reflexively, he pushed up and back with his legs, throwing the intruder off balance, and spun around, drawing back a clenched fist.

The maître d' didn't flinch, bracing himself for a fight. As soon as Mac realized who it was, he raised his hands, palms open. "Whoa, hold on! Didn't know it was you, Antoine," he said with a half-bow. "Gallant of you, Mon'Ami. My compliments."

Antoine stood his ground and glanced at Genevieve.

"I'm fine, Antoine," she smiled weakly, dabbing her eyes with a napkin.

"Very well, Mademoiselle," the Frenchman replied, reluctantly backing away from Mac with an I'm-watching-you scowl.

She dabbed her eyes again. "You said our life together would be wonderful this time?"

He smiled warmly. "Yes."

"And you said I should stay?"

"Yes," he nodded, "with T.J. and Marion."

She sniffled. "You already asked them?"

Mac chuckled. "A week ago."

She smiled. "Rather presumptuous of you, don't you think?"

"Mmmm," he shrugged. "More like hopeful, I think."

"We'll take it slow?"

"Like we just met for the first time."

"And you'll spend lots of time with Cameron?"

"Nothing would make me happier."

She gave him a smile and said, "Okay."

With the word, he felt relief and happiness fill him in equal measure. "So," he grinned, "when can I ask you out on our first date?"

"It's been five years," she replied with feigned impatience. "What have you been waiting for?"

9

"Two things fill me with constantly increasing admiration and awe, the longer and more earnestly I reflect on them: the starry heavens without, and the Moral Law within."

– Immanuel Kant

"People must interrogate their most fundamental assumptions. Only thus could they think and act correctly, see things as they truly were, get beyond false opinion, and arrive at intimations of that perfect intuition that would make them behave well at all times."

– Karen Armstrong

"People are illogical, unreasonable, and self-centered. Love and trust them anyway. If you do good, people will accuse you of selfish, ulterior motives. Do good anyway. The good you do today will be forgotten tomorrow. Do good anyway. Honesty and frankness make you vulnerable. Be honest and frank anyway."

– Kent Keith

"…and we should end the quarter with a budget surplus, even after accounting for the new field positions in Central Africa," Geneva Station Chief Viktor Kleinmann concluded.

"Fine," grumbled Schoen, getting up from the conference table. Plotting, fighting, conquering – *that's* what he craved, what he was *bred* for, not this soul-numbing administrative tedium.

The Station Chief stood and as they walked out together, said, "When should I tell Herr MacCrarey to report to Brasilia?"

"One week," the Under Secretary-General replied as they passed the receptionist's desk.

"Ach mein Got! Ein tochter!" Helga exclaimed. "Fünf jahr alt? Wunderbar!" Spying her boss, she said excitedly, "Herr Kleinmann! Herr MacCrary haben ein tochter!"

Schoen was about to hand Kleinmann a folder when he stopped cold and slowly turned. "What did you say?"

"A daughter," she repeated. "Five years old. From the States. He didn't even know!"

He cursed and mumbled to himself, "Another one to kill."

Helga's eyes grew wide. "What did you say?" she gasped.

"Where is he?" Schoen demanded.

She looked to Kleinmann who held up his hands in a don't-look-at-me gesture.

"*Take* me to him."

Helga picked up the phone with a trembling hand.

Schoen snatched it out of her hand and slammed it down on the desk.

She gave a cry of astonishment and jumped up from her chair, backing away. Kleinmann scurried off down the hall as Schoen started around the desk. "Take me to MacCrarey," he said in a slow, menacing voice. "Now!"

"J, ja, mein Herr!" she stammered. "Th, this way," she pointed and hurried to the elevator, pressing the button over and over. It seemed to take an eternity for the elevator doors to open, and another eternity for them to open on Mac's floor.

The Under Secretary-General grabbed her by the hair. She shrieked as he dragged her into the hallway. "Where is his office?"

She pointed, her hand shaking, and he pushed her back into the elevator. "Leave," he growled and stormed down the hall. Reaching the office door, he kicked it open and stepped inside.

Mac looked up from his desk. With a cocky grin, he said glibly, "Herr Schoen, how good to see you. I'm afraid I have bad news for you. I'm still alive."

"And now there are two of you," Schoen hissed.

Mac's grin faded. He slowly rose and came around his desk, hands balled into fists. "If you even *think* of hurting her, I'll kill you."

The corners of Schoen's mouth turned up. "You have been given another mission," he said icily.

"Why is it whenever you say 'mission' it sounds as if we're at war?" Mac replied contemptuously.

"And why is it that you speak of 'war' as if it were an evil? War is as much a part of us as breathing or breeding. As necessary to the spirit as sustenance is to the body. It cleanses society of lessor beings and coalesces power unto those strong enough to deserve it."

Mac considered his words carefully. "You make the mistake of many, Gerhardt," using his first name to garner his ire. "War is the way of savages. What makes us human is our struggle to transcend such barbarity. And besides…the UN isn't the Third Reich, and this isn't the 1930's."

Schoen took a step forward. "Isn't it?"

Mac didn't move. "Tell me what the mission is," he said, trying to control his temper, "and be gone. Your departure is such a welcomed event."

Schoen held out the mission file. "All you need to know is in there."

"You mean all you *want* me to know." Mac reached for the folder, but Schoen dropped it on the floor.

"Think what you like. I am only the delivery boy."

"Like hell."

"Report to Brasilia in seven days," he ordered.

Mac furrowed his brow and looked down at the file cover. "Brazil? UN missions in the Americas are almost unheard of."

"Good bye," Schoen said indifferently, "and good riddance."

Genevieve walked into the kitchen after putting Cameron to bed in Mac's guest room.

"Hey, you," she said, wrapping her arms around him as he stood in front of the stove. "I like a man who knows his place is in the kitchen."

Mac chuckled. "You might change your mind after you taste what I'm making."

"It smells wonderful," she smiled, leaning over the stove and looking into the sauce pan. "What is it?"

"Penne vodka," he answered as he stirred. "Here," he handed her the wooden spoon. "Turn the heat down and I'll get the penne," he said, lifting the top off a pot of boiling water.

Mac pulled an apron out of a drawer and opened the refrigerator. He took out a package of fresh penne noodles, set it down on the counter next to the stove, and wrapped the apron around Genevieve's waist. He tied a loose bow in back, resting his hands on her hips and kissing her neck.

"You smell wonderful," he said, pulling her against him.

She felt his body reacting to hers and smiled. "Easy. Sleeping daughter upstairs."

He sighed and smiled wistfully. "We didn't have to worry about that before, did we? We made love whenever we wanted to. And *where* ever, including the kitchen, if I recall correctly?"

Genevieve blushed. "It was everything it should be with you." She paused and asked, "Has there been anyone else?"

"No. There never could be."

His answer surprised her. Mac was a handsome and powerful man. "In all these years, you've never been with another woman?"

"No one, Genevieve."

She leaned forward and kissed him on the cheek.

"Would you like some wine?" he said self-consciously.

"That would be nice," she smiled.

He slid the sauce pan off the burner, took her hand, and led her into the dining room. She gasped when she saw the table – linen, china and silverware, flowers and candles, an opened wine bottle and crystal glasses.

"How did you do all this while I was putting Cameron to bed?"

"It's easy," he said, picking up the wine bottle, "if you plan everything out."

"Planned?" she said with a suspicious smile. "Is there an ulterior motive here I should be aware of?"

"Moi?" he said innocently, filling the glasses with a smile that quickly faded. "Actually, I'm going on another assignment. Thought it best to break the news over a nice dinner and good wine." He lifted his glass. "To romantic evenings and joyful homecomings."

"And no more good-byes." She took a sip of the wine. "Mmmm. Very good. What is it?"

"Cerise. A cherry port from Traverse."

"I came all the way to Europe, the center of the world for wine, and you open a bottle from back home?"

Mac chuckled. "Sorry. Thought it was kind of romantically nostalgic. How about I take you on a tour of the wineries around Lake Geneva next weekend?"

"That sounds wonderful."

The dinner conversation was as charming and pleasant as they could ever remember it.

They laughed. He told her how beautiful she was. She told him stories of Cameron. They shared dreams and talked about tomorrows to come. As he poured the last of the wine, she said, "Tell me about your new assignment."

"A UN advisory mission for the government of Brazil. I have to be in Brasilia early next week. Apparently, some settlers are being attacked by native tribespeople in the western Amazon. We're supposed to investigate and report back with recommendations on quelling the violence."

"How long will you be there?"

"Not sure. The details I have are sketchy. Could be a week, maybe two. But," he added with a less-than-convincing smile, "should be pretty routine."

"After Llasa? J.J.? Cyprus? I don't believe anything will be routine anymore, or safe."

Mac swirled the wine around in his glass. "Maybe that *is* the routine."

"Ever think about leaving? Going home to Traverse?" she asked.

"Only every time I look at Cameron," he smiled.

"Then quit," she said, taking his hand. "Come back home with us."

His smile faded. "I can't, Gen. The Clan has put their faith in me."

"Aren't you afraid?"

"No. Not anymore."

"I am," she said softly. "I don't want to lose you again."

"And I don't want to lose you." He smiled and got up from the table. "C'mon, let's sit by the fire. I'll make us some coffee."

She walked into the living room, grabbed some pillows off the couch, and tossed them in front of the hearth. Making herself comfortable, she wondered what she and Cameron would do while Mac was gone.

A cupboard opened in the kitchen and closed. Coffee beans poured out and a grinder whirred. And soon the delicious aroma of percolating coffee wafted into the living room.

Mac walked in a few minutes later with two china cups and a plate of English shortbread cookies and Swiss toffee on an antique silver tray. He set it down in front of the hearth and handed Genevieve one of the cups.

"How ironic," she said, "that five years ago you thought your life so meaningless you tried to end it, and now you risk it for others." He didn't answer. She kissed him on the cheek again. "I'm sorry I asked you to quit. Your nobility –" She giggled. "That word sounds so out of place these days, doesn't it? But, I can't think of a better one. Your nobility is a part of you…it's part of what makes me –" She caught herself before saying the words aloud. Not now, not when she needed to be strong.

Mac sensed what she was struggling with and asked, "Can I read you something?"

With relief and regret she smiled and nodded.

Mac threw another birch log onto the fire and took a small leather-bound book off the mantle. As he leafed through the pages, Genevieve looked over his shoulder and noticed the book was filled with Mac's handwriting.

"No peeking," he teased. She giggled. When he found the right page, he said apologetically, "It needs some more editing. I'm not very good at poetry. This type doesn't rhyme by the way. It's more a stream of consciousness." He glanced at what he wrote. "Maybe this was a bad idea –"

Genevieve leaned over and kissed him. "Read," she whispered.

He nodded, cleared his throat, and tentatively began.

"Morning is dawning.

The sun is cresting over Tropica.

From the bow, I plunge into the warm salty sea.

Through the crystalline shimmering waters my body falls.

Far below I see what I've longed for since longing came to me.

My breathing stilled, my heart pounding, deeper and deeper I fall.

All is risked to live in this moment. No yesterday, no tomorrow, only now.

Still deeper I go. No thought of retreat. Finally, I reach it – lost gold and burnished silver. Sparkling emeralds and rubies. Yet all pales beside you.

You are the beauty poets honor, the passion men long for.

Love's dream touched within you."

The words lingered in the silence that followed, and the fragrance of tropical breezes and warm, lapis lazuli seas slowly faded away until once again they were sitting before a fire on a cold winter's night.

"That was beautiful," Genevieve said softly. She wrapped her arms around his neck and pulled him towards her, pressing her lips against his.

Mac took in her taste, the scent of her skin, and whispered, "I love you."

With but a moment's hesitation, she forsook her fears and spoke the words she'd so wanted to say. "I love you. I've loved you since that summer's day we met in Traverse."

Mac stood up and held out his hand. She looked into his eyes and saw the love and longing behind them. She took his hand, and he pulled her up.

She took him into her arms and they held each other for a long while. Pulling apart, they held hands and walked silently down the hall to the guest room. Mac carefully opened the door and looked in. Silver-gray moonlight spilled in through the window and fell upon a little bundle of blankets. Stepping to the bed, he pulled back the blanket to reveal a tangle of silky blonde hair. He gently ran his fingers through it, amazed all over again that this wondrous little girl was his. The love he felt for Cameron was so simple, so natural, it must have been inside him all his life waiting for her to come along.

Genevieve touched him on the shoulder and held out her hand. Leading him out the door and down the hall to his bedroom, she sat him on the bed and stepped back. Slowly, she unzipped the back of her dress and slid it off her shoulders and over her hips. Letting it fall to the floor, she undid her bra, watching Mac take in her body – from full pouting breasts to curvaceous hips and firm thighs. Stepping to the bed, she unbuttoned his shirt as he slipped off her panties. Taking his hands, she pulled him to his feet and began unbuckling his belt. Kneeling, she slid his pants and boxers down and guided his fully aroused penis between her soft, moist lips. He moaned with pleasure and pulled her up, their lips meeting in a loving, passionate kiss. They laid down on the bed and he kissed her neck, her shoulders, her breasts, and when he reached her stomach he gently spread her legs apart and kissed the inside of her thighs. Slowly, his lips inched upward until he touched the soft curly hair between her legs. He tasted her soft, salty wetness and breathed in her musky scent. His tongue caressed her clitoris, gently at first, then faster, the muscles in her abdomen contracting with waves of passion.

"Get inside me," she breathed.

Their arms and legs intertwined and he pressed his throbbing penis against the silky, moistness between her legs. She reached down and guided him inside her. Passion consumed their torsos as they moved together, aborning anew in a timeless place of touch and emotion – she, the mysteries of the ages, velvet to the touch, riding the swells of passion; he – the tall, proud ship driving for the coast of Tropica; they – traveling upon waves drawn up by winds unseen, their crests growing higher and troughing deeper, their hearts beating to wild native drums.

"I love you," he whispered.

"I love you," she echoed.

Passion and love, ecstasy and joy, cresting and troughing, cresting and troughing, faster and faster until their bodies crashed upon the sparkling sand, thundering together in the frothy surf of unbridled pleasure.

The warm, salty waves slowly receded, their joined spirits lingering side by side on the glittering beach.

"I love you," he whispered.

"I love you," she echoed.

The End

"There are only four questions of value in life: what is sacred? Of what is the spirit made of? What is worth living for? And, what is worth dying for? The answer to each is the same: only love."'

– Jeremy Leven

Look for *Novum Orbis Regium*, the sequel to *Traverse* by W. A. Holdsworth, coming in 2019!

About the Author

W. A. Holdsworth was born in Chicago in 1961 and lived in several states before settling in Michigan. He spent his summers in Traverse City and still vacations there every year, as does the protagonist of his novel Traverse. Mr. Holdsworth attended the University of Michigan and Oakland University, earning an engineering degree and serving as President of the engineering school's honor society. After two years with General Electric, he enrolled at Michigan State University and earned an MBA. The following 30 years were spent working first as a management consultant, as President of a professional association, and as a Director for one of the largest counties in the U.S.

Not much of a reader as a youth, he began listening to Books On Tape during business trips. He soon became an avid reader of classic and contemporary adventure novels, and indulged his life-long interest in history, science, philosophy, and religions. It wasn't until his late thirties that he began writing while working and raising a family. A fan of the Arthurian legend, he wanted to bring the story of Arthur and Camelot into the modern world with a novel that was both exciting and meaningful. The result was Traverse, and its sequel Novum Orbis Regium. He is now writing the next book in the trilogy.

www.ingramcontent.com/pod-product-compliance
Lightning Source LLC
Chambersburg PA
CBHW051644180726
48284CB00006B/1862